NATURAL CAUSES

ALSO BY JONATHAN VALIN

The Lime Pit
Final Notice
Dead Letter
Day of Wrath

NATURAL CAUSES

Jonathan Valin

Congdon & Weed, Inc.
New York

Copyright © 1983 by Jonathan Valin

Library of Congress Cataloging in Publication Data

Valin, Jonathan.
  Natural causes.

  I. Title.
PS3572.A4125N3   1983   813'.54   82-23590
ISBN 0-86553-073-4
ISBN 0-312-92560-3 (St. Martin's Press)

Published by Congdon & Weed, Inc. 298 Fifth Avenue,
New York, N.Y. 10001

Distributed by St. Martin's Press 175 Fifth Avenue, New
York, N.Y. 10010

Published simultaneously in Canada by Thomas Nelson
& Sons Limited 81 Curlew Drive, Don Mills, Ontario
M3A 2R1

Printed in the United States of America by
The Haddon Craftsmen
Designed by Irving Perkins
First Edition

To Katherine

NATURAL CAUSES

1

I was trying to install an air conditioner in my office window when a short, bearded man in a three-piece suit walked into the room.

"I'll just be a minute," I said, waving a Phillips screwdriver at him. "Have a seat."

"Take your time," the man said in a jovial voice. He walked over to one of the captain's chairs by the desk and sat down. "I don't know how you could get by without one in this heat."

"That's what I told myself this morning." I fastened the last two screws in the casement, plugged the thing in, and turned it on. The air conditioner shuddered once then began to chug and hum noisily. A stream of warm, fetid air came pouring out the vents. I sniffed at it and frowned.

"It takes awhile for the coolant to circulate," the man said with amusement.

"Yeah?" One of the windowpanes began to shake. "What about the noise?"

He shrugged. "That you'll have to live with."

I sat down behind the desk, wiped my palm on my pants leg, and held out a hand. "Harry Stoner, part-time electrician."

"Jack Moon," the man said, shaking hands. He pulled a

card out of his coat pocket and held it up in front of me, like a cop flashing his buzzer. His name was printed on it above a familiar corporate insignia. I stared at the emblem for a second; the company had been in the papers a good deal that summer, because of a rather nasty class action suit filed against it. But I would have recognized the logo anyway—it was embossed on every bar of soap I'd ever bought.

"You work for those bad folks at United American," I said.

"Ha, ha," he said distinctly. He laid the card on my desk. "Keep it. The way things are going it may become a valuable charm, like the hexes on Pennsylvania Dutch farmhouses."

I smiled at him. "It can't be that bad."

"A thousand letters a day after the 'Clean & Fluffy' fiasco. Boycotts all over the Bible Belt. It's bad."

"I read where you'd taken some legal action of your own."

He rubbed the nape of his neck. "Yeah, well, we didn't have a choice. It turned out that a couple of competitors were spreading the rumor that 'Clean & Fluffy' was the work of communist conspirators. It seemed to help their business."

"Is that what you're here about? Your reputation?" I said, picking up the card.

"Nope." Moon plucked a pair of turtle-shell glasses from his jacket, flipped them open like a gravity knife, and stuck them firmly on his nose. The glasses were round and thick; Moon's face was round and thick, swarthy and acne-scarred above a curly black beard. He looked a little like a Hassidic rabbi in mufti—small, genial, with something lively and clever in his dark brown eyes. "United wants to take you to lunch, Mr. Stoner."

"They do, do they?"

"They do." He reached into his pocket again and pulled out a folded document. "But first there's the little matter of selling us your soul. It's just a formality. Sign at the bottom."

I examined the document. It was an agreement not to discuss United's business with any other company or agency. "I have a standard contract of my own," I said, as I scanned the fine print.

"I'm sure you do," Jack Moon said pleasantly. "And we will be happy to sign one of your contracts after you've signed ours."

"Yeah? What's this about?"

Moon put a finger to his lips. "It's a secret," he said.

We went to lunch—to the Maisonette, no less.

"As long as United is paying, why not?" Moon said over a bowl of vichysoisse. "You'll find that we're a very easy company to get along with."

"Is that true?"

"No," he said, spooning the soup into his Cupid's-bow mouth. "I lied. I'm supposed to say that to put you off your guard."

"Are you always so agreeable?"

"Always," he said and slurped the soup. When he was finished, he laid the spoon gently on the saucer, propped his elbows on the damascene tablecloth, and locked his hands beneath his chin. "I like you, Harry," he said. "You're a real Cincinnati square." He flipped his pinkies out and drew a square in the air.

"I thought you guys were the ones with the reputations for being squares."

"Oh, we are," Moon said. "At least, most of us are. Like our competition says, ninety-nine and forty-four one hundredths percent pure."

"I guess you fall into that other fifty-six hundredths percent."

He laughed. "What can I tell you?" he said, unlocking his hands and opening them expansively. "It's a job and I was tired of living the life of a starving actor."

5

"You were an actor?"

"You don't think I was born like this, do you?" he said, pinching the lapel of his suit. "Sure I was an actor. Off-Broadway in New York. I wasn't a very good actor, but I enjoyed the work."

"Then why did you stop?"

"Got married, had a kid, got civilized, I guess." Moon looked uneasily at the cart of seafoods that a waiter had rolled up to our table. "A man's got to eat, doesn't he? And for a little guy I've got a big appetite."

Moon dug into a cold lobster tail. "I'm always hungry," he said, as he chewed. "Only it's the wrong kind of hunger. That's why I'm living here, instead of in New York. That's why I didn't make it as an actor."

"Look on the bright side—that's probably why United hired you."

"Yeah," he said with a nod. "But they made a mistake. I'm not United material."

He certainly didn't seem to be, from what I knew about the company. But then I didn't know much. For an organization that owned most of the city and a good deal of the rest of the world, United American was a remarkably low-profile outfit. Their products were visible everywhere; the inner workings of the soap factory were veiled in bubbles. My impression of the corporation, before I'd met Moon, was of one vast minion of sedate, gray-suited, clean-shaven, clean-living men, working in ecumenical harmony—like a band of angels or the C.I.A.

"What do you do at United?" I asked him.

"Sell soap. What do you think?" He patted his lips with a linen napkin and called for the check. "I'm in U.A. Teleproducts, which is a separate corporation from the brands manufacturers. We make the shows that sell the soap."

"Soap operas?" I said.

"We prefer to call them daytime dramas. I'm the executive producer on one of the shows—a little number called 'Phoenix.'"

"You guys are going to run out of sunbelt boomtowns one of these days," I said.

"Oh, hell, we might as well have called it 'Little Rock' for all it has to do with the sunbelt. We were just looking for a typical American city, full of alcoholics, nymphos, drug addicts, bitches, and twins."

"Twins?" I said.

"Always," Jack Moon said as he signed the check. "Everyone in soap opera has a twin. In fact, someone ought to write a thesis on it. You know, the *doppleganger* in the American Southwest or the theory of parallel universes on daytime television. We've got to have twins, in case we kill the wrong character off and the audience wants us to bring him back."

"I see."

"Well," Moon said, "are you ready to sign now?"

I laughed. "Hell, why not?"

"Dandy," he said, rubbing his hands together. "Then we can go talk to the big boy about our little problem."

"And what problem is that?"

Moon stood up. "I think I'd better let Frank tell you," he said. "He's so much more impressive and dignified."

7

2

We walked down Ninth Street to United American headquarters. It was a large, ugly, unadventurous building, Spartan in its plainess.

"From Bauhaus to outhouse," Jack Moon said, staring up at the unadorned rows of windows. "The place looks like a giant tool shed."

"At least it's modest," I said, thinking of the chrome and glass extravaganzas uptown.

"Oh, it's modest, all right. It's modest the way Orson Welles was modest when he stuck his name at the end of the credits in *Citizen Kane*. This is the height of immodesty, man. Presbyterian chic."

We walked in through the Ninth Street entrance, past a homely, middle-aged receptionist, over to a bank of elevators. The place really was as conspicuously unadorned as a Presbyterian church—no logos, no paintings. Just plainly lettered signs and arrows and a couple of scraggly rubber trees parked in empty corners.

"See what I mean?" Moon whispered. "This is a megabillion dollar corporation and the reception area looks like a suburban bank."

"Why did they do it this way?"

"They don't want anyone to get the idea that they're

8

not just plain folks," Jack said. "It's their idea of unpreten-tious."

The elevator smelled like a fresh roll of toilet paper. When I asked Moon why, he said, "It's the brands. They're located on the lower floors and they've got product dis-plays in each of the lobbies. What you're smelling is the combined essence of U.A.—a little toilet tissue, a dab of laundry soap, a touch of bath oil beads. It's the sweet smell of cleanliness, Harry, the very odor of sanctity."

When we got up to the tenth floor, Jack gave me a push in the small of the back and said, "You're on your own, now, fella."

"Where are you headed?"

"Oh, I'll be around, if I'm needed. You just go over to the secretary, Jodie, and tell her you're here to talk with Frank Glendora. I'll see you afterward. I've got the terri-ble feeling I'm going to be appointed tour guide for this trip."

He wandered off down the carpeted hallway and I walked over to the reception booth, where a young woman with teased red hair was reading a copy of *Soap Opera Digest*. She looked up at me and her eyes got big.

"God!" she said, holding the magazine to her mouth. "You're so large!" She tittered like Goldie Hawn. "I mean, are you a football player or what?"

"I'm a private detective."

"God!" she said again and shook her head in disbelief.

Jodie was apparently one of those secretaries who need a secretary of their own—cute but rattlebrained. I gave her my name and told her who I wanted to see.

"Oh, God, Mr. Glendora," she said. "Is he in trouble or something?"

"I don't think so," I said.

The girl pressed a buzzer on an intercom and said, "Mr. Stoner to see you."

"Send him in," a man said.

"It's at the end of the hall to your right," Jodie said.

I started slowly down a corridor lined with office doors, looked back at Jodie, who was craning her neck to watch me, then picked up my pace. Toward the end of the hall, I had to step around a couple of guys in vests, who were talking about the contents of a folder that one of them was cradling in his arms. They lowered their voices as I got near them and stopped talking as I passed by, eyeing me with something akin to the wonder in Jodie the Secretary's voice. I glanced at my shirtfront to see if I'd left a button undone or spattered myself with cocktail sauce. But I was presentable. It wasn't really me, I decided; it was the novelty of a stranger in town.

I passed another guy at a water cooler, who gave me the same "Bad Day at Black Rock" look. But I'd grown fond of it by then.

"Where's Frank Glendora's office?" I said to him just to see how he'd react.

He pointed wordlessly at the double doors in front of me.

I stepped up to the doors and knocked.

"Come in," a man called out. I walked in.

Glendora's office was large and tastefully decorated. There were posters on the walls, framed in glass. Broadway playbills, opera festivals, gallery showings. A set of shelves built into the east wall was filled with editions of plays. I went over to the desk and sat down on a tan, tufted arm chair. The man sitting behind the desk stared at me for a moment.

"You're big," he said in a whimsical voice.

"So I've noticed."

Glendora smiled to himself. He was a good-looking man in his late fifties. Very thin and gray, with sad eyes and large, uneven teeth. Perhaps it was all the talk of Presbyterian decency, but something about Glendora's face reminded me of Billy Graham's haggard, resolute handsomeness: they both had the same burnt-out look of suffering for a cause.

10

"Did Jack fill you in on things?" he asked.

"Only on this." I handed him the agreement.

"You signed it?"

I nodded.

"Good," he said with a sigh of relief. "I like to have things in writing. Force of habit, I guess." He read through the agreement quickly, said "good" again, then laid it down on his desk.

"We've got a problem," he said, staring sadly into my face. He spoke very slowly and deliberately, like a man reading aloud from a difficult text.

"You've also got your own security people, don't you?"

"It's not that kind of problem. I suppose you know that we've been suffering through a crisis of sorts."

"You mean the flap about your soap?"

Glendora frowned. "It's all so very silly that I don't know what to say. However, the suit is a fact, and it must be dealt with. And so," he said with another sigh, "is this Quentin Dover thing."

"Is that what you need me for?" I asked. "This 'Quentin Dover thing?'"

He nodded. "It's important for you to understand our position in this matter. If it weren't for the pending court action and the unfortunate publicity surrounding the suit, we would probably be much less concerned about Quentin. I mean, in a business sense only. Naturally we'd be concerned. We're always concerned when one of our employees dies."

"He's dead?"

"Yesterday. Or, at least, that's when they found his body—on Monday. In L.A. My understanding is that he'd been dead for some time."

"And what did he die of?"

"No one seems to know at this point. Of course, an autopsy was performed, but the preliminary findings were inconclusive. His body . . . it had decayed. Right now the Los Angeles police are officially terming it an accident.

Death of natural causes, precipitated by a fall in the shower."

I glanced at the agreement I'd signed and then looked up at Glendora's sad-eyed face. He was having trouble getting to it—the reason why Quentin Dover's death needed investigation—so I decided to make the next step easier for him. "I take it there is some reason to believe that his death was not an accident."

"I'm afraid so."

"And what is that?"

Glendora looked embarrassed. "This is difficult for me, Mr. Stoner. I am not a gossip. Moreover, I believe that every man has the right to live his own life in any way he chooses. I know we have the reputation for being an ultraconservative organization, with all that that implies. And while the company would undoubtedly prefer its employees to be ethical people in every aspect of their lives, all that it demands is that they be ethical, productive workers. Quentin Dover was a brilliant writer and a very charming man. I, personally, liked him enormously. And if it weren't for certain circumstances, I would just as soon let the poor, troubled soul rest in peace." He said the last part with quiet dignity, as if he were literally speaking for himself. He was so convincing that I had to remind myself that he hadn't gotten that office on the tenth floor by questioning company policy.

"I have heard some reports, mostly from members of the production team, that Quentin . . . well, that he didn't always comport himself the way a man should."

I hated to make him say it, since it obviously embarrassed him, but I couldn't conduct an investigation on the basis of euphemisms. "Are you saying he was a homosexual?"

"I don't know what he was," Glendora said. "No man is just one thing or another, anyway. All I know is that the company feels that we can't afford even a small scandal at this time. God knows we've had enough bad publicity as it is. In order to forestall that possibility, we would like you to conduct an independent investigation of Quentin's death. Of course, if there is reason to suspect something more than a scandal, we would expect you to consult with the proper authorities at the proper time."

I smiled at him. "Who determines that, Mr. Glendora? The proper time?"

He gave me an icy look. "Let me make this as plain as I can. We are not engaging you to perfect a conspiracy to obstruct justice. *I* am not hiring you to do that, nor have I suggested it at any time. Do you agree?"

What could I say? "I guess so."

"No," he said firmly. "That's not good enough. I want it understood that you are being hired to conduct an investigation to determine whether Quentin's death might compromise our company's image and standing. We are not hiring you to cover anything up. On the contrary, we want to determine the truth of the matter."

I almost said, "And if that truth turns out to be disagreeable?" But I didn't. I just said, "I understand."

"Good," Glendora said. "We will make arrangements to fly you out to L.A."

"There are a couple of problems with that. I'm not licensed to practice in California, and I don't have any contacts on the L.A. police force."

"We will make arrangements," he said again.

"Dover lived in California?"

"He lived in Indian Hill. He sometimes worked on the coast—both coasts, actually. His wife and mother are here in the city. You will undoubtedly want to talk with them and with the members of Quentin's team. I'll have Jack arrange that for you. Jack will be your contact here and on the coast. And of course I will be available if you should need me." He folded his hands on the desk. "I guess that covers it. All except for your salary. We will

13

pay you twice your normal rate, plus all reasonable travel and other expenses. Is that agreeable?" He extended his right hand.

"It's downright generous," I said, shaking with him.

"Good. Welcome to the fold, Mr. Stoner."

3

I found Jack Moon sitting, cross-legged, on a visitor's bench beside the secretary's booth. He patted the cushion beside him and I sat down.

"So how'd it go?" he asked.

"All right. Glendora says I'm part of the fold."

He grinned at me. "You sold out, huh? Well, I guess everybody's got his price. What did he offer you? Gold, jewels, women?"

"Just plain old dollars."

"Yeah? How many?"

I glanced at him. His pally voice said that he was only kidding, but something in his clever eyes really wanted to know. When he saw that I'd figured that out, he ducked his head.

"Guess it's none of my business. Did His Nibs have anything to say about me?"

"You're my contact."

"I figured," he said without enthusiasm. "Well, you must have a few questions you want to ask, so let's go down to my office and start cleaning up the mess that Quentin left behind him."

I had a few hundred questions I wanted to ask Jack, but when we got to his office—a small, windowless room furnished with a Steelcase desk and a padded desk chair and one visitor's chair—the first one that came to mind was, "What kind of man is Frank Glendora?"

"Frank?" Moon scratched his curly black beard. "Frank is one of those guys who didn't miss his calling in life. He's a born company man. White, Anglo-Saxon, Protestant, sober, pliable, loyal, and discreet. United hired him out of college at the end of the Second World War, and he's never forgotten the favor. Or ever let anyone else forget. Frank's got what you could call a case of hard-core gratitude. The company gave him a home when times were hard and that makes anything the company wants to do O.K. by him. Jesus, you should hear him when he gets started on the subject. It's like it never occurred to him that some of us don't want to stick around for thirty-five years of regular promotions and Blue Cross, just to end up as head of production for a corporation that sponsors 'The Young Interns.' "

"He's United's head of production?"

Moon nodded. "Yeah. Why are you asking about Frank?"

"No reason," I said. But I had a reason. I was trying to figure out what Frank Glendora really expected me to do if I unlocked the wrong door and found that scandal he seemed to be afraid of.

"He's relatively honest," Moon said, "if that's what you're wondering about. He can be a bastard when the stakes are high enough, but then who can't?"

"All right," I said. "How about Quentin Dover? How honest was he?"

Jack sat back in his chair. "Ah, Quentin," he said. "There I can speak with some authority. You know, I worked with him. He was head writer on 'Phoenix.' "

"Was he a good writer?"

Jack threw his hand at me in disgust. "Naw, he was a terrible writer. A hack. What you got to understand, Harry, is that 'good' doesn't enter into it when you're talking about daytime TV. Frank and Helen aren't interested in good; they're interested in the old 41/42."

"And what is that?"

"Forty-one or forty-two minutes of playable story, every day of the year, year in and year out, with no summer reruns. In that respect, Quentin was a great writer. Or, at least, he was up until a few months ago. Quentin was a rarity—a man with no mind of his own, no artsy pretentions, and no sense of shame. He was perfect for daytime."

"How was he during the rest of the day?"

Jack grinned maliciously. "He couldn't pour a cup of coffee without taking a stiff drink first. He was thirty-eight years old and he'd already had a quadruple bypass. Does that give you any idea? Quentin Dover was Type-A incarnate. He was a walking basket case. He once told me that he took fourteen different pills every day. Fourteen! He carried a thermometer in his coat pocket. He couldn't pass a blood pressure machine in a drug store without slipping a quarter into it. His life was one long stifled scream."

"Glendora seemed to think he was charming."

"Glendora didn't have to work with him every day," Jack said bitterly and stared at his little desk with scorn. "Yeah, sure he could be charming. Most neurotics are. He had an act he went into when he was around the big boys. Frankly, I don't know how he brought it off. For a man without a shred of real confidence, he could put on the damndest show of self-assuredness you ever saw. They say money talks; well, if it does, Quentin had the accent down to a tee. He was a name-dropper, a gossip, a jet-setter without wings. You should have heard him go on about Back Bay Boston or about his days with Armand Hammer or about the time he escorted a starlet to a hot-tub orgy in Hollywood. He had the accent, all right. And that's what guys like Frank love to hear. It gives them a little goose, like paging through the *National Geographic*.

17

That's what Quentin was to them: a trip to the respectable unknown, with a glimpse or two of naked savages along the way."

"It's the not-so-respectable unknown that they seem to be afraid of," I said.

"I'm afraid I can't tell you anything about that," Moon said. "Outside of work, Quentin and I didn't do much socializing. You see, we weren't in the same league— money-wise. And money was all-important to Quentin."

It seemed to be rather important to Jack Moon, too. But I didn't make a point of it. Like he'd said, he had a big appetite and the job just didn't satisfy his hunger.

He must have recognized the rancor in his voice, because he straightened up in the chair and gave me a weary look of apology. "You don't know what it's like, Harry," he said. "Having to nurse these talentless bastards all day long. That's all I do—run a daycare center for neurotics. It gets old after awhile."

"I thought you were the executive producer of the show?"

He laughed biliously. "Executive producer is just a fancy name for go-fer. I'm United's boy at the plant, that's all. The show is run by Helen Rose. She's the producer, and the only person she's responsible to is Frank. I'm along for the ride—to pat Helen's hand for her when it needs patting and to count Quentin's pills for him when he loses track. Shit, do you know how much money Quentin Dover was making?" He didn't wait for an answer. "Better than half a million dollars a year."

I stared at him. "For writing soaps?"

"For writing soaps," he said with disgust. "They pay me twenty-six grand, Harry. So don't expect me to show much pity for Quentin. He had his house in Indian Hill. And his Rolls-Royce. And his centerfold wife, who had the brains of a Playboy bunny and fucked like one. They had the crew out to the house one Christmas Eve, and that woman got so loaded that she knocked over the tree. But she looked good doing it. I'll give Quentin that. And that's all I'll give him. He had what he wanted—all that money could buy. And if he's dead now because he bought the wrong stuff, well . . . that's tough."

"What kind of stuff?" I asked him.

"They found him dead on the bathroom floor in the Belle Vista. He'd been taking a shower and he apparently slipped on the soap and fell through the glass shower curtain and bled to death. Now, understand, this is a guy who couldn't take a piss without saving the last few drops in a sample bottle. This is a guy who'd phone his internist to see if there'd been any calls. You going to tell me that Quentin Dover slipped on soap? And then lay there for almost two whole days without anyone knowing where he was?"

"What *did* he slip on?"

"His own obsessions, probably. Quentin was always looking for the easy way out. Anything that could kill the pain and the worry and ease the burden of having to make all that dough. Hell, you read the papers. So do the L.A. coroners. It's just a matter of time before they figure things out. He'd probably been drinking; he bought his way into the wrong crowd; somebody fed him a little too much Dr. Feelgood; and he croaked. It happens every day—to much nicer people than Quentin Dover. And if he didn't work for United, nobody'd give a shit."

"Not even his wife?"

Jack shrugged. "You'd have to ask her."

That's what I decided to do. I had Moon phone the woman to let her know that I was coming out to talk to her about her husband. While he was arranging the meeting, I found a phone in an empty office and called the L.A. police to see what they had on Dover's death. They didn't have much or, at least, they weren't saying much. The officer I spoke to—a Lieutenant Escobar—read me a prepared statement, the gist of which was that Dover had

19

died of loss of blood, following an accident in the shower. When I asked him what had caused the accident, he gave me the usual runaround.

"That hasn't been determined, yet. We're waiting for the results of a chemical analysis of his internal organs. It may take weeks, even months."

"Why so long?"

"He was in pretty bad shape," the cop said. "You know, he'd been dead for several days."

"Is there any chance that it might not have been an accident?"

"We've more or less ruled out homicide."

"Could it have been a suicide?" I asked.

"Death by natural causes is what it says on this piece of paper," the cop said with a sigh.

"Then why are you running those tests?"

"It's standard procedure," he said. "Look, are you a relative or what?"

"I'm a Cincinnati P.I. My name is Stoner and I've been hired to look into Dover's death."

"Hired by the family?"

"That's privileged information," I told him, which really burned him up.

"You said your name is Stoner?" he said, and I could hear him scratching my name down on a pad. That's what they do when they want to put the fear of the Lord into you—take down your name.

"Harry Stoner," I said. "I'm registered with the Ohio Police Commission, if you want to check me out."

"O.K., Harry. We might just do that."

I'll bet, I said to myself. "In the meantime, do you think you could get me a copy of the autopsy report?"

Escobar snickered. "That's privileged information," he said and hung up.

If United was pulling any strings in L.A., Escobar hadn't heard about it. Which was both good and bad. Good, if it meant that the company wasn't meddling in the official investigation. And bad if Glendora couldn't find me a contact or an informant on the L.A. force. Of course, there was no way to know what United was up to on the basis of one phone call. And I wasn't about to take Frank Glendora's outraged protestations of corporate innocence at face value.

I was pondering the difference between an "independent investigation" and a conspiracy to obstruct, when Jack Moon tapped me on the arm.

"I just got through talking to Marsha Dover," he said. "She was pretty drunk, Harry. And pretty upset."

"You think I should hold off on the meeting?"

"I don't know," he said. "At best the woman's a foul-mouthed hick. And the sun don't rise on the days when she isn't drunk."

"I guess I'll take my chances then."

"How about the trip to L.A.? When would you like to do that?"

"As soon as possible," I said.

"There's a red-eye at eleven."

"Book us on it, Jack. And while you're at it, see what Glendora can do about finding me someone to talk to at the LAPD."

He said he'd get right on it.

4

I stopped at home before driving out to Indian Hill—to pack an overnight bag and a Dopp kit. After I finished packing, I put a quick call into my lawyer, Laurel Gould. She didn't offer any advice that I hadn't already given myself, but it made me feel better to know that Laurel was around to help in case *I* slipped on a bar of soap.

By the time I'd finished with Laurel and started off for my meeting with Marsha Dover, it was close to five-thirty. A brief August thunderstorm slowed traffic down on northbound 71; so it was almost six when I got to the Dover estate.

I drove past an empty gatehouse, down an oak-lined drive, and parked in a gravel turnaround by the garages. An acre away from me, a boy on a lawn tractor was mowing grass in front of a hedge wall. It looked as if he'd been interrupted by the storm and was just finishing up. The air echoed with the sounds of the mower. The rain had stopped by then, although I could still hear it falling in the branches of the oaks. Somewhere on the estate someone was playing rock music on outdoor speakers.

The house was huge. Three stories, with dormers on the top and gambrel-shaped windows on the second story.

The windows on the first floor were bayed and flanked by louvered shutters. Two fieldstone chimneys stood at either end of the long shed roof, with a third chimney projecting from its center.

A flagstone path led from the garages to the front door. I walked up it to the stoop, pressed the doorbell, and waited. No one answered. I pressed it again, and when no one answered again, I put an ear to the door and listened. There wasn't a sound coming from inside the house. All the noise was out on the lawn.

The roar of the mower got louder. I turned around and saw that the boy had driven up to within a hundred feet of me. He hopped off the tractor and walked over to the stoop. He was about sixteen, tall, skinny, and tan, with a red bandana tied around his head for a sweatband.

"Are you looking for Mrs. Dover?" he said.

"Yeah. Do you know where I can find her?"

"I think she's around back, by the pool. Just follow the path through the garden. You can't miss it."

"Thanks," I said.

"Yeah." He swiveled on one foot, as if he didn't really want to stop talking and go back to work. "She sure can use the company. She's real low about Mr. Dover. Mr. Dover's mom was here most of the day with her."

"Is she still here?"

"No. She left about an hour ago."

"You live in the neighborhood?" I asked the kid.

He pointed to the distant hedgerows. "Right over there. That's where we live."

"Well, thanks," I said again.

The boy looked disappointed as he turned back to the mower. "I don't really do this all the time," he said. "I'm just helping out until Marsha gets her head together." He was going to have that conversation whether I joined in or not.

I left him talking to himself and followed the path around the east side of the house into a topiary garden of rosebushes. There was a marble fountain in the center of the garden, ringed with shrubs. A despondent Cupid sat atop it, hands crossed, legs crossed, looking as if he were about to fetch a sigh and resign his post. The music I'd been hearing was coming from the top of the stairs.

I climbed the staircase and found myself standing on a large, tiled terrace abutting the rear of the house. A heart-shaped swimming pool was sunk in the tiles, its calm waters reflecting the stormy sky. An umbrellaed patio table sat beside the pool. The umbrella was closed and beaded with rain. A brass liquor cart was parked next to the table, with bottles of whiskey, an ice bucket, and several heavy crystal glasses on its top shelf. Two small PA loudspeakers were propped on the lower shelf; and it was from them that the music was coming. Between the pool and the umbrella table, with the speakers at her head and an uncorked, half-empty bottle of Jack Daniels within arm's reach, a blonde girl was lying on a woven lounge chair. She was holding a rain-spattered silver sun-reflector beneath her chin, and she was wearing silver aviator glasses on her nose. She was very tan—too tan for a Cincinnatian—apparently drunk, and jay naked.

The girl had long, beautiful legs and round, picture-perfect breasts, without a strap mark to mar the tan or a stretch mark to flaw her skin. Her hair was sun-bleached —very light, almost the color of sand—and what I could see of her face was breathtakingly pretty. Small mouth, darker than the surrounding skin. Small, shapely nose. Strong bones in her cheeks. She was more than pretty.

I stood at the edge of the terrace and watched her, not knowing what to say. For awhile I didn't think she realized I was there. Then she lowered the sun-reflector, spilling rainwater on her breasts and down her flat tummy. She tilted her glasses back on her forehead and gazed at me. Her eyes were dark blue, almost purple, and clabbered with whiskey.

"Connie?" she said in a boozy, downhome voice.

24

She tried to prop herself up on one arm, slipped, and caught her elbow in the webbing of the chaise. The sunglasses fell down, too, landing sideways on her nose. "You're not Connie," she said and wrenched her arm loose.

"No. I'm not Connie."

The girl picked a towel up off the tiles and draped it around her body. I'd never seen a body like that outside of a magazine, and the experience made me a little dizzy.

Seeing me hadn't done a thing for the girl. She reached for the bottle of bourbon, took a swig, and said, "Well, who the hell are you, then?"

"Harry Stoner. I'm here to talk to you about your husband. Jack Moon told you about me this afternoon."

"Jack?" the woman said, passing a hand through her golden hair. "Jack's in California."

"No. Jack's in town. He called you this afternoon. Remember?"

The girl gave me a puzzled look. If that was a stumper, I figured I was in for a long night.

"It's kind of gloomy to be sunbathing," I said—just to say something.

"What the fuck do you know about it?" Marsha Dover said sullenly. "Quentin bought me a book that said there were always good tanning rays in the afternoons. Even when it's overcast. Besides, it didn't seem to bother you any when you were standing over there with a hard-on."

She had a point. She also had one of the saltiest tongues I'd heard this side of the Marine Corps. The combination of that face and body with that tongue was bizarre and a little disconcerting, like finding out that the Mona Lisa was a WAC.

"Do you mind talking to me about your husband?" I said, trying to start something up.

"What if I do?" the girl said with sodden petulance. "Nobody gives a shit about my feelings, anyway. Just because I'm not a genius doesn't mean I haven't got feelings.

25

Quentin didn't marry me because I was a fucking genius. And somebody sure as hell better let his momma know. That woman has been on my back since I married Quentin—about how Quentin's got a reputation to keep up and about how I gotta dress right and I gotta talk right and I gotta do the sort of things she wants me to do. Well, I'm fucking sick of it!

"Quentin's reputation." The girl laughed bitterly. "He never gave a shit. Why the hell should I? And if Connie's so goddamn strong, how come *I* was the one who had to go to L.A.? How come *I* was the one who had to stare at his rotting body? I'd have plain loved to have seen Connie do that. Momma's little precious." She began to laugh again. "She'd have wet her pants."

I let her laugh herself out, then tried to start things up again. I knew it was hopeless—the girl was just too drunk—but, judging from what Moon had said and what I'd already heard, talking to Marsha Dover was always going to be relatively hopeless. Like the girl had said, she was no genius.

"You were in L.A. yesterday?"

She took another swig of bourbon and belched. "Yeah, so what?"

"Do you know what Quentin was doing out there?"

"Getting his kicks," she said.

"I thought he went out there on business."

"Maybe he did," she said. "That's what they tell me, anyhow."

"The police?" I said. But she wasn't listening to me. She was miles away, adrift on a sea of bourbon.

"I just wanted ta' call my Momma," the girl mused. "That's all. But, no. Connie says I can't. She says she doesn't want any of them showing up at the funeral and spoiling it for everybody. I haven't seen my Momma or Poppa in three years. I got a right. What's she expect me to do? Read some goddamn book on the stages of grief, like she did? I said to her, 'Connie, I'll tell you something.

You best lay off of me or you're going to be mighty sorry.' I'm not blind. I know a thing or two. And the bitch knows it, too." The girl glared at me savagely.

"She damn well knows it!" she said again. She turned her head and looked at the bottle of whiskey. "Maybe I'm not perfect. Maybe I'm not the perfect wife. Quentin wasn't anybody's fool. I told her, 'He knew he was getting damaged goods. And he was damn happy to have them. And you know it, too!' Quentin knew what I was. And I knew what he was. We both had our faults. But we loved each other. Shit, yes, we loved each other." She picked up the bottle and hugged it to her breasts. "He loved me. And she can't change that fact or take that away from me—no matter what she says about doctors or probate. My Momma ain't gonna let anybody probate my ass. Quentin wouldn't have let her do it, either." She began to cry. "He loved me."

I felt like holding her—to calm her down and give her back a sense of companionship. But she wasn't the kind of girl I could touch like that. It wouldn't have meant the same thing. At least, it wouldn't have to me.

"I'm sorry he's dead," I said. "It must have been a terrible shock for you."

"It was," she said through her tears. "You shoulda seen him. Connie wouldn't look. She wouldn't even look at the damn photographs. But *I* looked. They made me look. Only thing I recognized was his mouth. The rest of it . . ." She covered her mouth with her hand and gagged.

"Don't talk about it," I said.

"Gotta talk about it," she whispered. "If I don't, I fucking will go nuts. Keep dreaming about it. The way he looked. It made me wanna die, too, seeing him like that. Going to die, anyway, like Quentin said. She wouldn't give a shit. Nobody would."

Marsha Dover looked forlornly across the terrace. "Look at this place." I looked down at the beautiful little garden. "I never wanted it. Not any part of it. Quentin wanted it. No." She shook her head. "That's not true. I wanted it. I just don't want it anymore. And that's the truth. It doesn't matter anymore. None of it."

She sat up on the chair and the towel fell below her breasts. I almost had to catch my breath—she was that beautiful. "I shouldn'ta left," she said softly. "Shoulda stayed at home like Momma said. I was just a dumbass kid, balling bikers and living my own stupid little life. Shoulda stayed in Indianapolis. It's where I belonged. I got no place to go now. Lost my only friend in the world."

"Maybe you could go home for awhile," I said. "Stay with your family."

She shook her head. "They wouldn't have me back. Treat me like I'm dead, 'cause of what I did. 'Cause of Quentin.

"Can't go back," she said with sudden anger. "I changed too much. Quentin changed it all. Too hard, now. I'd break . . . break whatever I touched."

She held the whiskey bottle out and stared at it for a second. Then she threw it toward the edge of the pool, where it cracked against the concrete apron.

"Oh, Christ," the girl said in a heartbroken voice.

She got to her feet and the towel fell away completely. Marsha Dover stumbled crazily across the terrace and walked straight through the broken glass. She winced when she stepped on it but kept going, trailing blood behind her.

"Hold on," I shouted at her.

She just kept walking—right into the pool. She bobbed in the water, her blonde hair floating about her head, then began to sink in a vortex of bubbles and hair and lazy swirls of blood.

"Jesus!" I said under my breath.

I hopped over the lounge chair, ran across the terrace, and dove into the pool. The girl kicked viciously at me when I tried to pull her out. But I managed to get a choke hold on her and drag her to the shallows.

28

She cursed and screamed at me. "Get off me, you fuck-ing ape! Let go of me, goddamn it!"

Then she got sick, doubling over and coughing up pool water and bourbon. Then she passed out in my arms, leaving me knee-deep in puke and blood and chlorine, with the smell of bourbon rising around me like a mist.

5

I found a sliding glass door at the back of the house and managed to get Marsha Dover through it and onto a couch inside. After bandaging the cuts on her feet with strips I'd torn off the towel, I phoned Jack Moon and told him what had happened.

"Jesus," he said. "She really went bonkers, huh?"

"Yeah. Thanks a lot, buddy, for helping to arrange things."

"Sorry," he said. "But I did warn you she was drunk."

"Well, you didn't warn me strongly enough. Now what the hell are we going to do?"

"I could call Quentin's mother, I guess."

"I don't know if that's such a hot idea," I said. "Marsha doesn't seem to be crazy about the woman."

"You got any other suggestions?"

I thought it over. "O.K. Call Mom. I'll wait here until she arrives."

"You're going to miss the plane."

"Then we'll catch one in the morning, Jack," I said and hung up on him.

I sat down on a recliner across from the couch and closed my eyes. I was probably ruining an expensive chair with my wet clothes, but I didn't care. What the girl had done had shaken all that kind of caring out of me. I sat there for a few minutes, while Marsha Dover snoozed her drunk away. Then I turned on a table lamp, took a decanter of whiskey off a mahogany sideboard, and drank from the bottle.

It was first-rate Scotch. Everything that Quentin Dover had owned had been first-rate, including the little number on the couch. Getting sick had taken about three months off her tan, but she was still beautiful to look at. Beautiful and not a brain in her head—an exquisite little fucking machine.

"Jesus," I said aloud.

I walked out to the terrace and found a robe, crumpled up by the liquor cart. I brought it back inside and covered her with it. Asleep she looked about sixteen. She was probably no more than twenty-four or five, anyway. Just a dumb cracker from Indianapolis. I'd had a Hoosier friend who used to call it 'India-no-place.' That's probably what she'd called it, too. India-no-place. I brushed the wet hair off her face, and she moved her head slightly and sank deeper into the pillows. I sat down again on Quentin Dover's tuxedo chair and watched her sleep.

I'd drunk a good bit of the Scotch by the time Connie Dover arrived. I heard a car drive up to the garages and crunch to a stop in the gravel turnaround. Then I heard someone fumbling at a latch. Lights began to go on all over the dark house, refracted by the cut-glass panes of French doors and the crystal baubles of chandeliers. The woman came marching toward us on a wave of refulgent light. When she got to the back room, she stood in the archway for a moment, fists on her hips, and stared sternly at her daughter-in-law.

She was a smart-looking woman in her fifties—thin, thin-breasted, with fine, frosted blonde hair parted in the middle and knotted in back, at the nape of her neck. A wing of hair had fallen across her cheek and she brushed it savagely with her hand.

"I should have known this was going to happen," she said angrily and switched her gaze from Marsha to me. She had cold blue eyes and her skin was as pale and powdered as Marsha's was tan. "Are you Stoneman?"

"Stoner," I said.

"You do good work, Stoner," she said sarcastically.

"I wasn't hired to look after your daughter-in-law."

The woman tossed her head at me, as if that were beside the point. "Come on. Let's lug the sack of guts upstairs."

I carried Marsha Dover up to a bedroom. Her mother-in-law turned down the covers on the bed and I put her on the sheets.

Connie Dover stared at the girl for a moment. "She's a beautiful thing, isn't she? Beautiful but, oh, so dumb." She flipped a blanket over her body.

"Maybe you should call a doctor."

"Why? Have they discovered a cure for stupidity now?"

"Her feet," I said. "She cut them pretty badly."

"She'll be all right," the woman said. "Her problem isn't with her feet anyway. It's up here." She tapped her head. "And in her groin."

She flipped off the light and we walked back down the staircase.

"I suppose she flashed her rear end at you?" Mrs. Dover said. "That's her usual routine."

"She was pretty drunk and pretty shaken up."

"And tomorrow she'll be sober and contrite, and tomorrow night she'll be drunk again. It never stops. I don't know how Quentin could stand it. That girl's got a personality like house current. On again, off again. When she's on, she's little Miss Polymorphous Perversity. When she's off, she's what's left over when you take her toys away. Which isn't much, believe me. In either case, she's a child

32

and has to be treated like one." The woman gave me a pointed look. "She's not to be trusted, you know. She's an inveterate liar. Quentin rescued her from a life of dismal poverty, and she repaid him with public drunkenness and countless adulteries. God knows how many men she must have had. She probably qualifies under state law as a public utility."

"You really like her, don't you?" I said. "I mean deep down inside."

The woman eyed me coldly. "That's not funny. I'm trying to do you a favor, Stoner. Jack tells me that you've been hired to investigate my son's tragic death. I don't know what there is to investigate. The police have already ruled it an accident. But if you're going to go traipsing through Quentin's life, I can at least put you on the right track. To listen to Marsha, you'd think I was a monster and my son forced her to live a life of sinful luxury, away from the bosom of her family. Her family! Well, if you ever want to make a case for heredity affecting I.Q., take a good close look at that brood."

"And what was your son really like, Mrs. Dover?"

She stood very still, at the foot of the stairs. "He was a bright, witty, generous man," she said and her eyes teared up. "He was good to everyone. And it's a sin for anyone to say otherwise."

Connie Dover began to wobble unsteadily on her feet. I reached for her arm.

"I'm all right," she said quickly. "I'm quite all right." She wiped the tears from her eyes with her fingertips. "Really. You can release me. I won't fall."

I let go of her arm, and she braced herself against the stairpost.

"It's just been such a terrible week," she said. "And I'm worn out."

"Do you feel up to talking to me? I have a few questions I'd like to ask. But I could come back some other time, if you want."

33

She dropped her hand from the post and drew herself up quickly. "I'd be happy to talk to you. In fact, there is nothing I would rather do, especially after what you must have heard from Marsha. We'll go to the kitchen. I need a cup of coffee, and you look like you could use one too."

I also looked like something that would leave a stain on Quentin's brocade loveseats, and the kitchen stools were wood. I sat down on one of them, while Mrs. Dover brewed a pot of coffee on a free-standing Jenn-Air range. A huge, beaten copper chimney was suspended above the stove, with copper and silver pots dangling like tassels from its skirts.

The woman talked as she worked. "It's going to be lonely in this house without Quentin. It's really far too big for just two people. But then I had hopes that he would have children."

"There are none?"

The woman laughed mordantly. "No, there are no children—just Marsha. She was all the child that Quentin and I could handle. But then you saw for yourself."

"Yes," I said. I could see that Marsha Dover must have been a handful.

"You know, she's tried that kind of thing before," Connie Dover said. "That's why I didn't get upset about her feet. I wasn't being heartless—just sane. There were weeks when we had a different doctor out here every other day. I've just run out of names at this point. Names and patience. She wore my son down, Stoner, with pranks like that. She ruined his health and his well-being. It would have been different if she were deeply troubled, but Marsha's never felt anything deeply in her life. She's all shallows. It's one to her—attempting suicide, making love, getting drunk, whatever strikes her fancy."

"Why didn't Quentin divorce her?"

"He was afraid to divorce her," she said. "Afraid she'd really kill herself, instead of indulging in one of her

34

melodramatic charades. For some reason he held himself responsible for Marsha's drunkenness and her tantrums, as if it were their marriage that had unhinged her. He wasn't . . . rational when it came to Marsha. But then people in love seldom are. He loved her, you know. Quentin married her when she was very young—scarcely nineteen—and I don't think he ever stopped thinking of her as if she were the same beautiful little girl that he'd picked up in a bar. She was his version of *nostalgie de boue*. Also, she's got quite a build."

I smiled.

The woman poured the coffee into two cups. "She changed once she began to live here. Money changed her. License changed her. I warned Quentin it would happen. I told him she wasn't ready for this kind of life. I begged him not to marry her—just to keep her if he must. But . . ." She waved her free hand gently in the air. "He was very headstrong, my son. A very emotional, very impetuous man. He wanted the little hick and she was Baptist enough to get him to marry her first. Of course, after the ceremony, she turned as Episcopalian as the rest of us. She took one look inside the country club and decided that good manners meant getting drunk and sleeping around. It would have been funny, if she hadn't been part of the family. I never saw anyone change so fast. From a shy child who couldn't say two words without tripping over her own tongue to . . . well, to what you saw by the pool."

The woman brought the coffee over to the table and sat down across from me. "The last time I saw Quentin was right here at this table," she said softly. "On Friday afternoon. He and I had lunch at the house. It was a lovely meal. But then lunch with my son was always a joy. He was very excited that day. He was about to embark on a new project and that made him happy. That was why he was going to L.A.—to discuss the project."

"A project for United?"

"Probably. He didn't say. Personally, I was hoping it was the novel he had been working on for so long. But it was undoubtedly some TV thing. They're always so secretive about their little ideas."

"Did he go out west often?"

"Every week," the woman said. "His team was out there, near the studio. He'd fly to Hollywood on Sunday night, do the week's blocking for 'Phoenix', then come back home on Tuesday evening. Of course, I thought all that travel was too hard on him. You know, he was not in the best of health. But Quentin seemed to enjoy it. And, of course, he enjoyed coming back here. Coming home. His roots are in this city. Our family has lived here for generations."

"In this house?" I said.

"Close by."

I took a sip of the coffee. It was quite good. "Quentin left for California on Sunday?"

"No. He made a special trip that Friday night."

"Did he call you from L.A.?"

"He called me when he got in, from the Belle Vista, late Friday night. He always called when he went on a trip. He knew I'd worry if he didn't."

"What did he say?"

"That the flight had been bumpy, but that he was feeling fine. He said that he would probably be out of touch for a few days and not to worry if he didn't call again until Monday."

"Did he say where he was going to be?"

"I assumed a series of meetings. I remember that the last thing I said to him was not to forget to take his pills with him if he was going to be away from the hotel." She stared sadly into her cup. "The last thing he said to me was that he loved me."

There was a sound from the hall. We both looked up. Marsha Dover was standing in the kitchen door. She had wrapped herself in a bedsheet.

36

"You should be in bed, Marsha, darling," Connie said, making her face over into a cold mask.

"I was all alone up there and I had a bad dream about Quentin." The girl began to sob. "And I've hurt my goddamn feet."

"Mr. Stoner told me about that," the older woman said.

"Mr. Stoner?" The girl looked right through me, as if she'd never seen me before in her life.

The mother smiled in vindication. "You see," she said. She turned back to the girl. "We'll look after it in the morning, Marsha."

"I feel like shit," the girl said. "Will you come upstairs with me, Connie? I don't want to be alone. I'm scared I'll have more bad dreams."

"Of course, I will," the woman said briskly. "Aren't I always there when you want me to be?"

"Yes, Connie," she said in a subdued voice.

The Dover woman stood up. "I'm afraid I'm going to have to leave you, Mr. Stoner. My daughter-in-law needs me."

She walked over to the door and took Marsha by the hand, as if she were a child. I watched them walk off into the dark house—Marsha trailing her bedsheet behind her—and felt like laughing. But what had seemed funny in the kitchen didn't seem so funny when I got back to the car. On the way home, I was bothered by the feeling that I should have said something to Marsha Dover—something hopeful or kind. But for the life of me, I couldn't think of what there was to say.

37

6

Jack Moon called at eight the next morning.

"Did everything work out last night?" he asked.

I really didn't know how to answer him. I was still feeling like a derelict for not having said something to Marsha Dover the night before.

"Quentin's mother came over," I finally said. "The girl was all right when I left."

Moon laughed uneasily. "You say that like you think she's not all right now."

"It's just a feeling."

"Well, put your mind to rest. I talked to Connie a few minutes ago, and Marsha's fine."

"Good," I said.

"There's a flight out at eleven. You think you can make it?"

"I'm already packed."

"Great. Would you mind picking me up at home? Liz, my wife, needs the car this morning. The kid has Little League practice—some damn tournament in Fairmount. Some silliness." But he sounded as if he was going to miss seeing it.

I told him I'd pick him up.

At ten I picked Jack up at his house in Hyde Park. It was a modest little two-story with a brick porch and a small yard in front. There was a child's bike sitting in the middle of the cement walk. I pushed it onto the grass and walked up to the stoop.

A short, jolly-looking, red-headed woman in a Dartmouth sweatshirt and blue jeans answered the door. "He'll be right out," she said cheerfully. "My, you're tall, aren't you?"

"Six three."

The woman shook her head. "That's not what you're supposed to say."

"No?"

"You're supposed to say, 'I try to be.' That's what Bogie said to Martha Vickers in *The Big Sleep.*"

When I didn't say anything, the woman looked embarrassed. "I go to a lot of movies," she said with a shrug.

Moon came out the door, dragging a kid on a leather valise.

"Ride's over," he said and gave the boy a pat on the butt. The boy hopped off and grinned at his father.

"Ho-kay," Jack said, running both hands down the front of his suit coat. "Got everything, right?"

"Everything *I* need," the wife said affectionately.

They kissed and then Jack bent over and kissed the boy. "Have you two met?" he said as he stood up.

"We compared heights," the woman said with a grin.

Jack gave her a confused look, then made a face at me, as if to say, "That's the way she always is."

"This is my wife Liz. Liz, Harry Stoner."

We shook hands.

"What about me?" the little boy said, tugging at his father's pants leg.

"You?" Jack said, staring at him. "What about you?"

"I'm Nick," the boy said.

"I'm Harry."

"You a real detective?"

39

I glanced at his mother and said, "I try to be."

She laughed. "Take good care of my boy, Harry."

She herded her son back in the house, and Jack and I walked down to the car.

"Shit," he said as he got in. "The kid's going to be mad because I didn't make his game. That sort of thing's important to kids."

"To fathers, too," I said.

"It's a dog's life, ain't it?" he said morosely. "I'm in New York or L.A. three or four days out of every week. I tried to get Frank to transfer me to one of the coasts. But . . . no dice."

"How come?"

"United's office is here in the city. A multibillion dollar corporation and they don't even have a New York or L.A. branch. Not even a storefront." He settled back on the car seat and sighed. "Oh, well. There'll be other games, I guess."

He didn't say another word on the trip to the airport. In fact, it wasn't until we were airborne, somewhere over Indiana, that he shook off his melancholy and began to warm up. He was an odd man—a lot softer and a lot more the United type than he'd pretended to be. I wondered if he knew that about himself or if it was something he didn't want to know. If he didn't, it was a shame, because it was a large part of his charm.

"I'm sorry about Marsha," he said. "I don't really know her, and I never pegged her for a loon. A dumb hick, yes. A drunk, for sure. But not a psycho."

"She didn't even remember that you had called," I said dryly.

He shook his head. "Ah, Quentin. What the hell do you think he saw in her?"

"Are you kidding?"

"I mean beyond the T & A," Moon said. "How far can that take you, anyway?"

"You knew the man. I didn't."

40

"Yeah, I guess. But Marsha . . . she never quite fit into the grand scheme. I could see him marrying that body. But living with what was inside it—I don't know how he did it. Most of Quentin's prize possessions didn't talk dirty or throw up on the rug." He stared out the tiny window at the green, jigsawed earth. "She'll crack up one of these days. Right over the edge."

"Quentin's mother said that he'd loved the girl."

Jack shook his head again. "Quentin didn't know what the word meant. It was all self with him. You know the sin of lust? Lust of the flesh? Lust of the eyes? Pride of life? That was all Quentin knew about love or anything else. He was a creature of lust and doubt." Moon laughed. "Listen to me, I sound like the late Father O'Malley, my seventh-grade religion teacher. That's what comes of a Catholic boyhood. And that's why Nick goes to public school. What the hell, maybe he did love her. Maybe having to put up with all that shit was a kind of love. Or penance for not being able to love. You might talk to Helen about that. She's fairly shrewd about other people. And then she didn't have to count Quentin's pills for him or clean up his messes. You should talk to Walt Mack, his breakdown man, too."

"I'll want to talk to them both," I said. "And I'll also want to talk to the cops."

"I think we've worked something out on that score," Jack said. "It's going to have to be confidential, but there's a guy named Sy Goldblum in the Hollywood Division who's willing to fill you in on things."

I smiled at him. "How'd you manage that?"

"Just a little soap and elbow grease. Frank arranged it. He's been in the business a long time, and he's got a lot of pull."

"I'm impressed."

"We're an impressive outfit," Jack said. "We've got you booked into the Westwood Marquis. I'll be there, too. Walt and Helen are at the Belle Vista, holding a panicky meeting to decide what to do about 'Phoenix.' We've got to find another head writer this week. I'll have to sit in on some of the meetings. But I'll be around in case you need me. And I'll make sure that Helen and Walt are available at some point or other to talk to you."

The plane made a grinding noise and lurched. I flinched and Moon laughed.

"Take it easy, Harry," he said. "This is a 727—the safest plane in the skies. That was just the ailerons being lowered."

"Wasn't it a 727 that went down in New Orleans?" I said.

"It got hit by lightning in a hurricane, for chrissake. I thought you detectives were supposed to be tough guys."

"On the ground, Jack. Not in midair."

"White knuckle city, huh?" He leaned back in the seat. "I used to be like that—a couple of years ago. But I've logged so many air miles now that I look for the seatbelt when I go to the john at home. You'll get used to it. And if you don't . . ." He pointed at the air sickness bag tucked in the back flap of the seat in front of us. "This is my best suit, Harry. So don't wait for the light to go on, you know? They don't have one for Vomiting and No Vomiting."

"I'll manage," I said.

7

We landed at LAX at three-thirty Cincinnati time. After kissing the ground, I followed Jack to the luggage pick-up, where we got our bags. Then we took a cab north on the San Diego Freeway to Westwood. The Marquis was located across from UCLA on Hilgard. It was a swanky, modern-looking place with a smoked glass elevator tube running from the street to the lobby entrance—a matter of a few feet. When I asked the black doorman why they'd bothered to install an elevator that only went up one short flight, he grinned toothily and said, "Some people like to ride rather than walk."

I wanted to try the elevator, but Moon made me climb the stairs to the lobby. Inside, the Marquis was surprisingly old-fashioned and ornate. The walls were wainscotted in walnut; handsome oriental rugs were scattered on the hardwood floors. There was some very busy wallpaper by the elevators, but for the most part, the lobby was as trig and traditional as a seven-layer wedding cake.

We settled into two suites on the seventh floor. My suite consisted of two apartment-sized rooms, with two TV's— a big one in the living room and a slightly smaller one on a stand by the beds—four phones, including a wall unit mounted by the toilet; a wet bar, refrigerator, and dining

43

table off the living room; two desks; six chairs; two king-sized mattresses; and so many mirrors on the walls that I could have rented the place out as a funhouse. I saw myself everywhere I looked, from bath to bar. The mirrors made the rooms look larger, although they were plenty large as it was. They also duplicated every item in sight; and in a couple of spots, where the mirrors were set across from each other, they created an endless perspective of replication, like the famous shot in *Citizen Kane*. The suite was an egotist's delight, but it made me dizzy and a little sick to my stomach.

Jack seemed pleased with the accommodations. "Can't say we don't treat you right," he said proprietarily and waved his arm, which waved again in the mirrors.

"Just don't move around a lot," I said, shutting my eyes.

"You're probably still motion sick from the flight."

"Yeah, well the decor isn't helping things. Who designed this place? Narcissus?"

Jack laughed. "This place and most of Bel-Air."

"Could we get a drink, Jack?" I said. "Preferably in some dark and quiet place?"

"I think they cover the mirrors in the hotel bar until after the sun has set. I believe that's the law in this town."

"Fine. Let's go."

"You go ahead. I'll meet you in a few minutes. I want to call Liz and let her know that the insurance check won't be coming this trip. I also want to get in touch with Helen Rose."

"You might call your cop friend, too."

"Check."

I wandered down to the Marquis bar, which was relatively dark and bar-like, and ordered a double Scotch. I was working on my second round when Jack showed up. He'd changed from his suit into a pair of slacks and a sporty, short-sleeved shirt.

"When in Rome," he said, pulling up a chair. "God, I love L.A. It's the only place in the world where you

44

can be yourself and everybody else at the same time."

A waiter came up and Jack ordered a martini.

"And don't put any fruit in it, O.K.?"

The waiter smiled.

"You've got to watch that around here," Jack said. "You order a Tom Collins and they put half a cantaloupe in it as a garnish. Christ, they're proud of their produce."

"Did you talk to the cop?"

"Yeah. He's going to meet us here for a drink in an hour. And we're supposed to have supper with Helen tonight at the Belle Vista. She's really in a bitchy mood. She took Quentin's death as a personal insult, as if he'd deserted to The Other Side."

"She's pretty involved in the show?"

"Is the Pope Polish?" he said. "It's her whole life. Not a healthy situation. But she doesn't have much else going for her. Three or four divorces. A movie career that fizzled out. She eats, drinks, and dreams 'Phoenix.' "

"How about Quentin? How involved was he?"

"Not as much," Jack said. "It was his livelihood, and he took a businesslike interest in it. And, of course, he was vain about the drivel he wrote. But not as vain as the worst of them—like Walt. Let's not talk about Walt, O.K.?"

"Quentin's mother mentioned something about a new project he was working on. You don't know anything about that, do you?"

"Was it a TV thing?"

"That's what she thought."

"Beats hell out of me," Jack said. "It wasn't for us, I can tell you that much. And if it wasn't for us, it wasn't for daytime. Quentin had a little rider in his contract that gave us an exclusive option on his services as long as he was working on 'Phoenix.' And he loved that half a mil too much to queer the deal." Moon scratched his beard. "It'd be interesting, though, if he had been fishing around."

"How's that?"

45

"There's been some friction on the team. The usual back-stabbing and chicanery. I'll tell you, Harry, when the stakes get this high, it's amazing what people will do to keep their Mercs and Corniches coming in."

"I thought Dover had family money. That's the impression his mother gave me."

"I don't know," Jack said. "I don't think so. He certainly didn't give us that impression when we hired him. He seemed desperate for the job. Of course, all the writers act that way. The company counts on it. In a business where the quality factor tends to be on the low side, a healthy greed is the next best thing to a healthy sense of self-esteem. You can always count on greed. And, then, it breeds its own screwy ethic and its own aesthetics, for that matter. Learning that ethics is what this business is all about."

"Where did Quentin get his practice?"

"He worked some in nighttime television before hiring on with us. I've got a dossier on him, if you want to see it. He had his share of screen credits. Nothing major. Just solid, workmanlike stuff."

"Do you know how he started out?"

"I probably do," Jack said. "I've heard several different versions of his life story over the years. Let's see if I can make up a composite." He took a sip of his drink and put the glass down gently on a paper coaster. "Quentin either went to the Yale Drama School or to Harvard or to Northwestern, depending on whom he was talking to. Sometimes, he went to all three and was booted out of each for some adorable, boyish prank in which one was meant to see, like the glimmer of a flame, the hard, gemlike genius that was to erupt into 'Phoenix.' After the college years, he spent some lean times either as an actor or a playwright or a novelist. Once again, the big picture depended on his audience. But the features were usually the same. He had a tough go of it. His hard, gemlike genius went unappreciated. But he persevered, insinuating himself, somehow, into the world of the very rich, where

46

he charmed his way from estate to estate, all the while picking up the polish and skills that were to make him such a shrewd judge of human nature—as in the case of his wife. He did, in fact, seem to know an awful lot of gossip about some very rich people, which came in handy on the show. But I never quite treated his worldly wisdom as genuine. I don't know why, but Quentin never really impressed me as a truth-teller. Even his lies were lies. Anyway, to pick up the saga again, Quentin made his way to Hollywood on the stomach of a well-known actress. Or was it on the back of a rich Broadway producer? Or on the petticoat of the Broadway producer's wife? In rare instances, it was on the merits of a screenplay he had written about an actress, a Broadway producer, and the producer's wife. Quentin was a great one for threesomes. The screenplay, which I've seen by the way, was a transparent version of A Double Life, and it was never optioned or produced. In spite of this paradox, Quentin's fortunes were on the rise. He was soon writing scripts for TV serials. It was tough making do on a couple hundred grand—he actually said that to me once—but he kept at it, hoping for a break. And two years ago, the break came in the person of Helen Rose, who hired the great bag of wind as head writer on 'Phoenix.'

"And that," Jack said, downing the rest of the martini, "is the true story of Quentin Dover."

"You wouldn't happen to have a picture of the prodigy on you? I haven't seen his face, yet."

"I think I might."

I thought he was kidding, but Jack dug into his wallet and pulled out a snapshot of a lean, fleshless, vaguely reptilian-looking man. He had thick, black, shiny hair, combed straight back from the forehead without a part, sunken cheeks, a hawklike nose, a pencil moustache, pointed chin, tiny mouth, and the dark, elliptical, heavy-lidded eyes of a lizard. The photograph was inscribed, "To Jack—All the Best."

47

"He was a real looker, wasn't he?" I said.

"A dead ringer for Nosferatu."

"How come you kept the photograph?" I said, handing it back to him.

"That kind of ugly is rare," he said and tucked the snapshot back in his wallet. "It goes right through to the bone. And believe me—the picture doesn't do him justice. He was much worse in the flesh, although a lot of people—including Helen—wouldn't agree. Women seemed to find him attractive. He had the sort of ugly face that's almost as striking as a real beauty."

"If you say so," I said.

"Well, look at Marsha, for instance."

He had a point, though Marsha hadn't struck me as a particularly discerning judge of anything.

"He looked a lot older than thirty-eight," I said.

"His heart did that to him. He used to be kind of pudgy before his attack. After that, he could barely look at food. And then all the booze dried him out pretty good and killed his appetite, to boot."

"For a sick man and a hypochondriac, he had some bad habits."

"Yep," Jack said. "He picked his vices foolishly. But then most of us do. He'd rationalize the booze by saying that it raised his HDL cholesterol and stimulated his circulatory system. As for the sleeping pills and tranquilizers and Demerol . . . well, I guess he found some quack who was not only willing to prescribe them but to recommend their abuse. He always had his reasons, although I don't think he really believed in them. He was scared—that was the real reason."

"Scared of what?"

"Dying. Failing. Succeeding. Take your pick. Different people will give you different answers."

"I'm asking you, Jack," I said.

He pulled the swizzle stick out of his martini glass. It was a piece of plastic shaped like a cutlass, with a lemon rind impaled on its tip. "He didn't have any guts, Harry. I told you that. He didn't have anything inside. He was all sham and bluster. And he was in a business that depends entirely on personality—on the show of complete and unassailable self-confidence. Hell, nobody knows what show is really going to sell more soap. It's all a guessing game. And the man who makes the most dough is the man who can convince everyone else that he's the best guesser. Quentin had Frank and Helen convinced, but he couldn't fool himself. Jeez-Marie's, man, there was half a million bucks riding on Quentin's ability to fine tune his nervous system. Maybe a quarter million more come contract time. That's a helluva load. You asked me what he was afraid of. I think he was afraid that somebody would find out that he was running scared." Jack pulled the lemon rind off the sword and dropped it into an ashtray. "And now that we've hired you, maybe somebody will."

8

Halfway through his second martini, Jack got an attack of the munchies and ordered a plate of shrimps. They didn't go particularly well with my Scotch, but I ate a few anyway, just to put something in my stomach. I really had been feeling addlepated after the plane ride; and it was half-past seven, Cincinnati time, so the jet lag was creeping up on me, too. Neither the plane ride nor the jet lag seemed to bother Jack Moon. He ate and drank and chatted amusingly about Liz and Nick. We were just finishing the last of the shrimps when a tall, tan, strikingly handsome man in a silk safari shirt and khaki shorts walked into the bar.

I took a look at him and said, "Is that someone I should know?"

"They all look like movie stars out here, Harry," Jack said, biting the head off a shrimp. "He probably hops cars at the Brown Derby."

The guy said something to the bartender and when the bartender shrugged, the man turned to face the room, parked his elbows on the bar rail, and said, "Harry Stoner?" in a very loud, very deep voice. Everyone in the place looked up.

Jack dropped the tail of his shrimp on the plate. "I guess

he *is* somebody you should know. That must be Goldblum."

"Good Lord," I said. "Is he your idea of confidential?"

Jack laughed. He stood up and waved an arm at the
man. "Over here, Sy."

Sy Goldblum pointed a forefinger at us and came strid-
ing over to the table. He was a large man—about six two,
heavily muscled on his arms and legs. His physique was
the only thing about him that reminded me of a cop, and
even that was too good for a guy who spends most of his
time sitting in a patrol car or behind a desk. The rest of
him was pure Hollywood—thick razor-cut brown hair,
blue blue eyes, a neatly trimmed moustache precisely one
shade lighter than his sideburns, a half dozen gold chains
around his neck, and a couple of diamond pinkie rings
sputtering like neon on his manicured fingers. He'd left
the top four buttons of his safari shirt open—to give everyone a good look at his hairy pecs.

"You must be Stoner," he boomed, as he pulled up a
chair. "Sy Goldblum."

I nodded at him.

"And you're Moon?" he said, glancing at Jack.

"Yeah." Jack gave me a quick look. "If you want me to
leave, Harry . . ."

"I guess that's up to Sy."

"No problem," Goldblum barked. "I could use a beer,
though. Just got back from Chavez Ravine and I'm all
dried out."

"I'll get you one," Jack said and walked over to the
bar.

"Is he standing in a trench?" Goldblum said, staring at
Jack. "Little men are a pain in the ass. Always trying to
make up for being short."

"That right?" I said. "You were on special duty at the
stadium?"

Goldblum laughed loudly. He wasn't completely dried-
out, because his breath smelled like a bottle of Pabst with

a cigarette butt floating on the bottom. "Hell, no. I went to the game."

"How'd they do?"

"How d'you think?" he said with a grin. "The Dodgers can't be beat. They're too good. Won a few bucks on 'em, too."

"That's great."

Goldblum wrapped an arm around his chair and leaned back lazily. "So you're from Cincinnati, huh?"

"That's where I'm from."

"What a joke town. I spent a couple of weeks there one afternoon. It was the pits. Couldn't wait to get back here and catch a few rays."

"You from L.A.?"

"Nobody's *from* L.A., man," Goldblum said. "I'm from Butte, Montana. Came out here seven years ago, after a hitch in the Marines. Tried to break into the movies. Did some stunt work. Had a few bit parts. Maybe you saw me? I was in a couple of 'Happy Days' and one 'Barney Miller.' "

"I don't own a TV."

Goldblum gawked at me as if I were from another planet. "Now *that* is weird. You know about TV, don't you? A little box with a screen? Shows pictures that talk?" He clapped me hard on the arm. "Just kidding, Harry. Maybe they haven't got TV in Cincinnati, yet. You look for it in the papers."

"What happened to your acting career?" I asked.

"Aw, it went right in the toilet. Nowheresville. I got an agent. Changed my name. Took an ad out in *Variety*. Nothing worked."

"What did you change it to? Your name?"

Goldblum looked abashed. "To Sy Goldblum," he said. I laughed.

"Yeah, I know," he said miserably. "But there are a lot of Jews in the business. No offense."

"I'm not Jewish."

52

"Good," he said. "I thought a kike name might help. Now I'm stuck with it."

"Why don't you change it back to what it was before?"

"To Seymour Wattle? No, thank you. Besides, having a kike name doesn't hurt in this town, if you know what I mean. Your pal, Moon, isn't a hebe, is he?"

"No, he's a wop."

"Good," Seymour said. "I get along good with wops."

Jack came back to the table with Seymour's beer. Seymour snatched the bottle out of Jack's hand and patted the chair beside him. "Have a seat, Shorty."

Jack grunted and sat down. "Well, did I miss anything?"

"Only the story of Seymour's life," I said.

"Hey!" Wattle said, giving me an angry look. "Don't call me that. I'm Sy Goldblum, now."

"Sorry."

Wattle drained the beer in one gulp. A couple of drops leaked onto his shirt. When he noticed them, his face reddened. "Shit, this thing cost me seventy-five bucks on Rodeo Drive. It's pure silk. Some dago design." He glanced at Jack and said, "No offense."

Jack said, "None taken."

"Shall we get down to business, Sy?" I said.

Wattle nodded. "You want to know about Dover, right?"

"Right the first time."

"Well, I'll tell you," he said, leaning forward and cribbing the empty beer bottle in his hands. "I don't have much. The guy was found dead on Monday by a maid in the Belle Vista. Some Mex cunt. As near as we can guess, he'd been dead since early Sunday morning—maybe thirty-six, forty hours. I wasn't in on the investigation, but I've seen the lab photos and the boy was a real mess. He'd apparently been taking a shower and lost his balance and fell right through the glass curtain.

"Broken glass is the worst," Wattle said, peeling the label off the beer bottle with his thumbnail. "Give me a shotgun any day. Shit, the guy was sliced to ribbons. Belly open, guts hanging out. One eye dangling on his cheek. Even his pecker—"

"That's enough!" Jack said in a commanding voice. Then he ducked his head in embarrassment. "I'm sorry. I knew the man, that's all."

"Well, you wouldn't have recognized him anymore," Wattle said. "What wasn't cut up or off was scalded by the shower water or half-eaten by maggots."

Moon's face turned white.

"I think we can skip the clinical details," I said to Wattle, who was enjoying Jack's reaction.

Wattle laughed. "O.K. by me."

"You all right?" I said to Jack.

He nodded weakly.

"What caused the fall?" I asked the cop.

"We don't know. Could have been he lost his balance and slipped in the tub. The guy had a heart, so it might have been that. He was also a juicer, so it could have been any number of things."

Since I was looking for a scandal, I said, "Could he have OD'd?"

"We couldn't find any tracks on his arms, but that's not the only place you can shoot up and the rest of him was too messy to tell. If he was stoned, it probably wasn't on H."

"How about blow?"

"It's possible," Wattle said. "But that wouldn't change anything. Whether he was stoned or drunk or sober, he still slipped and fell."

"What about the rest of the room? Was there any indication that somebody had been there with him, before or after?"

Wattle shook his head. "He was alone. His suitcase was open on the bed."

"As if he were packing?"

"Or unpacking," Wattle said.

54

"How come the maid didn't come into the room before Monday morning?"

"Dover left a message at the desk on Friday when he checked in that he didn't want any maid service or phone calls until he said different. Since he was a regular at the Belle Vista, they went along with it. The only reason the Mex maid went into the room on Monday was because somebody complained to the management about the stink."

"Did he say why he didn't want any calls?"

"Nope. Just wanted to be alone, I guess."

I turned to Jack. "You buy that?"

He looked at me uncertainly. "I don't know. It's possible."

"You don't have any idea what Dover was doing between Friday night and Sunday morning, do you?" I asked Wattle.

He shook his head again. "The desk clerk checked him in on Friday at five-thirty P.M. Dover had dinner in his room. Left the tray outside his door. Then went for a drive in a rented car. He must have come back after twelve, because the kid who works the Belle Vista lot had already taken off for the night. The night clerk claims she didn't see him come back in. But she was on break between twelve-thirty and twelve-forty-five. Anyway, the car was parked in the lot on Saturday and stayed there all day. It was in the lot on Sunday, too. And on Monday, when the body was found."

"Did you check the odometer?"

"Yep. Nothing special. Sixty miles."

"Did anybody see him on Saturday?"

"Nope. But then nobody was looking for him, either. He didn't eat in the hotel, so it's probable that he went out. But we have no idea where or whether someone was with him. All we know is that he didn't take the rental car."

"How about phone calls?"

"He made a few local ones on Friday night. And one long distance one to Cincinnati."

"That would have been to his mother," I said.

I stared at the half-eaten shrimp on Jack's plate.

"What's the matter, Harry?" Moon said.

"There isn't very much to go on, Jack."

"It was an accident," Wattle said. "That's what I've been telling you."

9

Before Wattle left, he turned to Jack and said, "You footin' the bill?"

"For what?" Jack said.

Wattle tilted his head and gave Moon a long, hard look. "For what do you think, Shorty?"

Jack paled. "I thought this had all been arranged."

Wattle shook his head. "You're not going to try to stiff me, are you? Man, I'd hate it if you tried that."

Jack glanced at me and I said, "Pay the man."

"How much?" he said to Wattle.

"A hundred ought to cover it. If you want more, it'll cost more. And in cash. I don't take Visa."

"I don't know if I have that much on me."

Wattle sighed heavily and patted Moon on the wrist. "C'mon, Shorty. Don't make me mad. It just isn't worth it."

"Take it easy," I said to Wattle. "I'll pay the bill."

Wattle lifted his hand from Jack's wrist. I got a hundred out of my wallet and handed it to him. He folded the money up with one hand and tucked it in his shirt pocket.

"There," he said with a tight little smile. "Didn't hurt a bit. No hard feelings?"

"None," I said.

He looked at Jack. "No hard feelings, big guy?"

Jack managed to force out a "No."

"That's just swell," Seymour Wattle said. "I like doing business with people who like me." He got up, patted his shirt pocket, and gave us a Boy Scout salute. "See you around, fellas."

He strode out of the bar. Jack watched him with hatred.

"Forget it, Jack," I said to him.

"Fucking asshole," he said.

"He's just a jerk cop."

"Yeah?" Moon's face had turned red. "I guess you think I should have socked him."

"I think you should have paid him a hundred dollars."

"He's the kind of guy you're used to dealing with, isn't he?" Moon said.

"Do you mean, he's my kind of guy, Jack?"

"I don't know what I meant." He rubbed his red cheeks with both hands. "I'm sorry I said that. I should have said something to him."

"Look, this is his bar on his street in his town. The way he sees it, he's got squatter's rights." I got tired of my own explanation halfway through it. "Let's forget it, O.K.?"

"Yeah," Moon said without conviction. "It was just the way he talked about Quentin's body—the pleasure he got out of it." Jack stood up. "We better get going. Helen's expecting us at the Belle Vista at seven-thirty."

We walked out to the street. "I'll get you that one hundred dollars in the morning," Jack said. "I'll cash a check at the desk."

Although I was getting tired of his indignation, I said, "All right."

The doorman hailed a cab for us. Jack told the cabbie, "The Belle Vista." And he didn't say another word on the way over.

By the time we pulled up in front of the hotel, Jack had grown up again.

58

"Why'd you call him Seymour?" he asked me, as we stepped out of the cab.

I told him the story of Seymour's career in movies and he laughed.

"Christ, that's typical. I wonder how many lives people run through before they end up in this city? Three, four? It's like Hindu hell. If you can't make it in Butte or Des Moines, you live your next life waiting for a casting call in Studio City. And when the karma dries up, you're reborn as a cop or a parking lot attendant in Westwood." He turned to the doorman—a handsome Chicano kid in livery, standing in front of a long, canopied bridge. "You want to be in movies, don't you?"

The kid smiled. "You bet."

Jack smiled back at him. "Well, I guess we all do," he said. "After all, I wasn't born to be the executive producer of 'Phoenix.' It's guys like Frank Glendora who have the luck. They want one thing and they get it. The rest of us keep riding the wheel."

Moon tipped the kid a quarter and we walked across the bridge, over a gully of flowers, and through a pair of French doors into the hotel lobby. The lobby was nothing more than a short breezeway with a second pair of French doors propped open on the far side of the room. A prim woman in a floral print dress was sitting at a desk beside the second pair of doors. She stood up when we came in.

"Can I help you?" she said pleasantly.

"We're here to see Helen Rose," Jack said. "Tell her it's Jack Moon."

"I'll ring her room."

While the woman was phoning Helen Rose, I walked over to the second pair of doors and took a peek at the hotel grounds. There was a small cobbled court behind the lobby, with long buildings surrounding it on three sides. The buildings were in the Monterey Revival style—stucco, lath, and concrete, with low, hipped roofs of red clay tiles and wrought-iron trim on the doors and windows. Stone walkways angled off the court, running past the spare white buildings and back into the grounds. The walks were narrow, tree-lined, and heavily ornamented with shrubs and flowers. The place had the look of a private garden. And the smell of a garden, too. The mixed fragrances of the flowers were like a taste on the tongue—a sweet, thick, maraschino flavor of oleander, jacaranda, and bougainvillea.

"It's pretty, isn't it?" Jack said over my shoulder.

"Yes."

"It's like a conservatory out there. They even have name tags on the trees and flowers."

"Mr. Moon?" the woman at the desk called out.

Jack and I turned around.

"Miss Rose would like to talk to you. You can take it on the phone in the corner."

Jack walked over to the corner booth and I went up to the desk. The woman smiled at me. She had a pretty, slightly aloof-looking face that fit beautifully into that pretty, exclusive garden spot.

"Do you like our hotel?" she said.

"It's lovely."

"Yes," she said with pride. "It affords our guests a measure of privacy that's unusual in this city. I mean, of course, outside of a private residence in Bel Air."

"You must meet a lot of famous people."

"A few," she said mildly, as if she weren't interested in pursuing the topic.

"Where do all the paths lead?"

"To different quarters. We have a number of separate accommodations, tailored to the needs of our guests."

"I suppose you could get lost out there."

"Not really. There are signs and, of course, the grounds are walled. So you couldn't go too far wrong."

"Are there any other entrances?" I asked. "I mean, other than the lobby?"

The woman gave me an odd look. I was beginning to sound like a detective. I could hear it myself.

"There are no other entrances, although there are locked gates in the walls."

"I'll have to take a stroll."

"By all means," she said without enthusiasm.

Jack came back to the desk and touched me on the arm. "Excuse us, won't you?" he said to the woman.

She said, "Certainly."

Jack pulled me aside. "Helen is in one of her moods. Things didn't go well today with Walt—the little prick. He's angling for Quentin's job. And when Walt angles, he does it with a meathook. And then the taping got fouled up this afternoon—some flap over one of the scripts."

"Does that mean dinner is off?"

"What that means," Jack said, "is that we're in for another bumpy flight. Helen is really a very sweet person. But she's got a tough job and she cares very deeply about the show. Too deeply for her own good. When things go wrong . . . it gets to her. And between Walt, Quentin, and the flap on the set, a lot has gone wrong this week. Plus she's got to meet with Walt again tomorrow morning and with the network and agency people in the afternoon. Between you and me, the show has been slipping in the ratings lately, and we're all a little afraid that we may not make it through next spring."

"You mean you might get canceled?" I said.

"Or re-slotted." Jack gave me a nervous look. "This really isn't for public consumption, Harry. I'd appreciate it if you'd keep it to yourself."

I was surprised that Jack had kept it to himself for so long. It seemed like the sort of thing I should have been told. "Could that have been why Quentin was thinking about another show—the fact that 'Phoenix' was in ratings trouble?"

Jack shook his head. "I think that's a red herring, Harry.

61

There's nothing in the world in smaller demand than the services of the head writer of a canceled soap. If the show died, Quentin died with it."

"Perhaps he was planning to get out before the ax fell."

"And kiss goodbye to half a mil? Be serious. Besides, Quentin was contractually obliged to stay on the show until the end of this thirteen-week cycle. And believe me, United has no sense of humor when it comes to contracts."

I thought of the one I'd signed and sighed. "Maybe his mother was wrong, but there had to be some reason why he came out here on Friday afternoon instead of on Sunday night, like he usually did."

"Well, I don't know the reason, but I seriously doubt if it was another show. Maybe you should talk to Quentin's agent, Harris Sugarman. Or maybe Helen can help you. His trip could have had something to do with 'Phoenix.' "

"Let's go talk to Helen, then."

"O.K.," Jack said ruefully. "But remember, I warned you that she's in a bad mood."

"You warned me once before about Marsha Dover. Am I in for another suicide attempt?"

"Helen's a good Catholic. She might take a life, but she'd never take her own."

"That's promising," I said.

We walked through the French doors onto the court, then turned left down a path lined with palo verdes and jacaranda. The path took us behind several buildings and ended in another court of grass and blue wildflowers. There was a small stone pavilion in the middle of the lawn, with a bowl-shaped fountain sitting on a pedestal in its center. It reminded me a little of Dover's topiary garden, with its statue of Cupid. At the far end of the court, a serpentine wall—twelve feet high and dripping English ivy—ran from one side of the grounds to the other. Huge oak trees towered up behind it, casting long, leafy shadows on the pavilion and its fountain. Something moved

62

against the wall, picking up a piece of the fading sunlight and tossing it brightly in the air. I went over to the wall and looked.

It was a hummingbird—no larger than a butterfly—hanging above a bell-shaped flower. It darted away as I came close to it, disappearing through an iron gate set in the wall. Through the gate, I could see a street and several cars parked in the shade of the oaks. I rattled the gate, but it had been locked with a key.

"C'mon, Harry," Jack said. "Helen's waiting."

We walked south beside the wall to the corner of the court. A stucco building ran the length of the eastern edge of the pavilion. If it weren't for the number of doors and windows set in its facade, the building wouldn't have looked anything like a hotel. Jack went up to one of the doors and knocked.

"Just a goddamn minute!" someone inside hollered.

Jack smiled at me. "Fasten your seat belt," he said.

10

A few minutes passed, then a small, skinny woman in a yellow poncho and black, ankle-length skirt opened the door. Her hair was as thick, curly, and colorless as a Kewpie doll's, and like a Kewpie doll's it was massed in girlish bangs above a lean, hollow-cheeked face. There was nothing doll-like about the woman's eyes, however. They were brown and bloodshot and circled with dark, wrinkled flesh. The combination of that little-girl hairdo and those bruised eyes gave Helen Rose the weepy, suffering, mortified look of an abused child.

"Oh, Jack, honey," she said in a pained, husky voice. "I'm sorry for shouting like that. But I've had Walt here all day long, and I just don't know what to do anymore."

"You're going to sit down and have a drink," Jack said, taking charge. "And then you're going to have something to eat."

The woman smiled at him affectionately. "Baby, what would I do without you?"

Jack walked into the room, picked up the phone, and ordered two double martinis. "Scotch for you, Harry?"

"That'll be fine," I said.

"And send us some menus," Jack said into the phone.

64

"Who's your attractive friend?" Helen Rose said, giving me a look.

"Harry Stoner." I held out a hand.

"Helen Rose."

We shook hands.

"You're the detective, aren't you? I don't think I've ever seen a detective before, unless one of my ex-husbands had me tailed by one. As they used to say in the movies, you've got an interesting face." She turned to Jack and said, "Hasn't he got an interesting face?"

Jack grinned.

The woman turned back to me with a playful smile. She had very white, very even teeth; and her smile made her look years younger. "You'd make a good heavy. Wouldn't he, Jack?"

Jack laughed. "I don't know about that."

"Don't be disagreeable," the woman said. "I say he'd make a good heavy, and I'm always right. Aren't I?"

"Always," Jack said.

She winked at me and walked over to one of a pair of white sofas set in front of a tile fireplace. A log was burning on the andirons, filling the room with a warm, cedary smell. It was a big room, decorated in shades of white and pink.

"You have no idea what I've been through today," Helen Rose said to Jack. "Jesus, Mary, and Joseph, give me strength. Do you know what our friend told me? Or should I say demanded?"

"What?" Jack said irritably.

"He told me that he was going to quit and take the rest of the team with him, unless we gave him Quentin's job."

"He's bluffing," Jack said.

The woman flapped one of her hands equivocally. "Maybe. Maybe not. You never know with a *fegalah*.

"Never fuck a fag, Harry," she said, looking up at me.

"I don't intend to."

She laughed abruptly. "Christ, what a mess! Maybe he's bluffing. Who knows? He says he's been carrying Quentin for the past two years, and now he wants to get paid for it."

"He probably has been," Jack said.

"That's beside the point," Helen Rose said. "And he knows it and you know it and so do I. He's got us over a barrel, Jack." She looked up at the high, beamed ceiling. "Quentin, damn you, why did you do this to me? Why did you leave me like this? Just when I needed you?" She shook her head and looked down at the plush, white carpet. "That's not fair. I'm sorry, Quentin. I'm sorry that you're dead."

"Did you go to Mass this morning?" Jack asked.

"At nine. I lit a candle for him." Helen Rose sighed. "Oh, well. I guess we'll just have to give Walt what he wants."

"Helen, he's not the only fish in the sea."

"Then *you* deal with him," she snapped. "In case you've forgotten, Jack, I've got the network coming in tomorrow. We pulled a thirteen last week. A thirteen! What am I supposed to say to Sally Jackson? 'Sorry, dear, but we don't have long-term to show you? Or a team to write one?' My God, she'd pull the plug as she left the room. This is the tenth week we've been below a seventeen. What am I supposed to do? *You* tell me."

"The brands are standing firm," Jack said.

The woman grunted. "Yeah, sure. For the next thirteen weeks. And then what?"

"It's blackmail, Helen," Jack said angrily.

"Oh, wake up, Jack!" she said with disgust. "He's chief breakdown man. And the subwriters are a bunch of sheep. They probably will bolt, if Walt tells them to. Hell, what do they have to lose? We've got a thirteen share! Right now, he's all we've got. And furthermore, he's got the long-term document."

"Quentin said that he and Walt were working on the document together."

66

"I remember," she said. "And Walt spent the entire afternoon telling me a different story. You know what? I believe him. And so do you, Jack. You just said so a minute ago. So let's not have any more talk about blackmail, sweetie. Or about who wrote what for whom. Let's just get on with it, O.K.?"

The woman turned her head to me. "It's been a bad day for 'Phoenix,' Harry. A bad day for all of us. I'm sorry for the shop talk."

"That's all right," I said. I'd found the little of it that I'd understood interesting.

"Have you seen the show?" she said pleasantly.

"No."

Her face fell. "He doesn't like the show, Jack," she said. "I can tell from his voice—he doesn't like the show."

"Helen," Jack said long-sufferingly.

"What is it? The writing? I'll admit that the writing hasn't been up to par lately, but that was Quentin's fault—damn him. Is it the production? We've got a new line producer, and she just doesn't know how to block a scene properly. Did you see all those isos today, Jack? Not one two-shot in the lot. Christ, how is the audience going to get involved, if they can't see that the characters are involved? Walt went on for an hour about it. And he's right. He's absolutely right. She's got to go, Jack. Is that what it is, Harry? Is it the production values?"

She sounded so earnest that I was almost afraid to tell her the truth. "I don't own a TV."

"Oh," Helen Rose said. Then she started to laugh in a loud, gutty voice. "That's different."

The waiter came with our drinks. Jack organized the dinner orders, then the three of us sat down on the white couches.

"Just what is it you're looking for?" Helen said, taking a sip of her martini.

"I'm not sure," I told her. "I think I'm supposed to be looking for a scandal."

She snorted with amusement. "Well, baby, you've certainly come to the right place. We not only produce soap operas, we live them. Isn't that right, Jack?"

"Some of us do," Jack said.

"Don't be such an old woman," Helen chided him. "Harry looks all grown up. You're all grown up, aren't you?"

"Yep."

"So how can I help you with your scandals?" she said with faint suggestiveness.

"You can tell me about Quentin Dover, since he was apparently the guilty party."

"Guilty of what?" Helen said. "We're all guilty of something, you know. What did Frank Glendora tell you that Quentin was guilty of?"

"Of not comporting himself the way a man should. I believe that was the way he put it. He'd heard rumors."

Helen raised an eyebrow and Jack nodded at her. "What a schmuck that Walt is," she said. "Christ, Quentin's only been dead for four days and he's already taken a shovel to his headstone."

"So you think Walt is the one who's been spreading the gossip?" I said.

"Who else? It's his specialty. That and fist-fucking." She covered her mouth with her right hand. "Oops! Did I say that?"

"I'm afraid you did," Jack said dully.

"It's this martini—it's too damn dry. Well, Mr. Detective, Frank Glendora would believe that Jesus Christ Himself was a whoremonger, if Jesus Christ happened to get on the wrong side of the United American Corporation. He's a goddamn Sadducee, that's what Frank is."

"Helen," Jack said in warning.

"Oh, shut up, Jack. You know it as well as I do. Frank is a genteel, well-educated thug. Which is not to say that Quentin didn't have his little faults."

"Such as?"

68

The woman looked at me crossly. "Have you been listening to me or what? I'm not about to spread shit all over Quentin's grave, no matter what Glendora says. I happened to have liked the man."

"Then it seems to me that you ought to tell me what you know about him, because all I've heard so far has been negative."

"Oh, it has, has it?" Helen gave Jack a bitter look. "Settling a few scores, are we, Jack, honey?"

Moon ducked his head in embarrassment. "I just told him the truth."

"How could you tell, Jack? You're so bought and sold yourself."

Moon turned beet red. For a brief moment I thought he was going to strike the woman. The moment passed and he sat back silently on the couch.

Helen Rose looked at him and frowned. "I shouldn't have said that. I'm sorry. You're a saint, Jack. You know how I get."

"I know," he said.

"I'm just a bitch, Harry. A worn-out bitch, and you happened to catch me at the wrong time." Her eyes got a little moist. "Forgive me, Jack?"

"Consider it forgiven."

She wiped at the tears, but they'd dried up on their own. "Maybe I should tell you about Quentin, after all. It'll be my good deed for the day."

"I'm listening," I said.

"I'll bet you are. Little pitchers have big ears. And so do big pitchers."

"I'm not spying for Frank, Helen," I said. "I told you exactly what I wanted to know."

She nodded. "If you spend enough time in this business, you get a mite suspicious, Harry. Just a mite. That was one of Quentin's virtues. He was among the few people that I've known in this industry who was never deliberately cruel. He didn't always tell the truth," she said with a small smile. "But he was always gracious. Such manners! Such policy! He was Ronald Coleman, for chrissake. A gentleman to his toes."

Jack snorted with laughter and Helen threw a hand at him. "What would you know—you're a man."

"A few minutes ago you were calling him a liar," Jack said.

"I was angry," she said and shrugged. "All right, sure, he was a liar. But such wonderful lies! The places he'd been, the people he'd known!"

"Or pretended to have known," Jack said.

"You're missing the point," the woman said. "Of course he was a fake. In this business, that goes without saying. You're just too damn idealistic, Jack. That's your whole problem. You keep thinking you're going to turn a corner and find . . . I don't know, justice or something. That's not the way it works out here. Under the tinsel is the real tinsel and under that are the lies."

"And dollars," Jack said.

"Sure, and dollars. What are you in it for? The laughs? Quentin was one of the most gracious men I've ever met. There was an innocence about him."

Jack snorted again.

"All right, call it a corruption. What do I care? But there was something there—something that didn't change."

"I'd call it greed," Jack said.

"Sure, that was part of it. But what was he greedy for?"

"For money. What else?"

"You see," she said. "You don't know what you're talking about."

"All right, then, what *was* he greedy for?"

"For the life he was pretending to lead."

"Bullshit!" Moon said.

"Of course it was bullshit!" Helen Rose said. "It's all bullshit, Jack. I keep telling you that. You and Quentin were more alike than you think. You see, I've accepted it—that it's bullshit. All I've got is the show—no family, no real friends. Just the show. And when it goes, I'll go. Bang!" She snapped her fingers loudly.

Both Moon and I jumped.

"Jesus, Helen," Jack said. "Don't talk like that."

"You're hopeless, Jack," she said wearily. "But you're hopeless in a different way than Quentin was. That's why he was charming and you're just diffident and kind. He was a romantic, for chrissake. He didn't believe in his lies—he was obsessed by them! See, there's the difference. You're not obsessed, Jack. You're not driven. You don't know what it's like to be that hungry. Quentin did."

"We've all been hungry, Helen," Jack said stiffly.

"Not like Quentin," she said. "He told stories, all right. Especially after his heart attack. But whether they were true or not, he wanted them to be. He *needed* them to be. That was his weakness and his charm. There was a great well of loneliness inside that man that all the money in the world could never fill. I consider it quite a triumph that someone that unhappy could carry on with such style. And his stories were part of that style—a way of bridging the gap between what he knew he was and what he always wanted to be."

"And what was that?" Moon said sullenly. "What he always wanted to be?"

"Why a star, Jack," Helen said, cupping her face in her hands. "Isn't that what we all want to be?"

11

The waiter came with the food, which he set up in the living room on a folding table. Between courses, I asked Helen Rose if she knew why Dover had come out to L.A. on Friday rather than on Sunday.

She said, "No. It wasn't for 'Phoenix,' though. I can tell you that much. We were in New York over the weekend—Frank, Jack, and I—meeting with those wonderful brands folks."

"You were in New York last weekend?" I asked Jack.

"On Friday and Saturday. Frank and I went back to Cincinnati on Saturday afternoon."

"Ooh! Are we suspects?" Helen said. She'd put away an entire bottle of California's best over dinner, and she was showing it.

"I don't have anything to be suspicious about," I said honestly. "Dover told his mother that he was coming out here to meet with some people about a new project. I thought you might know what it was."

Helen Rose's face darkened as if a cloud had just floated overhead. "A TV project?" she said.

Jack waved his hands at me behind her back. But I ignored his warning. "That's what she thought."

"That son-of-a-bitch!" Helen said and threw her fork

72

down so forcefully that she cracked the plate.

"Oh, Christ," Jack said under his breath.

"That little worm! That fucking little traitor! We're in trouble because he couldn't come up with a goddamn story line and he's getting ready to jump ship! There's gratitude for you." Helen whirled around in her chair to face Moon. "Did you know about this, you bearded little bastard?"

"Now, Helen," he said throwing up both hands in defense.

"Don't 'Now, Helen' me, you weasel! You knew about this, didn't you?"

"I did not," Jack said. "Furthermore, I think the whole thing was one of Quentin's fabrications."

"You would," Helen said furiously. She turned back to me. "What exactly did Quentin's mother say?"

"That she had lunch with Quentin on Friday afternoon and that he mentioned a new project. Quentin didn't say whether it was for television or not. That was just his mother's guess."

"Well, I've met the bitch, and she was a damn good guesser when it came to Quentin." She pointed a finger at Moon and jabbed him with it—hard—in the belly. "I want you to find out about this, you hear me, Jack? I won't tolerate this sort of thing from my staff. You hear me?"

Moon leaned forward and stared her in the face. "The man is dead," he said between clenched teeth. "What the fuck difference does it make?"

"It makes a difference to me," Helen said. But she seemed shocked by Jack's tone of voice; and when she spoke again, her own voice sounded thick and pained. "I liked him, Jack. Christ, do I have to give that up, too?"

"Nobody made you take this job, Helen," Moon said. "You wanted it—remember?"

"You shouldn't talk to me like that," she said.

Moon leaned back in the chair and made a contrite face. "You're right. I'm just sick of Quentin Dover. We

73

wouldn't be in this mess, if it weren't for him."

I hadn't wanted to get involved in their 'Phoenix' problems. After signing that contract, I figured the less I knew about United's secrets the better. But it was beginning to look like I didn't have a choice. It was also beginning to look like there was a great deal about Quentin Dover that I hadn't been told.

"Perhaps you'd better fill me in on this," I said to Jack.

"Let Helen tell you," he said morosely. "I haven't got the stomach."

"Helen?" I said.

"What's to tell?" she said hollowly. "He dried up. For one year and six months he was a rock. He never had an excuse. He never needed one. He got the job done."

"Or Walt did," Jack said.

"What difference does it make? We had a long-arc story line, meaty breakdowns, and good scripts. Whether Quentin was writing the long-terms or supervising their writing or just finessing them, they were coming in on schedule. Six months ago, it all stopped."

"Why?"

She laughed unhappily. "Do you think if I knew why I wouldn't have done something about it?"

"Well, what did Quentin say?"

"What writers always say when they dry up. That he didn't believe in the story. That the breakdown people weren't cooperating. That the conferences weren't helpful or specific enough. He always had an answer."

"The truth was that he was all squeezed out," Jack said. "And he knew it. There just wasn't any more toothpaste in the tube."

"Christ, that's callous," Helen said. "It was a lot more complicated than that. He had open heart surgery six months ago, and when he came back he just didn't have the same resources of energy."

"You mean he'd run out of lies."

"Jack, where do you come off saying things like that?"

74

she said. "What did the man do to you? He thought he was going to die, for chrissake. And that wife of his was throwing fits every day. The whole fabric of his life was coming apart."

"And all he did was smile and procrastinate graciously."

"What would you have had him do? He was used to being in control, and the power was slipping through his fingers."

"And I'm supposed to care about that?" Moon said.

"I don't know what you care about, Jack," she said. "But it's not enough to say that he'd run out of lies or toothpaste."

"You were just furious at him a minute ago!" Moon shouted.

"Oh, grow up." She turned to me. "He was worn down, Harry. And then we pulled a switch on him. He'd written a document before the surgery and we'd accepted it. But goddamn *General Hospital* came out with their 'Ice Princess' story, pulled a 40 share, and suddenly every soap on daytime had to have a fantastic adventure of its own. We had a story conference here in L.A. three months ago, and I laid it on the line to him. He had to come up with a new document."

"Yeah, and he said it would be no problem," Jack said. "That he'd have it done in two weeks."

Helen nodded. "We kept setting deadline after deadline, all the while vamping with material from the old document. By then the ratings had dropped. The network began to complain to United. And United began to complain to me. I hopped on Quentin's back. And now . . . now he's dead."

"Helen," Jack said gently.

She'd begun to cry. Real tears, this time. "I killed him," she said. "I hounded him to his death—the poor, sweet bastard. I made his last months a living hell. Christ, how we fuck with other people's lives."

75

Jack put Helen Rose to bed. I'd wanted to ask her a few more questions, but she'd had it for the night. Frankly, I didn't see how she would possibly make it through the next day—she seemed that raw and depleted.

But when I said something about it to Jack, he didn't seem concerned. "Don't worry about Helen, Harry. She's used to living on the ragged edge. She's a helluva lot tougher and more cagey than she looks. Don't believe for a minute that she meant everything she said tonight about Dover, by the way."

"She was lying about him?" I said.

"Not exactly. She's a schmoozer, not a liar. She believes in what she's saying while she's saying it, but the belief doesn't go very deep or last very long. Look at the way she behaved tonight. One minute she's screaming about how Quentin betrayed her and the next she's crying because he's dead. Her feelings don't make any sense until you remember that she's playing the part of a producer—a man's role. With Helen, you learn to listen through the bullshit—the 'darlings' and the 'babys' and all the melo-dramatic, self-congratulatory scenes. You sift through it and try to figure out what's really bothering her, because that's who she's always talking about. Herself. I mean her real self—the part that she thinks she has to hide. In this case, she's just gone through a hellish three months with a troubled show. So dying has been on her mind a lot. That's what she was really crying about. The show, not Quentin."

I could accept that the woman had been talking about herself most of the time, that the innocence and screwball integrity she'd read into Quentin's life were apologies for the compromises that *she'd* had to make in order to sur-vive in a world where even the cops and the bellboys would do anything to become stars. But I wasn't com-pletely willing to accept, with Jack, that she hadn't meant what she'd said. She'd seen Dover from the top down; Jack had seen him from the bottom up. And she had enjoyed him for putting up the front that disgusted Moon. It made me realize that Jack had had a much tougher time adapting to Quentin Dover's world than he'd wanted me to believe. I'd already seen him have a tough time adapting to Helen Rose.

He must have been thinking about the same things, as we wandered back down the flower-scented paths of the Belle Vista gardens to the lobby. There weren't any lights along the paths, which surprised me a little; it was so dark that I could scarcely see him, even though he was standing beside me.

"Wouldn't you think?" he said softly, "that you could find a job that you actually enjoyed doing? That doesn't seem like much to ask for, does it? Just good, interesting work? And I don't mean something cushy or purposeless. I mean a normal, nine-to-five job that you were suited for, that fit what little talent you had. That doesn't seem like much to ask for, does it?"

"In one way, it doesn't," I said. "In another, it's asking a lot." I thought of what Helen Rose had said about Jack expecting to turn a corner and find justice.

"Frank Glendora's got it," Jack mused. "So does Helen. And so did Quentin Dover. He just changed the rules some and lied his way into a suitable position. He *was* a good liar—I can't take that away from him. And I'm not."

He said it sadly, as if he were pronouncing a sentence of doom on himself.

"Would you like to have a nightcap, Jack?" I asked.

I could see his teeth glimmer in a smile. "Yes. I think I could use one. I've been wondering, though."

"Wondering what?"

"Wondering how you ever became a detective."

I laughed. "I wonder about that, too."

12

It was three-thirty A.M., Cincinnati time, when we got back to the Marquis. Jack was pretty stewed and so was I. But mostly I was tired.

"You're a good guy, Harry," Jack said, clapping me on the back. "A good guy. I used to be a good guy, too, until I joined this goddamn circus."

"Oh, c'mon, Jack," I said. "You're still a good guy, and you know it."

He threw his hand at me. "That's what you think. I'm a rat. A rat in a tinsel maze. And what I don't understand is how come what you do doesn't make a rat out of you. How is that?"

"Let's talk about it tomorrow," I said with a yawn.

"You think it's a flaw in my character? A fatal flaw?" He began to laugh. "You know what the worst sin is?"

"Keeping somebody up past his bedtime?"

"Naw. That's venial. It's sloth, Harry. You know, sloth? Acedia? Going along with it when you know it isn't right? Going along with it because you're too scared not to, because you need the security of a job, of a few measly bucks."

"Then we're all sinners, Jack. And I'm going to sleep."

I left him berating himself in the hotel lobby and took the elevator up to my room. There was an envelope marked "Message" under the door. Frank Glendora had phoned at eight P.M. to check up on me. I was glad I hadn't been there to take the call. I had nothing to report, except that Quentin Dover was still safely dead. I chucked the envelope in a wastebasket, lay down on one of the king-sized beds, and fell asleep.

There was another message envelope on the floor when I woke up at nine the next morning. This one was from Jack Moon, telling me that he'd already gone to the Belle Vista for a meeting with Walt Mack and Helen and that I should join them there for lunch around noon. After what I'd heard about him the night before, I was looking forward to meeting Mack. As far as I was concerned, the Dover case was a subculture freak show and, by all reports, Mack was one of the main attractions. I didn't want to leave Los Angeles without taking him in—it would have been like going to Coney Island and skipping the rollercoaster ride.

I had a crate of California produce for breakfast—Jack hadn't been wrong about that—and after showering and shaving I phoned Harris Sugarman, Quentin's agent. The fact that Dover had come to L.A. two days earlier than usual was just about the only thing I had to go on. And what I'd heard the night before—about Quentin's problems on 'Phoenix'—made it that much more interesting. I got through to Sugarman's secretary and managed to talk her into letting me speak with her boss. The man had a soft, weary, vaguely dissatisfied voice that made him sound as if he'd just got done talking to someone he didn't like.

"What exactly do you want to see me about?" he said after I'd told him who I was and why I was in L.A.

"About Dover," I said.

"And what do you expect me to tell you? That the man was a saint?"

"I have some specific questions."

"Yeah, sure you do," he said grumpily. "All right. I'll have a drink with you. But I'm not doing it for Frank Glendora or for United. I'm doing it for a dead friend."

The way he talked, I had the feeling that most of his friends were dead. I arranged to meet him at the Belle Vista at eleven, then dressed and went down to the Marquis lobby.

Outside it was a bright, cloudless, beautiful August Thursday, without any of the Cincinnati stickiness that turns a summer day into a rite of passage between air conditioners. I caught a cab to the Belle Vista and instead of going straight to the bar, I spent ten minutes walking up Green Canyon Road—the street I'd seen through the gate in the hotel wall. Unless Dover had spent all day Saturday fasting in his room, he must have come out sometime, just to get a bite to eat. I thought, perhaps, he might have slipped out through the gate. But there weren't any restaurants on Green Canyon. It was a residential street, full of tall oak trees and private drives, circling up into the green walls of the canyon. I followed it for about half a mile, and when my ambition gave out, I walked back down to the Belle Vista.

On the way back I stopped at the gate and peered through it into the courtyard. At that time of the morning, the oak trees didn't shade the lawn, and the whole court was drenched in white sunlight. The smell of the flowers drifted through the gate like the aroma of spices from a kitchen cabinet. There wasn't a person in sight—on the street or in the court. And the only sound was the hammering of woodpeckers high in the oaks. The place couldn't have been more deserted if it were in the middle of Montana.

I followed the wall around to the parking lot in front of the hotel. It was a large lot, full of Porsches, BMW's, and several Rolls Corniches. Given all the cars, I was surprised again at how tranquil and unpeopled the place seemed to be. The very rich were also apparently the very demure. The only person in sight was the parking lot attendant—

a slick-looking kid in a white shirt and black pants, who was leaning against one of the struts of the canopy above the bridge. I walked over to him and he straightened up and smiled.

"Can I help you?" he said. He was the same kid whom Jack had tipped the night before—the one who wanted to be in the movies. I thought someday he might make it. He looked a little like a young Dennis Hopper, with a touch of Mexican blood.

"How come it's so quiet?" I asked him.

"House rules," he laughed. "Didn't I see you here last night?"

I nodded. "You've got a good eye for faces."

"What else is there to do?" he said with a shrug. "Except stare at the cars."

"Do you remember a man named Quentin Dover? He was a regular here, I think."

The kid gave me the kind of blank look that I'd learned to read over the last fifteen years. It was like the place on the menu where they say the price varies with the season. I pulled a twenty out of my wallet, and it started to come back to him.

"Sure, I remember him. He was the guy who croaked in 310."

"That's him, all right."

"You a reporter?"

I shook my head. "I'm a P.I."

"No shit," he said. "I thought maybe you were with *The Enquirer*. Sometimes they come around after somebody in show business croaks. They give good bread."

"Were you working here last weekend?" I asked.

"Every weekend," he said. "I don't mind. I see it as an investment in the future. Somebody might spot me, take an interest. You know?"

From the look of him I wasn't sure what kind of interest he meant. I supposed it didn't matter, as long as they gave good bread.

81

"Did you see Dover on the weekend?"

"I saw him here on Friday when he checked in," the kid said. "I got one of the rental cars for him that night."

"He went for a ride?"

"I guess."

"Did he have anything with him when he left? A briefcase or a valise?"

"Nope."

"Did you see him come back?"

"Naw, I checked out eleven-thirty, a quarter of twelve. But the car was back in the lot on Saturday morning when I came in."

"Did you see any more of him that weekend?"

The kid smiled. "Only on Monday, when Maria found the body. I took a couple of snaps, you know?"

"Just in case *The Enquirer* came around?"

He smiled. He was one sweet kid, all right.

"Is Maria working here today?"

"I think so. The cops hassled her some because her work permit expired. But I think the hotel fixed it up." He gave me a speculative look and said, "She's a good piece of ass, Maria."

"Where could I find her?" I heard myself say.

He looked at his watch. "It's ten-fifteen, so she's probably working the south quadrangle. They may be quiet around here, but they don't come any different than you or me. The sheets get just as stiff and sticky."

I guessed that was one way of saying that the rich put their pants on a leg at a time. I gave him the twenty and he slipped it into his shoe.

"You know Maria don't turn tricks while she's on duty," he said, straightening up.

My conscience got the best of me and I said, "That's not why I wanted to see her."

"Sure," he said with a smirk. "Well, if you need anything else, just let me know."

I walked over the bridge to the lobby, where the

prim-looking woman was sitting at the front desk.

"Hello again," she said cheerfully. "Are you here to see Miss Rose?"

"I'm going to meet her for a drink."

"Fine."

"Do you happen to remember what room she's in? I forgot to look last night."

"She's in 302."

"That's the south quadrangle?"

"Yes, sir."

I walked out the French doors into the first courtyard. The building behind it was apparently the Belle Vista's bar and restaurant. It had picture windows set in its stucco facade. Although the glass was heavily tinted, I could see the outlines of a few tables inside.

I followed the same pathway that Jack and I had taken the night before. In the daylight, I could see the signs that Moon had mentioned, identifying the genus and species of the exotic plants and trees. The midday heat made the smell of the flowers almost overpoweringly sweet and just the slightest bit rancid, as if the sun were burning the bougainvillea off their stalks.

I got to the southernmost courtyard and took a look around. Helen Rose's room was in the building on the left. The door was open and I could hear a buzz of conversation coming from inside. There was another stucco building on the right side of the court, with the gated wall running between. I walked up to the right-hand veranda and began peeking into windows. Most of the rooms were unoccupied. There is nothing quite as bleak and uninviting as an empty hotel room—even if it is in the Belle Vista Hotel. I was halfway up the walk when I heard the sound of a vacuum cleaner coming from a nearby door.

I looked inside 307 and saw a black-haired girl in a white uniform bent over a Hoover. She had a Sony Walkman on her head. It must have been playing salsa, because the girl was mamboing to the beat and slapping the nozzle of the vacuum cleaner on the carpet in time to the music. I knocked at the door, and when she didn't look up, I shouted "Hello in there!"

The girl jerked the Walkman off her head and shoved it into the pocket of her dress. Then she patted her thick black hair down, clicked off the vacuum, and turned around. She had black eyes and a high-cheeked, pretty, Indio face.

"Yes?" she said with a "j" instead of a "y." "Can I help you?"

The kid in the lot had been right about one thing—she was a sexy-looking girl. She had round hips and small, pointed breasts that were clearly visible through the thin fabric of her uniform. She gave me a quizzical look and tugged casually at her collar.

"Can I help you," she said again.

"I'd like to talk to you, Maria."

The girl frowned. "How come you know my name? I don' know yours."

"My name is Harry. I got your name from the kid in the parking lot."

"From Jerry, huh?" she said, as if it suddenly made sense to her. She eyed me curiously. "Wha'chu wanna talk about?" she said.

"About what happened here on Monday."

"You a cop?"

"Nope."

"Then wha'chu wanna know about that for?"

"I've got my reasons." I pulled another twenty out of my wallet and held it up to the light. It had worked on Jerry. And this one looked just as wised-up as he had been.

Maria sashayed over to me.

"What's that for?" she said coyly.

"For a little information."

"About Monday, huh?"

She was almost on top of me—so close I could smell her. She smelled interestingly of sweat and flowers. The girl

84

wet her top lip with the tip of her tongue.

"I like to help you, Harry," she said sweetly. "But I got work I gotta do. You know?" Maria's time was apparently valuable—like everyone's in L.A.

I waved the twenty under her nose. "I might be able to dig up a few more of these, for a little cooperation."

"I tol' the cops what I know," she said.

"I'd still like to talk."

She nodded slowly, mulling it over. "Maybe I talk to you," she said after a time. "But it'll cost'chu more than that."

"How much more?"

"I gotta think about it." She pivoted on one foot and eyed the twenty greedily, as if she wanted to eat it for a snack. "I gotta talk to a few people, you know? Check everythin' out."

If she'd just had some trouble with the cops, I could understand her cautiousness, although Jerry the carhop was probably the only person she would check me out with.

"You stayin' at the Belle Vista?" she asked.

"I'm at the Marquis."

"Oh, yeah? That's some nice place, man. Maybe I call you there tonight."

"Ask for Harry Stoner," I said.

She gave me a cagey grin. "Maybe we do more than talk, huh?"

"Maybe," I said.

She plucked the twenty out of my hand and tucked it in her bosom, deliberately giving me a look at her breasts. "Bring some of his brothers, O.K.? We coul' have a party."

Maria stuck the Walkman on her head and strolled back to the vacuum cleaner. She turned the Hoover on with her foot, bent down to lift up the nozzle, and wiggled her ass at me as she stood up.

"Mercy," I said to myself.

85

13

It was somehow reassuring to discover that extortion and sex were alive and well on the south quadrangle of the Belle Vista Hotel. The place had seemed staid unto death, before I met Maria the maid and her pimp, Jerry. I walked back up the flowered pathway, chuckling over my secret, and went into the bar behind the lobby courtyard.

It was dark and relatively empty at eleven in the morning. It was nothing special at any hour of the day—just a leather bar rail with chrome-spouted bottles lined up on mirrored tiers behind it. A large cocktail lounge was built around the bar, with horseshoe-shaped, tufted leather booth seats jutting out from the walls. I sat down at a booth near the door and a waitress came by to take my order.

"Scotch—up," I told her. "I'm expecting somebody at eleven, so if a guy comes in and asks for Harry Stoner, point him in this direction."

"Yes, sir."

The girl brought me a Scotch, and a few minutes later she brought me a paunchy, balding, gray-haired man in a blue pin-striped suit—like second prize in a raffle.

"You Stoner?" he said in a hostile voice. He had a big

walrus moustache that moved instead of his mouth when
he talked.

"I'm Stoner."

"Sugarman," he said abruptly and sat down across from
me. He was wearing huge square glasses with thick bifocal
lenses tinted brown on the tops. His dark eyes and big-
pored cheeks looked squeezed in behind them, reduced
in size by the lenses so that you could see a little bit of the
room on either side of his face.

"I'll take bourbon on the rocks," Harris Sugarman said
to the waitress. "Put it on *his* tab."

"Yes, sir," the girl said.

Sugarman pulled a huge cigar out of his coat pocket and
bit off the end. He picked the cigar tip out of his mouth,
dropped it in a glass ashtray, and wiped a few strands of
loose tobacco from his tongue. "You got until this is half
smoked," he said, lighting the cigar. He puffed on it a few
times, filling the booth with smoke.

"I want to ask you a couple of questions about Quentin."

"It's your dime," he said.

"Did you see him or talk to him this weekend?"

Sugarman chewed on the fat cigar. "Nope."

"Was Quentin working on another project for television?"

He shook his head.

The girl came back with the bourbon. Sugarman swallowed it in one gulp and wiped his mouth with the back
of his hand.

"Is that it?" he asked.

"No. I've got a few more."

"Then, I'll have another one of these," he said to the
waitress.

"Quentin usually came into L.A. on Sunday. Last weekend he came in on Friday afternoon."

"So?" Sugarman said.

"I had a talk with his mother and she thought he was

coming in for a series of conferences about a new TV show."

"She thought wrong."

"Could he have been working with another agent?" I said. "On some special deal?"

Sugarman laughed hoarsely. "No, sonny," he said. "He could not have been working with anyone but Sugarman. Quentin and I go back too far—to the dawn of time."

"That far, huh?"

He flicked the ash off his cigar and studied it like a watch. "You got about ten, twelve more puffs."

"I understand Quentin was having some trouble on 'Phoenix.' "

"Yeah. He was having a few problems. Nothing major."

"That's not what I heard."

Sugarman sighed impatiently. "What did you hear?"

"I heard that he hadn't produced a thing in six months. And that because of him the show was in ratings trouble. I also heard that he didn't write some of his own material, that he got his breakdown man to write it for him."

"You been talking to his enemies," Sugarman said.

"I've been talking to Helen Rose and Jack Moon."

"Let me explain a few things to you." The girl brought him another bourbon and, this time, he took a small sip. "You don't go talking to the producer and executive producer of a soap if you're interested in finding out the truth. Naturally they're going to blame the writer. It's automatic. Like the Army, the game is cover your own ass. And with Helen Rose that goes double. Why? Because she's a woman doing a man's job. She practically had to suck Frank Glendora's dick off to get the job in the first place. United does things by the book. Hell, they wrote the book. And, believe me, there ain't a chapter in it says you hire a washed-up production assistant to run a day-time show. Glendora broke the rules when he gave Helen Rose the job. He knew it and so did she. Now the show is kaput. You wanna figure whose fault it is? Look and see who had the most to lose."

"A half million dollars isn't exactly peanuts," I said.

"Quentin had other irons in the fire. Some real estate. A house in New Mexico. A mansion in Cincinnati. He would have done all right. He was a survivor, baby. Trust me on that."

"You sound like you knew him well."

"Since he was a kid," Sugarman said. He glanced at his cigar. "The meter's running."

"Why do you think he stopped writing six months ago?"

"His health. His wife. He had problems with a couple of investments. Things just piled up on him. It happens. He would have snapped out of it. He had a lot of moxie, Quentin."

"Moon says he was all bluff—that he had nothing left."

"Who the fuck is Jack Moon?" Sugarman said angrily. "How many songs has he written? How many knocks did he take? I've handled Quentin since he was a twenty-two-year-old kid fresh from the sticks. I watched him work his way up from nothing on sheer guts. No experience, no contacts, no looks, no excuses. Just desire, sonny. And if you think that's easy in this town, you're an idiot."

"I thought he had family money."

"You been drinking from a Sterno can? Who you been talking to? I'm telling you the boy had nothing but the shirt on his back. He was one step above a bum."

"Why'd you take him on, then?" I asked.

"He wanted it," Sugarman said. "That's why. There are those who want it and those who don't. I never met a kid who wanted it more. He'd do anything for it. And he did."

"What do you mean by that?"

"I mean he had to pay some heavy dues. Kapiche?"

Sugarman pulled at his cuffs. "Time's up," he said, swallowing the rest of the bourbon. He stubbed the cigar out, got up, and left.

A few minutes later Jack Moon walked into the bar. He spotted me at the table, came over, and sat down.

"Helen and Walt will be along shortly. We've concluded negotiations—or paid the extortion money, depending on your viewpoint—and now we have a new head writer. And a long-term document."

"Great."

"Why so glum?" he said.

"I just met Quentin's agent."

"Sugarman? He's a character, isn't he?"

"He's something more than that," I said, but I was thinking about Connie Dover. She'd certainly given me the impression that Quentin had been born to the life he led, although everyone else seemed to think that he'd either made it up out of whole cloth or eked it out like a farmer working the soil.

Jack Moon was thinking about Sugarman. He eyed me nervously. "Did Harris say something about the show?"

What he really meant was—did he say something about me? He had said something, but it wasn't worth repeating. "No," I said. "He just made an impression, that's all."

Jack smiled with relief. "He'll do that, all right. Sugarman's the old-style Hollywood agent, right down to the ten-dollar cigars. He's a dinosaur compared to the new breed. You should talk to one of them some day, if you really want a laugh. They're so laid back they have trouble standing up. At least Sugarman's got a sense of who and where he is. Of course, his sense of himself is a little dated—like late nineteen-thirties. But he's a step above the space cadets of today. What did he say about Quentin?"

"He seemed to feel that he'd been going through a phase."

"His blue period?" Jack said. "That's shit. Never trust an agent, Harry."

I laughed. "He told me never to trust a producer."

"That's typical. Most agents look on us as the enemy.

They foment an adversarial relationship with management just to give themselves alibis for collecting their ten percent. It's ridiculous. If a writer was smart, he'd deal directly with the production company and save himself a lot of money. What else did he say?"

"That Helen was to blame for 'Phoenix's' problems."

"Helen doesn't write the show. She produces it. Sure she can be difficult. I told you last night—she's got a live-in identity crisis. But, believe me, once she gets in the studio, she's all pro. She leaned over backward to give Quentin the benefit of the doubt. She put her neck on the line—and the show, to boot—to help snap Quentin out of it."

"Sugarman seemed to think that he *would* have snapped out of it. That it was mostly his health and Marsha that were bothering him."

"You don't snap out of a quadruple bypass," Moon said. "And if you don't believe me, ask his doctor. Or his druggist. You don't snap out of a rotten marriage, either. I don't think Quentin had any intention of dumping on Marsha. He was dried up, I'm telling you. There was nothing left inside."

"No inner resources," I said to myself. "What do you know about Dover's financial situation?"

"Just that he was making half a million dollars a year. Why?"

"Sugarman said something about bad investments."

Jack shrugged. "You'd have to talk to Marsha or to Connie about that. Or to Quentin's lawyer, maybe. As far as I knew, he was doing all right. Which is to say that he was only spending about twenty-five percent more than he earned. Like most of them out here, Quentin didn't know the meaning of the word 'enough.'"

Jack looked up suddenly. "Here they come—Olivia and Malvolio."

"What does that make you?" I asked him. "Sir Toby?"

"That was Quentin's role," he said dryly. "I am the Prince."

14

Helen Rose and Walt Mack walked over to our table. The woman was wearing a red blouse and dark blue skirt. Walt Mack was dressed in red and blue, too. He had on a dark red, kid leather sportscoat, a salmon-colored shirt with a thin black tie knotted at the collar, and blue jeans.

"I don't think you two have met yet," Helen said, squeezing in beside me. "Harry Stoner, this is Walt Mack—our new head writer."

"Congratulations," I said, holding out a hand.

Mack said thanks and shook with me. He was very thin and tan, medium height, moustached, nice-looking in a clean-cut, collegiate, Tony Perkins-like way. If I hadn't already been told that he was gay, I wouldn't have guessed. He had none of the usual mannerisms. The other surprising thing about him was his age. I'd expected a man in his late thirties—like Dover himself. But Walt Mack couldn't have been more than twenty-six or twenty-seven.

"Let's order quick," he said as he sat down. "I'm starving. And I've got to get back home by two." He turned to Helen. "Did you see the scene I wrote for Carlotta, the one in the bar?"

Helen smiled.

"Notice what she was drinking?" Mack said. "A double martini with an olive. I put that olive in for you, sweetie."

The woman laughed loudly. "She's got my booze. I wish I had her thighs. Did you see her in that bikini on the remote, Jack?"

Moon nodded. "Did you see Hal Walker? Christ, we've got to keep his clothes on, Walt."

"His and a few others," Helen said, raising an eyebrow.

"It's unattractive," Jack said.

"I still wish I had Carlotta's thighs. They look like they're made of steel. And that ass!"

"I hear she's been spreading it around some," Mack said.

"No," Jack said, looking hurt.

Helen nodded at him. "I'm afraid so. She's been shtupping Paul List, and she's six weeks pregnant. She came in last week and told me. It's supposed to be a secret," she said, glancing at Walt.

He grinned.

"Jesus," Jack said. "What are we going to do about that?"

"I'll handle it in the breakdowns," Mack said. "Don't worry, Jack. It's a blessing in disguise. We'll just have Hal rape her, as well as beat her up."

"Yeah, but Carlotta's the Bitch." Jack looked at Helen. "Do we want a pregnant Bitch?"

"I'm thinking about it," Helen said. "I'm thinking I love it. But then what do we do about Hal and Cecily?"

"Who cares about Cecily?" Walt said. "I've been telling you for months—she's boring. You saw the results of the test groups. Nobody likes her. I think we should pull a Danny Meeghan."

They all laughed and I said, "What's a Danny Meeghan?"

Mack smiled at me. "Excuse us, Harry. We're just used to talking shop. Danny Meeghan was a character on one of the soaps back in the mid-sixties and he has since become apocryphal. He was a popular young character for a while, then he started to fade—fast. The writers decided to write him out of the show. Usually that's easy enough to do. You send the guy out of town on a business trip or something."

"Far out of town," Jack said.

"But in Danny's case, that wasn't possible. He'd been crippled in a car accident in the backstory—so he was housebound. He could have been sent to a hospital; but that would have meant writing a long bit about him getting sick, and then there would have had to have been bits about how the other characters reacted to his illness. It would have taken forever, and the writers wanted him to go fast. So one day they had somebody wheel Danny upstairs to his room. And he never came back down."

I stared at him. "He never came back down?"

"Nope," Mack said. "He's been up there for the last fifteen years."

"Didn't anybody miss him?"

"Only his agent," Mack said. "You can do just about anything you want on a soap, Harry. The audience has got an astonishingly short attention span. That's why we do two or three minutes of prologue at the start of each show—to remind them of what they're watching."

"He just disappeared, huh?"

"It's a tough world," Walt Mack said. "They disappear all the time."

"About Cecily?" Helen said. "What kind of guarantee does she have?"

Jack said, "I think she's two a week. But she's up for renewal at the end of September."

"How fast can we get rid of her?" Helen asked Walt.

"Like that!" He snapped his fingers.

Helen laughed. "Be serious, Walt. Is she worth renewing for another thirteen at a guaranteed two?"

Mack groaned. "I think it's a mistake. She's boring; the

94

audience hates her; and so do I. I think we should get rid of her right away. A car hits her, and that's it!"

"You've got to learn that you can't have everything your own way, babe," Helen said a bit sharply. "You may hate her, but I've got a feeling that we're going to get a lot of mail if we give her the fast shuffle. That so-called audience sample has been wrong before."

Jack laughed. "We interview a few ladies every other month, Harry, to get feedback on the show."

"I'm still willing to take the chance on Cecily," Mack said.

"And I'll remember you said that," Helen told him. "All the mail goes to your office, Walt. Jack, make a note—Walt gets all the Cecily mail."

A waitress came over and took our orders. Then the three of them started talking about the show again. I was beginning to get an amusing sense of the group's dynamics, and Walt Mack was clearly its star. He was a fast, articulate, enthusiastic talker. And while I didn't always understand the reasons for what he said, he clearly had a reason in mind. If he had an obvious weakness, it was his reluctance to concede any of his points. He only had a few of them, which he kept coming back to, again and again, rephrasing the ideas each time, as if the objections that the other two had raised were merely matters of semantics. Next to him, Jack appeared to be a very deep thinker, indeed. He didn't say much, and when he did speak, it was usually to a question of fact. Helen was the most changeable of the three. She was, by turns, amused, touched, irritated, and intimidated by Mack's enthusiasms. In that respect, she was no different than she'd been the night before. But because I'd seen her at the end of an evening, I had a clearer sense of what was going on behind those changes. For all the passion he put into arguing his position, Walt Mack seemed uninterested in 'Phoenix' compared to Helen Rose. The only sense of involvement I got from him was with his own ideas, as if, to Walt, the whole conversation was a matter of hoarding your points and conceding as little as possible to anyone else. It made him seem his age or younger—jejune, vain, and a little stupid in the way that bright, young men seem stupid when they act as if a thought of their own, any thought, is precious because it could be their very last one.

I wanted to jump into the conversation myself and ask Mack a few things. Like why he'd apparently been spreading the rumors about Dover that had led to me being hired. And why he'd claimed that he'd been "carrying" Quentin for the past two years. But there just didn't seem to be any room for me to edge in.

Helen and Walt argued before lunch about something called a "crossover set." And as soon as lunch ended, they started again.

"We need it, Helen," Mack said. "You've been on my back for two years about the number of sets in the breakdowns."

"And you know why," she said. "We're running fifty grand over budget as it is, Walt."

"All the more reason to build a crossover set. It'll end up saving us money, Helen—that's my whole point—by cutting down on the number of sets we have to use."

She laughed unhappily. "I gave you Cecily. I gave you Carlotta. What more do you want, Walt?"

"I want it all, sweetie." He'd meant it to sound funny, but it didn't come out that way. Walt ducked his head and said, "Right now I want a crossover set. In town. Convenient to everyone. A place to meet. A restaurant. A bar. A gift shop. Something. Do you know what we have to go through to get people together now? Jesus, it takes two or three days to arrange a meeting and at least that many sets."

"I know," Helen conceded. "Let me think about it, O.K.?"

Walt raised his hands—palms up—as if *he* were

96

surrendering. "That's all I'm asking, Helen. Just that you think about it."

Moon shook his head disgustedly. "Sure," he said under his breath.

Mack glanced at his watch. "Christ, I've got to get going. It's a quarter of two."

"And we've got to meet the network," Helen said dismally.

Jack looked at me. "Jesus, Harry, I'm sorry. You didn't get a chance to ask Walt any questions."

Mack smiled graciously. "If you want to talk to me, Harry, you're welcome to come over to my place. It's only a few miles from here. I've got a call to make, but after that I'm free for the afternoon."

"If it wouldn't be too much trouble," I said. "I'll take you up on it."

"No trouble at all," he said. "Tell you what, I'll go collect the car and you can meet me in the lot. I've got a blue Porsche 928."

Mack got up, kissed Helen on the cheek, and left.

"What a pain in the ass!" Jack said once he'd walked out the door. "It's going to be like this from now on, Helen. The Walt Mack Hour."

"Maybe he'll change," she said without conviction. "I gotta go, too. Are you coming, Jack?"

"Just a minute. I'll pick up the tab."

Helen left and Jack went up to the register to pay the bill. As we were walking out of the bar, I asked him, "How come I got invited home?"

He smiled. "Well, Harry, either Walt's got an interest in you or he wants to appear cooperative to the right people. That boy knows which side his butt is buttered on, and it wouldn't do to upset the United brass. Jesus, to hear him in there you would have thought he was Quentin Dover reborn."

"Dover was like that?"

"A little slower, a little more considerate, a little more adept at hiding his ego. But he always had an answer—just like young Walt. Hell, they worked together for two years. I guess it would be surprising if *he* didn't show a family resemblance."

"See you tonight?" I said.

"Yeah. After six at the Marquis."

Jack veered off to the left, down the pathway that led to the south quadrangle, and I continued on through the lobby and out to the lot.

15

It took Walt Mack about fifteen minutes to get to his house by the beach. We drove down Sunset Boulevard to the Coast highway, then due south for a few miles to Pacific Palisades. Mack parked the Porsche in a little turn-off above a cove, then we walked up a flight of railed, salt-whitened stairs to a fenced compound. Walt unlocked the gate and said, "Watch your step. It's slick."

I stepped through the gate onto a plank court fronting a row of two-story bungalows. Each bungalow had its own entryway, running off the common court and up to the front door. Mack's house was the third in a series of five. They were all built in the same beach-house style—cedar shakes on the outer walls, flat shingled roofs, windowless first floors with redwood spilings underneath them, and huge sliding glass doors and balconies on the second floors, where the houses peeked over the fence and looked out on the ocean.

"Nice," I said.

Mack shrugged. "I want one in Malibu—right down on the beach. Maybe I'll get one now. It's been a dream of mine."

He opened the door and I followed him into a narrow tiled hall. There was a decorative mirror on one wall and a brass clothes tree on the other. Mack stripped off his jacket, draped it on the tree, then pulled off this tie and unbuttoned his shirt.

"Jesus, I hate wearing ties," he said, studying himself in the mirror. "Why don't you go upstairs and make yourself comfortable, Harry, and I'll get this phone call out of the way."

He pointed to a circular staircase off the hall. I walked up to the second floor. There was another hall at the top of the stairs with a doorway on either side of it—the right-hand door led to a room at the back of the house, the left to the room with the balcony. I turned left—into a small den with white, stippled plaster walls and a glossy hard-wood floor. There were only a few pieces of furniture in the room—a gray silk davenport; a low, candy red Parsons table in front of the couch; and a black Barcelona chair to the left of the table. The sliding glass door dominated the room. Through it I could see the cove on the other side of Highway One and, beyond the cove, the huge expanse of the Pacific Ocean, breaking on the beach in white, even, sunlit waves. It was the first time I'd seen the Pacific since I'd come home from 'Nam. I stared at it, listening to the rush and boom of the breakers.

Beneath me, on the first floor, Walt Mack was talking softly on the phone. The sounds of the ocean covered his voice, but now and then I caught a word. And once I heard him distinctly.

"Fine, Mother," he said. "Everything's fine."

I sat down on the Barcelona chair and waited for him to finish with Mom. There was only one picture hanging on the white walls—a huge lithograph called "Tele-phone." It was by Richard Lindner, and, like most of Lindner's stuff, it was deliberately overripe and repellent. This one featured two stylized grotesques—a man and a woman—talking to each other on phones. The woman had huge purple breasts, and the man wore a trenchcoat and slouched hat. I wouldn't have been able to live with it, but then I wouldn't have rushed home to call Mom, either.

After a time, Mack came upstairs. He stood in the entry-way and looked at me in a friendly, slightly curious way.

"You want a drink, Harry?" he said.

"Yeah, I'll take a Scotch. No ice."

Mack went down the hallway and came back a few minutes later with two glasses of booze. He handed one of them to me, then walked over to the davenport and sat down.

"You ever been to L.A. before?" he said, stirring the drink with his fingertip.

"When I was in the Army," I said.

"You were in 'Nam?"

I nodded.

He leaned back against the couch and took a sip of booze. Away from Helen Rose and Jack Moon, Mack seemed like a different man—a much quieter, much more phlegmatic personality. I thought perhaps the phone call home had taken something out of him. Or perhaps he just didn't know what to do with me.

"It's been a long couple of days," he said, as if he'd been reading my mind. "And I'm worn out. You know, it's a funny thing. I've waited years to get this break. Paid a lot of dues. And now that I've got it . . . " He stared out the window at the surf. "I wonder if it was worth the trouble."

"I thought you wanted the job," I said.

Mack stirred up a smile. "Sometimes it's hard to know if you really want something until after you've gotten it, if you know what I mean."

It sounded like the sort of thing you said when you'd strong-armed your way into someone else's job, but then I'd heard a lot of things about Walt Mack.

"You want to talk about Quentin, don't you?" he said.

"Yeah. I want to ask you a few questions."

He nodded thoughtfully. "I'm willing to answer your questions. But I'd like to ask you something first."

"What?"

"As I understand it, Quentin's death has been ruled an accident by the coroner's office. Is that true?"

"The preliminary autopsy indicated death by natural causes, yes."

"Then why are you investigating him?"

"I thought maybe you could help me answer that question," I said.

"Me?" He pointed to himself. "Why me?"

"Frank Glendora hired me because he'd heard rumors about Dover's private life. It's my impression that you were the one who'd been spreading those rumors."

Mack laughed nervously. "Who told you that—Jack or Helen? I'm sure it wasn't Glendora. I've only met the man a few times."

"It's no secret that you didn't like Quentin."

"There was nothing there to like," he said cooly. "Dover had a personality like a black hole. He sucked in everything around him and gave nothing back in return. I suppose some people found that fascinating or alluring or sad. I didn't. I wasn't taken in by his act, that's all."

"And others were?"

"Yes," he said with a bitter smile. "Others were."

"Dover came to L.A. on Friday of last week, instead of on Sunday. He made a special trip. Do you know why?"

"No," Mack said. "We hardly talked to each other, outside of weekly story conferences and occasional phone calls."

"Did he say anything at the last story conference—anything that might explain why he came in on Friday?"

"No," Mack said again. "I told you—outside of business, we didn't travel in the same circles."

"And he didn't get in touch with you this weekend?"

Mack glared at me. "Did somebody tell you that he did?"

I said no.

But he didn't believe me. "I can just imagine what Jack

and Helen have been saying. And they claim *I'm* the one with the big mouth!" He laughed scornfully. "The last time I saw Quentin Dover was a week ago Monday at the Belle Vista. And he didn't say anything. He just sat there, popping pills and smiling. He'd take another pill and smile a little more. He was a burned-out house, Harry. There was nobody home—just the rats in the rafters."

"What was the story conference about?"

"What they'd been about for the last twenty weeks—the fact that we didn't have a story line." He looked at me for a second. "Do you know anything at all about this business?"

"Not really," I admitted.

"Then maybe I'd better explain a few things to you—some fundamentals—so that you can get the picture. O.K.?"

"Fine."

Mack leaned back on the couch. "The head writer on a soap, Quentin, in this case, writes the long-term docu-ment—a ninety- or a hundred-page plot outline that pro-vides three to six months worth of story material for the subwriters. Without a document, the whole process is screwed. The breakdown writers, a group that used to include me up until today at about 12:15, expand on the long-term, by turning it into daily narratives, in which the plot is fleshed out and the dialogue is indicated. We don't actually write the dialogue; that's the job of the scriptwrit-ers, who turn the breakdowns into scripts—pure dialogue in dramatic form. Usually one of the breakdown people acts as chief breakdown man. That was my job before today. The chief breakdown man has a little more say about story, but the head writer has the overall responsi-bility, or he's supposed to have, for writing the document, seeing that the breakdowns are done, editing the scripts, and delivering all the materials in a satisfactory form to the producers. When things are run well, by an ex-perienced hand, it's a remarkably efficient way of doing things. It actually works. I've seen it work. I got my train-ing under one of the best writers in daytime, so I know what I'm talking about. When things aren't run well, as in the case of our boy, Quentin, it's like slow death. Without a document, we have to make the story up from day to day, vamp for weeks on end. It's not a healthy situation."

Mack hardly looked old enough to have had much expe-rience, yet he talked as if he'd been in the business for years.

"How did you get involved in 'Phoenix'?" I asked him.

"I started working on 'Restless Years' as a scriptwriter under Russ Leonard. Russ was a close friend of mine. When he was made head writer on 'Phoenix' in '79, he took me along with him as his chief breakdown man."

"Dover wasn't the original head writer on 'Phoenix'?" I said.

Mack laughed snidely. "They didn't tell you about that, did they, Harry?"

"No, they didn't," I said uncomfortably. "Was Helen the producer in '79?"

"Yeah," he said. "She's always been the producer. Jack wasn't made exec until right before Quentin took over in '80."

"Why did Quentin take over?"

"Oh, that's the good part," Mack said. "You know, Quentin Dover wasn't the first death on 'Phoenix.' No, sir. But they didn't tell you about that either, did they? They just told you that Walt was spreading scurrilous gossip about poor dead Quentin. Only Walt seldom talks to any-one higher up than Helen. So you tell me, Harry, how did big bad Frank Glendora hear all those awful stories?" He laughed again and jingled the ice in his glass. "I need another one of these. How 'bout you?"

"I'm fine," I said.

"Sure, you're fine, Harry," he said as he got up from the couch. "You're a real he-man."

He walked out of the room and came back with a full

glass and a bottle. He dropped the fifth on the Parsons table and raised his glass in a toast. "Cheers." Walt swallowed all of the whiskey. "Got to get primed for this one," he said, pouring another shot. "Always get primed for my Russ Leonard story. Where was I, anyway?"

"You said there was another death."

"Oh, yeah. It was Russ. He died."

"How?"

"Well, it wasn't in the bathroom. He had a little sense of style, Russ did. How did he die? Let me see. He died of loss of blood—I believe that was the coroner's verdict."

"Like Quentin?"

"Nooo," Mack said. "Not *like* Quentin, because of Quentin. Quentin and Helen."

"What does that mean?"

Mack took another swallow of booze and set the glass down hard on the tabletop. "I mean someone started up some nasty rumors about Russ. Isn't that a coincidence! A year into the show, and they started talking him down. Helen didn't like his long-terms. She said they didn't measure up. Enter Quentin Dover—Helen's 'story consultant.' Dear Quentin. Dear, sweet Quentin. He stepped on the scene like something out of Henry James—one of those charming, worldly-wise, rotten little bastards without a heart for anything but himself. He stepped in all paternal kindness and good manners. He was going to help straighten everything out, then go on his merry way, leaving a happy world behind him. It was like a visitation from a god. What bullshit! You know, I learned one thing from the bastard. I learned that you can get whatever you want if you just ask for it in the right way. There was a three-month transition period, while the rumors percolated and Quentin lorded it up. Russ held his breath and made nice-nice to Quentin and tried not to hear the names they were calling him behind his back. Then Helen put her foot down—right on Russ's neck."

"She fired him?"

"You got the picture, Har'," Mack said. "Smart as a whip. She not only fired him; she ruined him. She and Quentin buried him so deep in shit that nobody would ever touch him again."

"Why?"

"You've got to pile it on deep, Harry, when you're trying to cover something up. Hell, the show wasn't doing well enough. We had a seventeen share. Never mind that we were slotted against one of the top-rated shows on daytime or that we'd only had a year to get established. Those share points, Harry, they mean money. And money is life. I really believe that. Helen wasn't about to take it in the pants. But somebody had to. Who did that leave?"

"What happened to Leonard after she fired him?"

Mack sat back on the couch and tossed the rest of the bourbon down. His face got red and he blew noisily out his mouth. "Whew! I'm getting crocked. Sure I can't pour you another one?"

I shook my head.

"What happened," he said, sweeping the bottle off the table and tipping it with a click into the glass, "is that Russ went home and put on a record. Then he sat down on the floor and began to cry. You know how I know that? Because I got there before the tears had dried—right after Helen passed me the word about firing him."

Mack hugged the bottle to his chest and swallowed what he'd poured into the glass. "I called the life squad, of course. But it was too late. I knew it when I saw him, curled up on the floor. And you know what's funny? Helen cried her eyes out at the funeral—cried like a baby. Blamed herself for everything. Helen's a big spender when it comes to after-market guilt."

"How about Quentin?" I asked.

"The putz didn't even realize what he'd done," Walt said with enormous rage. He'd started to cry himself, but just tears—as if someone had passed an onion under his eyes. "When he found out that he'd inherited Russ's job, he was surprised. I mean really surprised! Alarmed is probably the right word. He'd just been bullshitting all along. But Helen and Russ—they'd taken his act seriously. All that visiting god crap. Russ actually thought Quentin was there to help. And Helen was banking on it. It gave her the courage to knife Russ. But Quentin . . . Quentin was just putting up a front. Doing what he did best— acting charming and competent and never dreaming for a moment that someone might put him to the test. That kind of self-delusion is criminal."

Downstairs, I heard the door open and someone called out, "Walt?"

"Up here, Dave," Walt said.

A lanky kid in a T-shirt and jeans walked into the room. He took a look at Walt's face and said, "Jesus, what happened?"

"Congratulate me, babe," Walt said. "I've just been made head writer on 'Phoenix.'"

16

Dave stood in the doorway, staring at Walt Mack. He was a handsome kid in his mid-twenties—hair cut short like Mack's, with the same bland, boyish, unexceptional face. "Perhaps you can explain what's going on," he said to me.

Mack had sunk into silence, his hands folded around the bottle at this chest. I glanced at him and said, "Maybe Walt should tell you."

"We were just having a talk, Dave," Mack said. "About Russ."

Dave raised an eyebrow. "Oh," he said. "I thought you weren't going to think about that anymore."

Mack shrugged. "Sometimes you can't help yourself." He looked at me. "Is there anything else you want to know, Harry?"

"Yes," I said. "Why didn't you quit after Leonard's death?"

"You mean, if I cared so much, why didn't I tell them how I really felt?"

"Something like that," I said.

Mack laughed, although I didn't see much of a joke. "That's not the way it works out here, Harry. Moral outrage doesn't put the bread on the table."

Or the Porsche in front of the beach house, I said to myself.

"I like my life," Walt said. "And why should I have committed suicide, too, just to make a point? Besides, there are other ways of getting revenge."

"Like talking down your head writer?"

Mack glared at me. "I already told you that I didn't spread any gossip that wasn't already being spread by your friends. I even tried to help the bastard out. Somebody had to look after things with Quentin in control or the show would have died months ago. He didn't really know anything about the business. He was worse than an amateur. He didn't even have an amateur's curiosity. All of his credits had been in prime time and soaps were a new world to him. He tried to fake his way through it for the first few months, but the other writers knew what was going on. And when he realized that we'd seen through him, he acted like a kid who'd been caught in a lie. I guess he thought that was charming—that we'd all feel sorry enough for him to help out. Who knows? Maybe we did. I doctored his long-terms for twelve months and did most of the weekly blocking, and he patted me on the back in that fulsome, paternal way of his. But that was all I ever got out of him—a pat on the back. He was shrewd enough to take all the credit for himself when things were going well."

"If he wasn't doing the work, how could he get away with that?" I asked.

Mack laughed again. "You really don't understand this business, do you? Helen had a lot invested in Quentin. Christ, she'd just driven a man to suicide because she thought Dover was worth the risk. You can't change head writers every other month, Harry. It makes you look bad, makes people like Glendora think that you don't know what you're doing. And Helen had a tough enough time getting the job of producer in the first place. Once she made the decision about Russ, she *had* to live with

Quentin. And then, in spite of his incompetence, he never lost his ability to charm the right people. Regardless of what was coming out of his typewriter, he could make the folks at United believe that he knew exactly what he was doing. It was a gift he had—his only real talent. But even Helen had to reconsider things after Quentin had his heart attack. There was something there before March—the semblance of craft. Afterward there wasn't even that much—just a twitch, a reflex. He might as well have been dead. He couldn't do anything but smile and take his medicine. The ratings dropped. Helen began to get pressure from the brands and the network. And before you could say 'Russ Leonard,' the rumors started up again. Only this time they were true. Quentin was a borderline personality. He was taking a lot of drugs and booze. And he was incapable of telling the truth. Or of facing it."

"The document that you gave Helen today was your work, wasn't it?"

Mack drew himself up on the couch. "That's almost an insult, Harry, old stick."

"Why did you write it?"

"Somebody had to or the show would have folded. It still might fold."

I stared at him for a moment.

"All right," he said. "I wrote it to finish him. I wrote it because Helen was desperate and, if I produced, it would have meant the end of Dover's career. Is that what you wanted to hear?"

"Is it true?"

Mack stared out the window. "Who knows?" he said.

"Jack seems to think that Quentin had a hand in writing the document."

"Jack's full of shit," Mack said. "Oh, Dover offered me money to help him out—a larger piece of the pie. But that was his only contribution."

"And you wanted it all," I said.

"I wanted what was owed me. And it wasn't just money, Har'."

"Did Quentin know you were working on a story line?"

Mack nodded. "I didn't keep it a secret. I told him three weeks ago. And I told him what I was going to do with it, too."

"How did he react?"

"He didn't," Mack said. "I told you—he was dead from the neck up. He just said, 'Do what you have to do.' And that was it. Later on, I found out that he'd gone to Helen after we'd spoken and told her that he and I were collaborating on a long-term and that it would be done by this Monday. Can you believe that? The man never lacked chutzpah, I'll give him that much. Maybe he thought he could charm me into cooperating with him at the last moment."

"Could he have?"

Mack snorted. "Not a chance."

I got up. "I'm going to have to get back to the hotel."

"Yeah, it was fun for me, too," Walt said sulkily.

"Take it easy, Walt," I said. "You got your points across."

He stood up and put the bottle down on the Parsons table. "I'll give you a ride back."

"You can't drive," Dave said. "You're too loaded."

"I'm all right."

"No, you're not." Dave looked at me. "I'll give you a lift. Where are you going?"

"The Belle Vista."

"O.K." He turned to Walt. "And you cheer up. We've got some celebrating to do when I get back."

"I almost forgot," Mack said with a smile. "I just got what I've always wanted."

It was a quarter of five when we pulled into the Belle Vista lot. As I crawled out of the Porsche, Dave said, "You want to do Walt a favor?"

"Not particularly," I said.

He smirked. "Then let me put it another way. Stay out of his life, schmuck. He has enough problems of his own without having to worry about Russ Leonard again. Or about fucking Quentin Dover."

He peeled out with a squeal of his tires, and I walked slowly up to the canopied bridge. Jerry, the parking lot attendant, saluted me; but I wasn't in the mood for his brand of high jinks. I'd already heard about enough high jinks for one afternoon. I brushed past him without a word and headed straight for the lobby.

"Be that way," I heard him say.

The woman at the reception desk gave me her practiced smile.

"Miss Rose, again?"

"I'd like to call her room," I said.

She plugged a line into a PBX and pointed to the booth in the corner. "You can take it over there."

I closed myself in the booth and picked up the receiver. Jack answered the phone. "Helen Rose's room," he said wearily.

"It's me," I said.

"Thank God. It's a relief to hear a sane voice. How'd it go with Walt?"

"I have to talk to you about that, Jack."

He must have heard the annoyance in my voice—I wasn't trying to disguise it. When he answered me, he sounded miles away. "What happened?"

"Well, among other things, I just found out about Russ Leonard."

"Walt mentioned him, did he?"

"The question I want to ask is why didn't you?"

"Why should I have?" Jack said. "What does Russ have to do with Dover's death?"

"I don't know if he has anything to do with it. It's just that I keep hearing things bit by bit, Jack. Like the fact that the show is in trouble, and that Mack delivered a long-term document that Quentin claimed he'd helped write, and that a man committed suicide after Dover took his job. It makes me wonder what else is in store: whether I've been hired to look into a possible scandal or to be guided around a few old ones."

"I resent that," Moon said angrily. "I'm an executive producer, Harry, not a sleuth. I told you what I thought you needed to know. Frank Glendora had the same facts that I have. If he thought Russ Leonard's death was important to the case, he would have told you."

"That's another thing that worries me," I said.

"Look, can this wait an hour? We've got the network here and I've really got to go back to the meeting."

"Go back to the meeting, Jack," I said.

"We'll get together at the Belle Vista bar at six," he said. "And I'll clear this thing up. I'll even call Frank if it'll make you feel better. I don't know what Walt told you, but I'd be willing to bet that it's not the whole truth. Or even most of it. He's got an ax to grind, too, Harry. They all have."

17

I spent an hour in the Belle Vista bar, drinking Scotch and waiting for Moon to finish with the network. At six-fifteen Jack showed up, looking as if he'd lost a friend. His face was haggard with fatigue, and he smelled through his coat of sweat and bone weariness.

"We need to get a few things straightened out, Harry," he said as he sat down beside me.

"I guess we do."

"First of all, I talked to Glendora and he wants you to call him. Tonight, if possible. If not, then first thing tomorrow. He says he left a message at the hotel yesterday but that you didn't choose to answer it."

I started to say something, but Jack waved an arm at me to shut up. "Let me finish," he said. "Secondly, I want to assure you that I haven't deliberately tried to mislead you. I don't know why I have to say this. I thought we understood each other."

I didn't say anything this time. He had obviously been stung by what I'd said on the phone, and I owed him a chance to speak his piece. From what I'd seen, he didn't often get that chance around Helen or Walt.

"As far as Russ Leonard goes," Jack went on, "Glendora didn't mention him because he didn't think that

Leonard's suicide had a bearing on Quentin's death. I didn't mention Russ because I'd just started working for United at the time of his death, and it didn't occur to me to tell you about him. I can't speak for Helen, but you ought to know that Russ was a good friend of hers and she took his suicide very hard."

"So Walt told me," I said.

"Did he also tell you that Russ Leonard was his lover? And that Leonard had severe personality problems, as well as a thousand dollar a day cocaine habit?"

"No," I said. "He didn't tell me about the drugs."

"Understand, I hardly knew the man. That's one of the reasons I didn't talk about him. Most of what I've heard, I've heard from other people—from Helen, Frank, and Quentin. However, I do know Walt Mack, and I can tell you right now that he is a dishonest and manipulative person, with some fairly hefty personality problems of his own."

"Such as?"

"Such as a long history of sordid sexual encounters that have resulted in several scandals that Helen—and Quentin, to be fair—helped bail him out of. There have been drugs, too. Walt is one fucked-up human being, Harry. And by all reports, so was Russ Leonard."

I said, "Mack seemed to feel that Leonard's problems stemmed from the way he was treated by Helen—that she made him the scapegoat for all her problems and that she and Quentin drove him to suicide."

Moon laughed bitterly. "Well, let me tell you that this scapegoat was so stoned most of the time that he couldn't even dress himself, that Helen begged him to see a psychiatrist and even offered to pay his way to a clinic where he could have dried out, that she only fired him after he'd threatened to kill her and himself."

"Why did he threaten to kill her?"

"The man was psychotic, for chrissake! He'd blown half a million dollars up his nose. He claimed that Helen was trying to ruin his career when she hired Quentin as a consultant on the show."

"Was she?"

Jack eyed me coldly. "Anyone else would have fired Russ Leonard months before that. Helen was trying to help him. Quentin was never supposed to end up as head writer on 'Phoenix.' He was brought on initially to lend Russ a hand until Leonard could get his life together. But Russ didn't see it that way. Or, at least, Walt didn't. Walt was always the more ambitious of the two. He pumped Russ up with so much paranoid hatred that Leonard finally blew his stack."

"Why would Walt have done that?" I asked.

"You met him, Harry," Jack said. "He only thinks of one thing—himself. And if you ask me, he deliberately played on Leonard's paranoia, hoping that Helen would end up firing Russ and replacing him with Walt himself. And it looks like he finally got his wish."

I asked Jack what I'd asked Walt Mack. "If he's such a rotten bastard, why do you deal with him?"

Jack shook his head, as if I'd missed the point of what he'd been saying. "They're *all* rotten bastards. Haven't you figured that out, yet? Russ, Quentin, Walt—they're all branches of the same tree. This is a tough business. Writers get chewed up and spit out every day. Remember, these guys have to write five hours worth of story every week of the year. That's like a novel a month. That kind of work load destroys people who aren't strong enough or vain enough or jaded enough to forget that what they're writing is as disposable as toilet paper. It takes a peculiar personality to bear up under that much pressure. And the fact that they all develop kinks and warps like stress fractures is to be expected. Russ Leonard made himself strong with drugs, until he fried his brains out. Quentin did it with constant lies and lots of booze, to kill the pain. And Walt does it by spreading poison about the other guy before he can be poisoned himself."

"Yeah, but Mack claims he wasn't the one who'd been spreading the poison about Quentin, that Helen and you were doing it. He also claims that Helen did the same thing when she wanted to get rid of Russ Leonard."

"What can I say?" Jack held up his hands. "Call Glendora. Ask him how he heard about Quentin's problems or about Russ."

"All right, Jack," I said. "But why couldn't you have explained all this to me in the first place?"

"I already told you—I didn't think it mattered. And then I don't like to spread gossip if I don't have to."

"You didn't hesitate with Quentin," I said.

"He was different."

"How different?"

Moon looked guiltily into my face. Weariness and the unpleasantness of having it out with me had loosened something up inside him—some constraint. I could almost see it giving way. "I used to like him," he finally said. "I guess that's why. I used to think he was an exception. But then I was new to the job and didn't really know my way around. If you'd asked me what I thought of Quentin Dover when I met him two years ago, I would have told you that I wished he'd adopt me. He was that goddamn convincingly paternal. It was as if there wasn't anything that he hadn't done or seen or heard about. I was impressed. Hell, we all were. He had everybody sold. Especially me."

He ducked his head as if he'd admitted something shameful.

"We all make mistakes, Jack," I said.

"Yeah, but I was the asshole who recommended Dover to Frank and Helen." He tugged gently at his curly black beard. "I really liked him at first, Harry," he said with regret. "The son-of-a-bitch really fooled me." Moon stared out the lounge window at the dark trees. "Somehow they always do."

117

Around eight-thirty, Jack stretched his arms and said, "I guess I'd better check in with Helen. She had dinner with Ted Griffith, our agency man. They're planning strategy for tomorrow's meeting with Sally Jackson."

"How's it been going?"

He shook his head. "Not good. We've just got too many strikes against us. Three head writers in three years does not make for continuity. And then we've got that thirteen share and a so-so document. Even United is going soft on this one. It's my guess that we'll get the ax. Not right away, but thirteen weeks down the road."

"What happens to you?"

"Who knows?" He patted the tabletop with his fingertips and smiled. "Could be I'll junk it altogether. I'm not really cut out for this job, Harry. I told you that."

"What will you do?"

"Maybe I'll try to make it as an actor again. Maybe I'll try something else. If I had a little money, the choice would be a lot easier. It wouldn't take much. Just enough to pay the mortgage and keep Liz and Nick happy. If I didn't have to worry about them, I'd have quit a long time ago."

"You're lucky to have somebody to worry about," I said.

"Yeah?" He smiled at me. "Maybe so. You know, just because I may not be working for United much longer doesn't mean that we couldn't have a drink now and then. You might have to pick up the tab . . . " He laughed, but I could see from his eyes that he was thinking uncertainly of his future. "Then again, maybe I'll stick. There's something to be said for a regular paycheck and Blue Cross. Jesus, I sound like Frank."

He got up. "So long, Harry," he said. "It's been a good night. Bad day, good night."

"So long, Jack," I said.

I watched him walk out of the restaurant into the garden. Then I went over to the register and paid my bill.

18

I took a cab back to the Marquis. There were two messages on the floor this time. One of them was from Frank Glendora, asking me to call if I got in before eleven, Cincinnati time. The other was from Maria Sanchez. It took me a second to realize that she was Maria the maid. There was a number on the message card. I dialed it from the bedroom phone, but no one answered. It was too late to call Glendora.

I laid down on the bed and tried to think about the Dover case. But I ended up thinking about Jack Moon, instead. His disappointment with Quentin Dover was like a boy's disappointment with his father, when he first discovers that Dad can act like a kid, too. Only Quentin hadn't ever stopped acting like a child or holding to a child's belief in the inviolability of his charm. He'd wanted everything for himself, including to be loved for his lies. And the amazing part was that he'd gotten what he wanted—that was apparently the way it worked in the TV biz. Ask in the right way and ye shall receive. But Jack, who could be boyishly charming himself, hadn't been so lucky. Helen and Walt and Quentin had forced him to grow up all by himself—to clean up their messes, while they played in the back-yard sandbox. That would have made me resentful, too. Made me wonder why some people seemed to be blessed beyond deserving. It was a shame, because, outside the job, Jack Moon was a likeable man. He was owed a break, and I hoped he'd get one, although I didn't think it was going to come in the world of daytime television.

I fell asleep on the bed and woke up two hours later to a ringing telephone. I glanced at the clock, which was showing half-past ten, and reached for the receiver. A woman with a soft Hispanic voice said my name.

"Yeah?" I said groggily.

"Is Maria," the woman said. "You know? From the Belle Vista?"

I sat up on the bed and tried to shake myself awake. "Yeah, Maria. I got a message that you'd called."

"I check you out, and it's O.K. So you wanna talk now? About Dover?"

"If you've got something to say," I said. "I'm willing to listen."

"Yeah, but how much you willin' to pay?"

"It depends on what you've got."

She didn't say anything for a moment. "I got somethin'. But is gonna cost you two hundred."

"We'll see. I have to hear it first."

She put her hand over the mouthpiece, and I could hear her say something in Spanish to someone off the phone. When she came back on the line, she said, "O.K. But'chu gotta come here. I don' have no wheels, you know?"

"What's the address?"

She gave me a street number in Pacoima. I wrote it down on a notepad that the Marquis had thoughtfully placed on the nightstand by the bed, along with a half-dozen glossy picture postcards of the hotel—to make all my friends jealous. "I'll be over there as soon as I can catch a cab."

Maria hung up. I stared at the notepad for a second, wondering if it was such a bright idea to go traipsing off into the Los Angeles night with a couple hundred dollars in my wallet. But I didn't see where I could afford to pass up a lead. Nothing else about the case had materialized, with the exception of the Leonard business—and that was the wrong scandal. I went into the john and splashed a little tepid water on my face, then picked up the phone by the toilet and called for a cab.

It took the cabbie about forty minutes to get to Pacoima on the Golden State Freeway, and halfway there I started to have second thoughts. To Maria, I was just a dumb gringo passing out twenty-dollar bills. That's probably what Jerry had told her, too—that I was easy pickings. Plus the girl had already talked to the cops, which meant that anything she told me was either going to be evidence that she'd withheld from the police or an outright lie. And I was in no position to know which was which.

By the time we arrived at her home, I had to force myself out of the cab. I took a look at the place and told the cabbie to wait.

It wasn't that awful, really. But then I didn't know what awful was—in Pacoima. From the outside it looked a little decrepit but respectable—like a clean old man. There was a palm tree in the front yard, its bark diamonded like a pineapple skin and peeled back on top, where the fronds hung above the rooftop. A small barrel cactus huddled in the dirt by the door, squat as a fire plug. The place itself was thirties Spanish modern. Stucco walls, rounded arches, wrought-iron trim, and the ubiquitous red tile roof. It wasn't very large—no more than three or four rooms. A cottage house. The dark little street was filled with them.

There weren't any lights showing through the windows, but I went up to the door anyway and knocked. A second later the door opened, scaring a scarab beetle that was standing by my foot. The bug lumbered off toward the cactus and I looked nervously over my shoulder at the cab.

121

Maria peeked around the door. When she saw it was me, she smiled.

"Hello, Harry," she said.

She opened the door fully and leaned against the jamb. She was wearing a red kimono with a blue and yellow parrot design. I didn't think she was wearing anything else beneath it. She smelled too ripe.

"Come in," Maria said.

I walked through the doorway into the living room. Maria closed the door behind us. A candle in a red glass globe was burning on a table parked against one of the walls. It sent a red glow throughout the small room, making the patterns on the few pieces of furniture shift with the flickering flame. The room smelled strongly of dust and cuminos—like a pepper tree.

"You think you could turn on a light?" I said to the girl.

She shook her head. Her lips were thick and heavily rouged with candy red lipstick. "I like to, Harry. But we don' got no electricity. They come'n turn it off a couple days ago."

Swell, I said to myself.

"You don' have to worry none. Is better this way."

Maria took my hand and pulled me over to a couch. It appeared to be covered in a pebbled blue material embossed with palm leaves. A cushion spring sang out as we sat down.

The girl stared at me for a second. Her teeth looked blunt and off-color in the candlelight. Without a word, she slipped the kimono off her shoulders and let it fall to her waist.

"I thought we were going to talk," I said.

"We coul' do both," she said.

Her breasts were small and brown, with dark areolas covering most of their tips. Her pubic hair was thick and black.

"Don'chu like me?" she said coyly.

"Sure, I like you. But let's talk first."

122

She pulled the kimono back up but didn't cinch it—just left it hanging open.

"You a gay boy?" Maria said, leaning back on the couch.

"No."

"You don' look like no gay boy." She ran a hand through her dark, tangled hair. "But is hard to tell, you know? Like Jerry. He go both ways, you know? Acey-deecy. Me, I'm straight, you know?"

"Great," I said.

"Maybe for the right kinda bread, I'm not. But nobody give me that kinda bread 'round here."

"You from here? From L.A.?"

She laughed. "Shit, no. I come up from TJ. Gotta make some bread, you know? Ain't nothin' goin' on down in TJ, man. Just same old, same old. You sure you don' wanna fuck, huh?"

"I'm sure," I said.

Maria sighed. She pulled the kimono shut and tied it at her waist. "You wanna do some smoke?"

I said, "No."

"You're some swinger, ain't you, Harry?" She got up and walked over to the candlelit table. "You ain't vice?" she said, looking at me over her shoulder.

I said, "No."

"I'm askin' you, man. You gotta tell me, now. The law say so."

"I thought you had me checked out."

"Shit," she said. "That Jerry, man. He's too damn cold, you know? Think he's got it all figured out. You don' answer my question, yet."

"I'm not vice. I'm not with the LAPD. I'm a private detective."

"Yeah?" She turned back to the table and pulled a fat yellow joint out of one of its drawers. She stuck it in her mouth, bent over the candle, and lit it—filling the room with a sweet, unmistakeable smell. "Who you workin' for."

"Some people who are interested in Quentin Dover."

Maria walked back to the couch, the joint smoking between her lips. She cinched the robe tightly, tucked it beneath her legs, and sat down. "Yeah? Wha'chu wanna know about him for?"

I didn't answer her.

She pulled the joint from her mouth. "You got the bread, pachuco?"

"I haven't heard anything yet."

"Wha'chu wanna hear?"

"When's the last time you saw Dover?"

"On Monday," she said with a smile.

"Before that."

"I seen him a coupla weeks ago. I seen him a lotta times, you know? He come to the hotel every week. Leave me big tips, you know, if I clean his room up good."

"You ever sleep with him?" It seemed like a natural thing to ask Maria.

"Once or twice," she said, to my surprise. "He ain't very good in bed, you know? He can't fuck 'cause he's too scared about his heart. So I suck him off a couple times. He says I'm a good girl. Says he usta fuck different chicks every night. But he can't do it no more, 'cause of his heart. Real macho, you know? I think it's bullshit. 'Cause once he gets kinda fucked-up. Starts tellin' me 'bout his old lady, you know? 'Bout how much she like to ball, and how he can't ball her no more, 'cause he's scared he's gonna croak. He says he's scared the bitch's gonna walk. She's been fuckin' 'round so much and other shit. I say, 'Why don'chu dump on the chick, man?' But he says he can't do it, 'cause he still loves her. Is bullshit, you know? I'm suckin' him off and he's sayin' he loves his old lady." She curled her lip in disgust. "Don' nobody love anybody like that. He's just fucked up, you know? Later on, when he comes he gets real nervous, man. He says, 'Forget what I say. Is just bullshit, you know?' I think he's scared it's gonna get back to his old lady—what he been doin' with me. I say, 'Don' worry. I ain't gonna say nothing.' He gives me a big tip."

Maria took a long toke from the joint.

"It's interesting," I said. "But it isn't worth two hundred."

She made a grunting sound and expelled a cloud of sweet, white smoke. "That ain't what I'm gonna tell you, man. I just throw that in, you know? Por nada."

"What are you going to tell me?"

She rubbed her thumb and forefinger together. "Is about what I see in his room. When I go in on Saturday."

"I thought no one had gone into his room until Monday."

Maria just smiled.

Somewhere in the dark house something made a creaking noise. The sound made me jump. But Maria didn't move.

"What's that?" I said.

"Nothin'," she said. "Is just my kid, you know?"

I wasn't sure I believed that, but I didn't know what I was going to do about it. I glanced through one of the dark archways leading to the back of the house. Then I pulled my wallet from my jacket and took two hundred-dollar bills out. Maria's eyes gleamed in the candlelight.

"All *right!*" she said softly. She reached tentatively for the money, as if she were almost afraid to touch it, afraid that it might vanish if she did. I held it back from her.

"Let's hear the story first."

She looked at me uncertainly. "You ain't gonna stiff me, are you, man?"

"Let's hear it, Maria."

She stared at the money for a moment then nodded. "O.K. But don' try no tricks, you know?" She wet her fingers and pinched the lit end of the joint a couple of times. When it went out, she stuck the roach behind her ear like a stubby yellow pencil.

"When Dover checks in on Friday," she said, "I'm off

duty. So I don' get the word about how he don' want no company. On Saturday morning I go see him—change the sheets, see if maybe he wants a little head. I could use the bread. Ain't got no electricity, you know? Anyway, I knock on the door and when nobody answers, I unlock it with my key and go in. There wasn't nobody there, man."

"You mean he'd gone out?"

"I mean there wasn't nobody there. There never was. I clean enough rooms to know when somebody been there at night. And nobody been in that room."

I stared at her. "Are you sure, Maria?"

"Sure, I'm sure. The bed ain't messed up. There ain't no luggage, neither. It freak'd me out some. I go up to the desk and ask about him, 'cause I think maybe Jerry's been playin' one of his dumb-ass jokes on me, you know, when he say he seen Dover check in. But Louise, she tell me he check'd in on Friday afternoon and say he don' wanna be disturbed."

"Did you tell her what you saw?"

"No, man. I don' tell nobody. I got a good job, and I don' say nothin' gonna fuck it up."

"You didn't tell Jerry?"

"No, man. I didn' tell nobody."

"Why didn't you tell the cops?"

"Nobody ask me about Saturday," she said. "Besides, I don' give nothing to them cabrons for free. Is just askin' for trouble, you know?"

I thought about it for a minute. "So he wasn't there on Friday night or on Saturday."

"That's what I been tellin' you, man."

"What about Monday? How did the room look then?"

"It still don' look like nobody'd lived in it, you know? I mean, the clothes, they been put away. But his suitcase was still sittin' on the bed and the sheets ain't messed up or nothing."

"Like he'd just come in?"

126

"Yeah," she said. "Of course, I don' get no real good look. Once I smell the bathroom . . . I just run."

"Did you see his body?"

"I don' have to," Maria said. "I know what that smell is."

"According to the cops, he'd been there since early Sunday morning. How come it took so long for someone to complain?"

"Man, that's the south quadrangle. It cost big bread to move in down there. I don' think there's nobody around 'til Monday morning."

"The place was empty? Both buildings?"

"Almost. August is a slow time, man."

"O.K., Maria." I handed her the two hundred dollars.

She held the money close to her breasts, moving her lips as if she were saying a bedtime prayer.

19

As I got up to leave, I heard another noise coming from the hall. I looked into the dark archway leading to the back of the house and saw a pair of eyes glistening faintly in the candlelight.

"What's going on?" I said uneasily.

Before Maria could answer me, a small brown boy came running into the light.

"That's what's going on, man," Maria said. "Come here, pachuco."

The little boy ran over to his mother and hid his face in her robe. He looked at me once—all brown eyes and brown shiny hair.

"Say hello," his mother said to him.

The boy hid his face again and shook his head. Maria brushed the hair from his forehead. "He's shy, you know?"

I nodded at her. "Thanks for the help."

She rubbed the two hundred-dollar bills together. "Is what it's all about. No bread, no electricity. No bread, no nothing."

I opened the door and stepped out onto the stoop. The cab was still sitting on the dark street corner, idling in a cloud of exhaust. I walked under the palm tree, down to the curb, and looked back at Maria's tired cottage. Then I got in the cab and told the driver to take me to the Marquis.

It was about two o'clock when I got to the hotel. I went straight up to my room and sat down at the desk by the bed. It was too late to call Jack, although I wanted to talk to him about what Maria had said. I figured I could get in touch with him in the morning at the Belle Vista. I wanted to do a little more snooping around there, anyway, to see if I could figure out precisely how Quentin Dover had managed to slip away unnoticed late Friday night.

If Maria could be trusted, that was apparently what he'd done. Gone out after supper in the rented car, returned after twelve, picked up his bags, then left again without anyone seeing him come or go. If he'd returned between 12:30 and 12:45, when the night clerk was on break, I could get him into the hotel. But it was a little tougher to get him back out. Fifteen minutes wasn't much time to return to the room through that dark garden, pack a bag, go back out through the garden, and catch a ride with someone waiting in another car. It could have been done, I supposed, if he'd known precisely when the clerk was going on break. But it would have had to have been run like clockwork. Moreover, it would have had to have been planned in advance.

Whether he'd come in and gone out through the lobby or whether he'd found some other way to enter and exit—through one of the gates—it *did* look as if the thing had been planned out. Or, at least, as if Dover hadn't wanted anyone to know where he was going. He'd made a special trip to L.A. three days earlier than usual. He hadn't contacted anyone on the 'Phoenix' team. He hadn't even called his agent, who claimed that they were long-time friends. He had told the desk clerk that he didn't want to be disturbed by visitors. And he had entered and left the hotel grounds with his luggage, unseen, in the middle of the night, leaving his own car parked prominently in the Belle Vista lot. Then he'd returned, surreptitiously, early Sunday morning. That sounded very much like a man who didn't want other people to know what he was up to.

As to which "other people," it occurred to me that if Quentin had been going behind his agent's and his producer's backs—if he had, in fact, been meeting with someone on Saturday about a TV deal that neither Sugarman nor Helen Rose knew about—he would have had a very good reason to keep his whereabouts secret. And given the situation on 'Phoenix,' he might have been desperate enough to risk anything in order to land another job. The fact that he'd come to California at all pointed to some sort of television connection. But I didn't really know how to confirm it, short of canvassing every agent and producer in town. And even then the chances of being told the truth were probably nil.

He *had* made those telephone calls when he'd arrived. Several local ones, according to Sy Goldblum a.k.a. Seymour Wattle, and one long-distance one to his mother in Cincinnati. He had also driven the rental car some sixty miles. If I could have found out whom he'd called in L.A. or whom he'd gone to see on Friday night (if he'd done anything more than drive around), I'd have been better able to answer the central question of where he'd been on Saturday. But the calls were untraceable; so was the car ride. And I was beginning to feel like I'd worn out my welcome in L.A. Quentin's friends and associates claimed that he hadn't been in touch with them—period. That left me with the one person I knew he'd been in contact with—Connie Dover. I'd barely scratched the surface with her and hadn't even gotten that far with Marsha. There was a fair chance, I figured, that one or both of them knew something that I wanted to know. In fact, Marsha Dover had claimed to know "things," compromising things. Although it might have been the liquor talking, it was worth a shot. Plus, Dover's lawyer was in Cincinnati; so was Frank Glendora. And I had questions I wanted to ask each of them.

First thing Friday morning, I called Seymour Wattle at the LAPD, Hollywood Division. I asked him if they'd had any further word on the autopsy findings, and he said no. Then I asked him about the phone calls Dover had made from the Belle Vista. The long-distance one had been made at seven P.M. Pacific time and had lasted for two minutes. The last local one had been made at approximately seven-thirty on Friday night. Dover had rented the car—a Dodge Diplomat—at seven forty-five, picked it up at seven fifty, and had driven off immediately after signing the rental agreement in the lobby.

When I asked Seymour if there was any possibility of tracing the local calls, especially the last one, he said, "Not a chance. The hotel phones are direct-dial within Los Angeles county. All you gotta do is punch '9' and make the call."

"How about the car ride?" I asked. "Any idea where he went?"

"Tell you what you do," he said. "Go downstairs, buy yourself a map of L.A. Get a compass. Set the point on the Belle Vista Hotel. Then draw a circle with a thirty-mile radius. *That's* where he went, man. Somewhere in that circle."

"Thanks for the help," I said.

"Don't mention it," Wattle said.

"I may have another job for you, Sy."

"Great. I could use the bread."

"Hit a losing streak at the ballpark?"

"Hell, no," Seymour said. "The track. Lost a bundle on a gray horse. I'm a sucker for a gray."

"Well, I've got a sure thing for you."

"I hear you," Wattle said.

"Ask around. See if you can find anyone who's done

131

business with our boy in the last few weeks."

"What kind of business?" Wattle said.

"The TV kind. A new soap opera, maybe. A nighttime show. Maybe even a movie."

"That's a lot of asking around."

"There's two bills in it for you. And if you come up with anything I'll see to it that you get a fat bonus."

"How fat?"

"Something in the four-figure range."

"Get right on it, man," Seymour Wattle said.

After I got done with Seymour, I called Jack Moon's room. There wasn't any answer, so I called Helen Rose's suite at the Belle Vista. Moon picked up the phone.

"Black hole of Calcutta," he said.

"I take it things are not going so well."

"You take it correctly." He put his hand over the mouthpiece. "Sally Jackson's here. From the network. She and Helen just had a little spat."

"What about?"

"This'll amuse you—Walt's document. You know, the one that he wrote all by himself?"

"What about it?"

"Sally claims he stole it from another show. She used to work with Russ and Walt on 'Young and Restless,' and she claims it's Leonard's work. Can you beat that with a pair of leather thongs?"

I started to laugh. "Where and when does it stop, Jack?"

"It never stops, Harry. *Plus ça change, plus c'est la même chose.* Or something like that." He laughed himself. "Can you believe that little putz? Jacking us up about a document he didn't even write? Bluffing Helen and Quentin and me, too? God Almighty, what a world!"

"What does Walt say?"

"He says—and I quote—'It may bear a superficial resemblance to Russ's work. So what? It's still good, solid material.' What the hell, he's probably right. They all steal from one another anyway. Quentin did it. And Russ did

132

it, too. It's like running a foundling home for plagiarists."

"What are you going to do about it?"

"What do you think?" Jack said. "Nothing. Oh, Helen will have a little talk with Walt, slap his hand. But it's too late to back out of the deal. The show just couldn't stand another writer change at this point. The brands are already nervous, and the network is just hanging on by their nails. Anyway, Walt's been on the team from the start, so we couldn't do without him in any case. And he knows it."

"Son-of-a-bitch," I said. "Do you think Dover knew what Walt was planning?"

"Naw," Jack said. "Actually, it's the kind of stunt that Quentin himself would have pulled—in his heyday. But he was too much of an egotist to think anyone else could bring it off. There *is* a kind of poetic justice about it, though."

He sounded pleased.

"So Walt didn't have a document of his own, after all?"

"Nope," Jack said. "He just buffaloed Quentin into thinking that he did. And fooled all the rest of us, too. Some sweet guy, huh?"

"A slice of marzipan," I said. "I've got some news."

"Oh, yeah?"

"Quentin wasn't in his hotel room on Friday night or Saturday morning."

"Yeah?" Jack said with interest. "How in hell did you find that out?"

"From a maid at the Belle Vista. She went into his room on Saturday—to clean up. And there was nobody there. No luggage, either."

"I'll be damned," Jack said. "Where was he?"

"Out trying to hustle himself up another job, I think."

This time he didn't try to talk me out of it. "Maybe, he was. I mean, if our new head writer can foist a four-year-old document off on us as his own work, then anything's possible."

"Where would he have looked, Jack?"

"Not at United," Moon said dryly. "Hell, at any of our competitors, P & G, General Foods, ABC. Or maybe at some freelance production company. The possibilities are endless."

"He was apparently going behind his agent's back, as well as behind yours. Could he have gotten away with it?"

"I don't know. I suppose he could have slipped out of the United contract on the grounds of poor health. And a lot of writers have more than one agent, although I'm pretty sure that Quentin dealt strictly with Sugarman."

"Why would he bypass his agent?"

"Why do you think?" Jack said. "Money. If he was dealing on his own, he'd have saved himself ten percent."

"Was he that hard up for cash?"

"I don't know. It's something to look into."

It was, indeed.

"I think I'm going to catch a flight back to Cincy this afternoon," I said. "I'd like to talk to Quentin's mother again. And to his wife."

"I'm sorry to hear you're leaving," Jack said with regret. "It's been fun, with you around."

"I'll stop over at the Belle Vista before I leave. Maybe we can have a drink together."

"Just name the time."

I took a look at the clock on the nightstand. "It's ten-thirty now. I'll meet you at noon. O.K.?"

"See you then," he said.

20

I called LAX and made a reservation for a two o'clock flight that would get me into Cincinnati International at nine-thirty P.M. Eastern time. Then I called Glendora.

I'd been holding off making the call for two days—primarily because I didn't have anything to tell him. Now I did. And I had a few questions to ask, too. Hearing that measured voice again reminded me of his sad-eyed, preacher's face.

"I was beginning to wonder what had happened to you, Harry," he said. He didn't sound angry, exactly—which is what I'd expected after I'd ignored his calls—more bemused, the way he'd sounded when he'd been talking about the 'Clean & Fluffy' snafu. "Is everything coming along all right?"

"I've uncovered a couple of things. If you want to wait until tomorrow, I'll tell you about them in person."

"You're returning to Cincinnati?"

"Tonight. I want to talk to the Dovers again. And maybe to Quentin's lawyer. You wouldn't happen to know his name, would you?"

"As a matter of fact I do. Seth Murdock. He's my lawyer,

too. Quentin kept singing his praises so highly that I decided to try him out."

Frank Glendora was probably the last person on earth whom Quentin Dover could still bamboozle. It was almost touching.

"I'll call Seth for you, if you'd like. Clear the way."

"Great," I said. "There are a few matters I'd like to talk over with you. Maybe we could meet for lunch tomorrow."

"I think I could take a lunch on Saturday," Glendora said, paging through a calendar. "Yes, I'm free. Shall we say twelve-thirty at the Maisonette?"

That would make the second time I'd been to the Maisonette in less than a week. The second time in ten years. "Sounds fine," I said.

"I'm sorry about that Russ Leonard thing. Jack told me that you were rather upset with him. And with me, too. It just didn't occur to either of us to mention it, what with Quentin so newly dead." Glendora sighed. "The family buried him on Thursday afternoon, by the way. I wish to God that we could bury this whole saddening business with him."

I didn't realize it at first, but he was asking me a question.

"Can we bury it, Harry?" he said straight out.

"I don't know, Frank. I'm not through with the case yet. I can tell you this much—I haven't come across anything that would compromise United's image yet. At least, nothing relating directly to Dover."

"That's wonderful," he said with relief, although I wasn't sure if he was relieved for United or for Quentin. Probably a little of each.

I told him I'd see him the following day and hung up.

I watched myself pack my overnighter in the bedroom mirrors. I'd gotten used to all those reflected versions of me by that point. When I was fully packed, I saluted myself one last time, put my bag outside in the corridor, and closed the door on that snazzy room full of telephones and shiny mirrors. I caught an elevator down to the lobby and checked out. As I was waiting for them to tally the bill, I took a look at the newspaper rack by the front desk and found a map of L.A. It had sounded silly when Seymour suggested it on the phone, but I decided that there was no harm in drawing a couple of circles with a compass. Anyway, it was a souvenir of an odd August week.

Once I'd paid my bill, I walked out to the smoked-glass elevator on the top landing. This time I couldn't resist. I stepped into it, feeling like an oversized parcel of mail in a pneumatic tube, pressed a button, and was lowered twelve feet to the sidewalk.

"Now you gettin' the spirit," the black doorman said with a grin.

I laughed.

The doorman flagged down a cab. I got in, carrying my suitcase in my hand.

"We be seein' you again, sir?" the doorman asked.

"I don't know," I said.

"Via con dios." He patted the door and the cab pulled out into traffic.

It was a sunny day—a little warmer than it had been earlier in the week. I hadn't noticed the heat before, even though it had been running in the low eighties. That Friday there was more moisture in the air and suddenly it felt hot. I took off my sportscoat and draped it over my arm.

"You goin' to the airport?" the cabbie said.

"Eventually. Right now I want to go to the Belle Vista Hotel."

We drove up Hilgard to Sunset. Bel-Air ran up the canyonside, north of Sunset. A maze of walls and gates and flowering trees and brief glimpses of white masonry, like glimpses of bare, beautiful flesh seen through a hedgerow.

The driver turned left on Sunset Boulevard and then

137

right on Green Canyon. We coasted under the towering oaks up to the walled compound of the hotel. I had the cabbie drive past the gate in the south quadrangle before letting me out in the lot. I was pretty sure that was how Quentin Dover had slipped away on Friday night—through the gate—unless he'd sneaked past the front desk or hiked across the gully of flowers that separated the lobby from the parking lot. There was no other exit.

I got out of the cab—suitcase in one hand, coat in the other—and walked up to the bridge. Jerry was leaning against a strut, staring at his reflection in one of his glossy patent leather shoes.

"Hi," I said to him.

"Hi," he said dolefully.

"Sorry about yesterday. I had a long afternoon."

"Oh, that's O.K.," he said. "It happens to everyone." He looked at my bag. "You leavin' us?"

"Yes. Back to Cincinnati."

"Yeah? Is that where you're from? WKRP-land? They got a good football team."

"That's one thing that can be said for it." I put my bag down on the pavement. "You want to make another quick twenty bucks?"

He grinned. "Do you need to ask? What is it? More questions about the guy who croaked?"

"Yeah."

"Shoot," he said.

"What time did you say you got off Friday night—the night that Dover took the car out?"

"About eleven-thirty, quarter of twelve," the boy said.

"And what time did you go back on duty the next day?"

"Nine-thirty in the morning."

"Where was the car parked when you came in?"

"Over there," he said, pointing to the south end of the lot.

"That's a long way from the bridge," I said.

"He probably didn't have much of a choice. All the

good spots get snatched up by midnight or one."

"So you figure he came back after one?"

"It's possible," the boy said. "Maybe he just parked down there 'cause he wanted to stretch his legs."

"He had a heart condition."

"Oh, yeah. That's right. I read that in the papers."

"What time did he leave on Friday?"

Jerry scrunched up his face. "About eight o'clock. Yeah, that's it. It was eight o'clock, 'cause he asked me what time it was."

"Like he had some place to go?"

He shrugged. "Like he wanted to know the time, mostly."

"He's gone four and a half, five hours, at least. Right?"

"Eight to one. Yeah, that's five hours."

"And how many miles did he put on the car?"

"Sixty-two," the boy said. "The cops made me check it out."

"What speed would you have to be traveling at to go sixty miles in five hours?"

Jerry laughed. "Pretty damn slow."

"So he went someplace," I said. "Got out of the car, spent three or four hours there. Then came back."

"Sounds good to me."

"And wherever it was, it had to be within thirty miles of the hotel."

"Thirty-one miles," Jerry corrected.

"Got any ideas?" I asked him.

"He could have gone to the ocean—that's nice at night. Watch the surf at the Palisades."

I thought of Mack's beach house. "Pacific Palisades is about thirty miles from here, isn't it?"

"Depends on what part you're talking about. Some of it's closer."

I made a mental note to check the mileage between the Belle Vista and Mack's home, although Walt didn't really fit into my scenario. "Where else could he have gone?"

"Up into the canyon," Jerry said. "Look out at the city. Nice view up there on a clear night."

"Was it a clear night?"

"Yeah. Now you mention it. It was real nice. No smog, . you know?"

"Who lives in the canyon?"

"Who do you think?" Jerry said. "The big bucks live in the canyon."

"The big TV bucks?"

"Yeah, and movies, too. They got homes all over the valley. Some of them got more than one, you know? A town house and a ranch—that kind of setup."

That was more like what I'd wanted to hear. Some TV or movie mogul might have asked Dover to spend the night at the ranch—take a dip in the pool, breakfast by the tennis courts, spend the day talking shop. So Quentin comes back to pick up his togs and his pills. But if that were the scenario, then I wondered why he'd bothered to check into the Belle Vista at all. Unless it had been a last-moment invitation or an uncertain one. And if so, then Quentin couldn't have counted on getting in and out of the hotel through the lobby. That route depended on split-second timing. Which left the gates.

"The gates in the walls," I said to the kid. "Do they leave them unlocked?"

"You mean here at the hotel?"

I nodded.

"Yeah, sometimes they do. During the day."

"How about at night? Late at night?"

"No," he said. "They lock 'em at night. You gotta have a key."

"Did Dover have a key?"

"How should I know?" the kid said.

He hadn't liked that question. I could hear it in his voice. It made me wonder if I'd found Quentin's concierge.

"Did you get him a key, Jerry?" I asked.

"No," he said. "I didn't get him a key."

"Are you sure?"

"Wha'd ya' mean, am I sure? Of course, I'm sure." He wiped his brow with the flat of his hand. "You expect a lot for twenty bucks. I shoulda warned Maria."

"Did she get him a key?"

"I don't know," he said. "No. She didn't get him a key. What the fuck's all this crap about a key, anyway? What sort of shit has that greaser been feeding you?"

I got twenty bucks out of my wallet and handed it to him.

"She's got a big fucking mouth," Jerry said disgustedly and stuck the twenty in his shirt pocket. "She should stick to sucking dicks with it. You know?"

"See you around, Jerry," I said, picking up my bag.

"Yeah, see you," he said dully.

21

The Belle Vista's cocktail lounge was crowded that Friday afternoon. I edged my way among tables, where tan men in optical gray sunglasses and open-collared Italian sports shirts sat beside women who looked as if they'd just stepped off tennis courts, bronze, sun-bleached, and fit. I held my suitcase at my side, hoping they'd think I was some kind of doctor. When I found Jack Moon, sitting in a booth by the tinted window, I squeezed in quickly beside him.

He looked at my suitcase and sighed. "So, you're going to make me fend for myself, huh?"

"You seem to have done all right on your own up 'til now," I said.

He smiled wistfully. "Yeah, but it was nice having someone around to talk to."

A waitress came by to take our orders. After she'd gone, Jack asked me when I'd be coming back to L.A.

"I don't know," I said. "I guess that depends on how things go in Cincinnati."

"You're going to talk to Connie and Marsha?"

I nodded. "And to Quentin's lawyer, too. Maybe I can figure out exactly what he was up to."

"You know I've been thinking about that." Jack folded

142

his hands on the tabletop and tapped his thumbs together. "Maybe he *was* trying to land another job in television. Maybe he thought it was the right time for a change, before things got so out of hand on 'Phoenix' that his reputation, such as it was, was completely ruined. Nobody had been badmouthing him publicly. All the talk was in-house. So he still had some credit in the industry, although a soap with a thirteen share doesn't give you much pull. But it might have been enough. God knows people have been hired for big money with much worse track records."

"What made you change your mind about him?" I asked.

Jack stopped twiddling his thumbs and looked at me. "Yesterday, when I was talking to you about Quentin, I realized with a sinking feeling that I was mad at him because he hadn't turned out to be the man I'd expected him to be—not because he'd fucked up on the job, but because he'd fooled me into thinking he was someone he wasn't and I was hoping for the best. Then this morning, when I found out that Walt was playing the same kind of games that Quentin had been playing, hoping for the best suddenly seemed like a ridiculous waste of time. Hoping for the best wasn't going to put the bacon on my table or help me make it through the day. So I said to myself, 'Sure, Quentin might have been angling for another job. Whatever made you think that he had enough loyalty left in him to do otherwise? Whatever made you think that he had any principles at all? It's time to quit kicking against the pricks, Jack, and start going with the flow.'"

"Then you've decided to stay in the business?"

"I guess so," Jack said with mild surprise, as if that conclusion hadn't occurred to him. "Hell, I'm thirty-five years old. Too old to try to remake the world or to keep hoping it's going to get better. I'm in a relatively safe spot. I guess I'll just have to learn to adapt to it."

"I wish you luck, Jack—whatever you do."

143

The girl came with our drinks. We picked them up and clicked glasses.

"We made a pretty good team, didn't we?" Jack Moon said.

"Not bad," I said to him.

I swallowed the rest of the Scotch and got up. "I'd better get to the airport."

Jack looked mournfully into his glass of whiskey. "Give me a call sometime, will you? If we don't see each other out here again?"

"Sure, I will."

"And I'll ask around for you. See if I can find out what Quentin was doing—whether he really did have a deal going on the side."

"I'd appreciate it." I pulled the suitcase out from under the table. "So long, Jack."

"So long, Harry," he said.

I stopped at the Belle Vista's front desk to clear up a few final questions. The prim woman with the aristocratic face wasn't very helpful, but I did manage to confirm that the night clerk did *not* take a regular break between twelve-thirty and twelve-forty-five and that the bridge between the lot and the lobby was the only way in or out, aside from the gates. Which meant that Quentin had, indeed, secured a key of his own. Probably from Jerry.

I looked for Jerry when I got to the lot. But he wasn't around. Another kid, just as slick and venal looking, told me that Jerry had gone home for the day. That was all right. Jerry's uneasiness about the key was almost as good as a confession. And I figured I could always hire Sy Goldblum to scare the truth out of him, if things reached that point.

I tipped the new kid a dollar to get me a cab. And when it pulled up, I got in and settled back for the long drive to the airport.

144

It took us about thirty minutes on the San Diego Free-way to get to LAX. The cabbie dropped me off at the American building, and I walked down the long, glassed-in corridor to my boarding gate. I was a little surprised at the number of people sitting in the waiting area. Chil-dren, nuns, straw-hatted tourists. It looked as if the plane was going to be full. I took that as a bad omen. They always went down when they were full of children, nuns, and happy tourists. Probably some cause-and-effect rela-tionship having to do with the weight of expectations and the buoyancy of fate.

I sat down on a hard blue plastic chair and parked my overnight bag at my side. Through the picture windows I could see jets gliding effortlessly down runways, their tail fins glistening in the sun. Up they went, into the yel-lowish Los Angeles sky. And with each successful takeoff, I saw my own chances of survival diminishing. A sign at the American booth said that the flight to Cincinnati wouldn't be boarding for another half hour. I tried closing my eyes, but the turbine roar of the jets and the faint chatter of the other passengers kept me from relaxing. A boarding area in an airport is a little like a waiting room in a dentist's office. Everyone tries to look unconcerned, but there's really only one thing on their minds. It was certainly on my mind. And I kept thinking that, this time, I wouldn't have Jack Moon along to hold my hand.

When I couldn't take it any longer, I picked up my bag and walked down some steps to a bar beneath the board-ing gate. They were asking a buck and a half for beer, but I didn't care. I drank two. And when that didn't cut the tension, I ordered a double Scotch. The bartender grinned at me.

"First time in the air?"

"It's always the first time for me," I said miserably.

"Why don't you buy yourself a magazine?" he said. "There's a newstand across the way."

He put the Scotch down on a paper coaster with airplane jokes printed on it.

I didn't feel like buying a magazine, and the idea of reading the airplane jokes horrified me. But I was going to have to do something to distract myself—besides drink. So I unzipped a pocket on the overnighter and took out the map of L.A. that I'd bought at the Marquis. I unfolded one page of it and tried to locate the Belle Vista Hotel—the center of my circle.

"What are you looking for?" the bartender asked me.

"The Belle Vista Hotel," I said.

He turned the map around, rattled it to straighten the page, studied it for a moment, and pointed to a tiny spot.

"There she is," he said. He rotated the map back toward me and lifted his finger from the paper.

"You got a pencil?" I asked.

He pulled one out from beneath the bar and handed it to me. I made a little 'X' on Green Canyon and looked at the legend at the top of the map. It was scaled one-tenth of an inch to a mile. Thirty miles made a three-inch radius. That was a lot of ground—some of it pretty damn expensive. As I was conducting my survey, the bartender leaned over and said, "I think your flight is boarding."

I looked up at him.

"You know they used to execute people for delivering news like that."

He grinned. "What were you looking for on the map?"

"What does it matter—I'm about to die." I folded the map up and stuck it back in the bag. "A hiding place," I said to the bartender. "Some spot that's about thirty miles from the Belle Vista."

"Which direction?"

"You got me."

He gave me a puzzled look. "Just any place?"

"Nope. Someplace special."

He shook his head, as if he thought I was plastered. "Well, we're about thirty miles from the Belle Vista," he said, as he walked away, "if that's any help."

I picked up my bag, walked up to the boarding platform, and got in line to meet my doom.

It wasn't until we were well off the ground, somewhere over New Mexico or Texas, that I began to think again. And one of the first things that came to mind was what the bartender had said about LAX. Maybe Dover *had* gone to the airport, I thought, to see somebody off or to meet somebody who was coming in. Or maybe he'd gone to Pacific Palisades. Or up into the canyons. Or to Pacoima, even—it was about thirty miles away, too. There was no point in speculating about it until I knew why he'd gone to L.A. in the first place.

22

Midway across America, I got drunk on airline booze and flew drunk—and relatively happy—all the way home. It is, in my opinion, the only way to fly.

The 727 touched down at Cincinnati International at a quarter of ten—fifteen minutes behind schedule. Under different circumstances that would have been cause for hysteria. But with three or four little bottles of Dewar's in me, I didn't even mind the bumpy landing. As we were coming in over Indianapolis, the plane made one of its odd, hydraulic hiccoughs, and the woman sitting beside me tensed up as if she'd seen her own death. I turned to her and actually said, "Don't worry, it's just the ailerons being lowered." She seemed unimpressed, in a polite way.

Once we'd landed and disembarked, I wandered out of the terminal to the long-term parking lot, where I'd left the Pinto, got the key out of my pocket, unlocked the door, chucked my bag in the back seat, and drove home.

I woke up in a sweat at eight-thirty the next morning. It felt like August again in my tiny bedroom—hot, sticky, and windless. And there wasn't a mirror in sight. Just the oriel window looking out on the Delores' parking lot. I got out of bed, went into the john, and took a long cold shower—to wash the sweat and booze out of my system. After I'd towelled off, I walked back into the bedroom and pulled the white pages off the nightstand shelf. I had three and a half hours to kill before I met with Frank Glendora, so I decided to put them to use. I found Quentin Dover's number and dialed it on the bedroom phone. A woman answered on the fourth ring.

"Yeah?" she said sleepily. It was Marsha Dover. I recognized the nasal twang of her voice.

"It's Harry Stoner, Mrs. Dover. Remember me?"

"No," she said.

I sighed. "I'm the guy who pulled you out of the pool on Tuesday."

"What pool?" Marsha Dover said. "What the hell time is it, anyway?"

"It's a little past nine."

"Jesus. Nine in the morning?"

"I'm afraid so."

"Jesus," she said again. "Who'd you say you were?"

"Harry Stoner. The detective? The guy that Jack Moon told you about? You know, I came over to see you on Tuesday. I pulled you out of the pool."

"Oh, yeah," she said dimly. "The good-looking one."

I wasn't sure if that was me or not.

I could hear the rustle of bedclothes. "So what can I do for you?" Marsha Dover said.

"I'd like to come out and talk to you about your husband."

"Quentin?" she said as if she could barely place the name. "Quentin's dead."

I stared at the phone for a second. "Yeah, I know. United hired me to look into his death."

"Why? It was an accident, wasn't it?"

"Maybe if I could come out there, I could explain it to you."

149

She thought about it for a moment. "Yeah, why not? You can come out."

"When?"

"I dunno—later. In the afternoon, all right?"

"See you this afternoon."

"Right, bye."

I could hear her struggling with the phone. It took her three tries to hang up. It certainly hadn't taken her long to hang up on old Quentin. Sober—or, at least, half-awake—Marsha Dover was a helluva lot less sentimental than she'd been when she was drunk. I wondered if that was why she drank—to put a little feeling in that beautiful body. Maybe Connie Dover had been right, about the girl being all shallows. She certainly didn't sound like the same person who'd attempted to drown herself in a suicidal fit of grief.

I scanned the phone book and came to Connie Dover's name. She had an address on Camargo. It was a high-society address, just like Quentin's. But that story had worn thin and needed mending. I dialed her number and she answered immediately—no mornings in bed for Connie.

"Yes?" she said. "Who is it?"

"Harry Stoner."

"Oh, yes? How are you, Stoner?"

"Pretty well. I was wondering if I could come over and talk to you again."

"Of course, you can. I'd be interested in hearing what you've found out about my son's death."

I wasn't so sure she'd be interested in hearing what I'd found out about her son's life, but I went ahead and arranged to meet with her anyway.

"We can share another cup of coffee," the woman said.

Connie Dover lived in a condominium development called Indian Village. It was a nice place, as prefabricated communities go—chic, multilevel buildings, arranged in

150

a semicircle like the pipes of an organ. The buildings were brick with cedar inserts and tall smoked-glass windows running from floor to roof. I figured the condos couldn't have been more than five or six years old, which meant that Connie had probably moved in just about the time that Quentin married Marsha. The change from mansion house to condo living must have been traumatic.

I parked on the street at ten sharp and walked up to the front stoop. Two smoked-glass windows flanked the entryway, with silver Levelor blinds hanging behind them. When I rang the bell, one of the blinds crinkled open for a second. It snapped shut and Connie Dover came to the door.

"Hello, Stoner," she said.

I'd forgotten how deep and acerbic her voice was. It went well with her pale, blonde smart-looking face—like a dash of bitters in a Manhattan. Although she was wearing slacks and a casual shirt, Connie Dover still looked dressed-up—perhaps because she had gold bracelets on her wrists and a gold pendant around her neck. Like the last time I'd seen her, her face was powdered ivory white and her hair was tied back in a bun.

She motioned to me to come in and I walked through the door. It was cool inside the condo and dark with the shades pulled. The parquet floor smelled of wax and air freshener—a heavy, manufactured, woodsy smell that reminded me of the Belle Vista's gardens. We went down a hall, past doorways opening on beautifully furnished little rooms, to the kitchen at the back of the house. That seemed to be Connie's idea of the proper place for me to be. This one was small and modern, with Poggenpohl cabinets and built-in appliances, gleaming spotlessly in the morning sunlight. I sat down at a white pine table, beside the rear window. Through the window, I could see the woven wooden fence that circled the development.

Connie unplugged a percolator and brought it and two

cups and saucers over to the table. She poured the coffee and sat down next to me.

"It's refreshing to see you in dry clothes," she said with amusement. "You look like a different man."

"How's Marsha been doing since Tuesday?" I asked.

"She is, as they say, 'bearing up.' In fact, she was bearing up the phone man when last I saw her. She thought he needed a drink. Marsha thinks the world needs a drink and a warm, tight place to rest its penis. That's her philosophy of life."

"Glendora told me that you buried Quentin on Thursday."

"Had to," the woman said dryly. "He died. I guess someone should have told Marsha."

"She didn't go to the funeral?"

The woman shook her head. "Miss was so overcome with grief that she drank a couple bottles of gin that morning. Her feet hurt her, you see. I told her to stay in bed. Better than having her whoops on the coffin. It was a simple and refreshingly dignified ceremony without her. Frank was there. And a few others. I thought you might show up."

"Why?" I asked. "I didn't know your son."

"Something about you, Stoner. You look like a joiner."

I laughed. "You seem to be 'bearing up' yourself."

She smiled sadly. "It's just the makeup, believe me. On the whole, I don't think I've ever felt worse in my life."

"I'm sorry," I said.

"Are you? I would have thought, after all the dirt you've been told, that you wouldn't care one way or another about Quentin."

"How do you know what I've been told?"

She smiled again. "Don't kid a kidder, Stoner. I know the people you've been talking to—almost as well as Quentin did."

"I don't know how I feel about him," I said honestly.

"A diplomatic answer." She picked up her cup of coffee and took a sip.

"How do you feel about answering a few more questions?" I asked.

She thought about it. "I will, if you'll answer a few of mine."

"Like what?"

"Like what specifically did you hear about my son? I think he's owed the chance to defend himself, even if it is by proxy."

"Fair enough," I said. "Opinion was divided. Helen Rose and Harris Sugarman liked him. Walt Mack and Jack Moon didn't."

"Harris is O.K.," Connie said. "He was honest with Quentin."

"And the other three?"

"Various species of crocodiles," she said. "Not Jack as much as the other two. Jack's just hatched. But Walt and Helen are fully matured reptiles."

"Helen liked Quentin," I said.

"Haven't you ever had a pet?" the woman said. "Helen was Quentin's pet croc, until she started snapping at him. Helen Rose doesn't like anyone for very long. It's just not her nature."

"And Walt?"

"I think I would pay to see him die. He is a viperous little faggot with a forked tongue and a malicious temper. He did everything he could to thwart Quentin, often successfully."

"He claimed he had his reasons," I said.

The woman frowned at me. "If you're alluding to the Russ Leonard thing, you probably don't know the whole story."

"I'm willing to listen," I said.

"All right." Connie laid her hand sideways on the table, as if she were exposing a poker hand. The gold bracelet

153

jangled against the wood. "Quentin was originally hired on 'Phoenix' as a consultant, which in the paltry code of televisionese is the nice word for 'heir apparent.' He would have preferred to take over after Leonard had been formally fired. But Helen Rose is not the kind of woman to make a tough decision gracefully. She told my son—on the day she hired him—that Leonard was out and Quentin was in. Then she spent three months trying to get Russ to cut his own throat publicly and spare her the embarrassment of canning him. That three-month transition period was the kiss of death for Quentin. He made enemies just by showing up. Russ's whole team was against him. Quentin wanted to quit right away, but he'd signed one of United's goddamn contracts. By the time he'd goaded Harris into trying to break the deal, Leonard had cut his wrists and the show had gone into limbo. Helen begged him to stay on at that point, promising him anything and everything. What choice did he have? He stayed."

"I was under the impression that Helen tried to help Leonard," I said. "And that Quentin was originally hired strictly to consult."

The woman laughed. "If feeding Russ Leonard cocaine was helping him, then Helen did all she could."

"Are you saying she was his connection?"

"She told Quentin that it was safer than letting Leonard hustle it on the streets. It's not at all unusual, by the way. Cocaine is a form of legal tender out there."

"For Quentin, too?"

"Certainly not," she said. "My son had too many health problems to make cocaine into a habit, although he might have tried it at one point or another. They all do."

"Do you think he might have tried it at the last point?"

"The thought had occurred to me," she confessed. "But what with the new project in the works and things looking up on 'Phoenix,' I can't see him dicing with death—

because that's what it would have amounted to in his condition."

"What makes you say that things were looking up on 'Phoenix'?" I asked.

She gave me a funny look. "You heard differently?"

"I heard that your son was having problems, yes. Serious problems. Walt Mack claimed that he'd been carrying Quentin for some time. And it's a fact that he hadn't produced any material since his heart surgery."

"He was working on a story line," Connie said defensively. "He told me so three weeks ago. And as for Mack, it was just the other way around. Quentin had been carrying him. Part of the deal that Quentin made when he agreed to stay on the show specified that he would have complete control over his team. Naturally, everyone assumed, under the circumstances, that he would let Walt go. But he didn't. He kept him on, drying his eyes for months after Leonard's suicide and cleaning up his sordid little messes for him whenever Walt fell into the sack with Mr. Wrong. Which was every other week. Between Walt and Russ and his own wife, Quentin was kept rather busy in the scandal-snuffing department."

"Why did he do it?" I asked

The woman shook her head. "I don't know. You would have thought that he'd have tired of them after a point. But he didn't. When I asked him why, he laughed and said he'd grown used to other people's troubles. I suppose helping out made him feel valuable. Quentin was always playing father or son to friends and enemies alike. Perhaps because his own father was such a failure."

"Would you care to elaborate on that?" I said.

"What's the point?" she said bluntly. "Just take my word for it—Jim didn't measure up in the guts department."

"He's dead?"

"Yes," the woman said.

155

"I think I should tell you that I've heard some confusing things about Quentin's background. Harris Sugarman told me that your son was down and out when he first met him. And Jack Moon said that he seemed desperate for the job on 'Phoenix.' But you gave me the impression that he was born to wealth."

"I never said that," the woman said after a moment. "I just said that he came from an old family. The money part was your idea."

She said the money part with a touch of scorn, as if money didn't enter into her idea of a pedigree.

"Then he *was* hard up for money?"

"He was when he started out," she said cooly. "No one ever handed him anything, either."

"So Sugarman said."

"Sugarman made his ten percent. Don't let the hype fool you." She stared at the oil spots drifting on the surface of her coffee. "Everyone got his share of Quentin Dover," she said in a way that made me think she was including herself as well. She'd started to look sad, for the first time since I'd arrived.

"He had a bad time?" I said.

"He had to do . . . certain things on the way up. They stayed with him." She blinked and a tear ran down her cheek, turning white with powder, like a tiny ball of snow. "And then he didn't pick the easiest row to hoe. But he had guts, Quentin did. I don't think you know how much." She wiped the tear from her face and rubbed it between her fingers, leaving a white, glistening smudge on their tips. She stared at the powder for a second. "You know, they say that cocaine is the drug of choice in Hollywood. But they're wrong. Money is the drug they're high on. It always has been. The getting and spending of money. It does things to your mind."

"To Quentin's, too?"

"To everyone's," the woman said.

156

"Sugarman said that Quentin was having financial problems."

Connie Dover drew herself up in the chair and shook her head slightly, as if she were still thinking about the things that Quentin had had to do to make it into life's charmed circle. "I'm sorry," she said. "What did you say?"

"Was he having some financial problems?"

"Not really," she said. "Keeping Marsha in booze and stomach pumps was always an expensive proposition. And he'd had some unexpected outlays. His house in New Mexico was damaged by a flash flood and that cost him a bundle to repair. In fact, Jorge Ramirez, his overseer, was here last Wednesday to give him an accounting. Also to drink a lot of Quentin's beer. I'm sure the New Mexican thing was costly, judging from the way they carried on. But Quentin had things under control."

"Then the new project wasn't crucial to him financially?" I said.

"No."

"If, as you say, things were looking up on 'Phoenix' and his financial situation wasn't desperate, then why was he looking for another job at all?"

"I said things were looking up. I didn't say they were satisfactory. When Quentin Dover took over on 'Phoenix,' the show had a seventeen rating and a fourteen share. In less than a year, he built that up to a twenty-one rating and a seventeen share. The only reason that 'Phoenix' started to slip was because Helen Rose capriciously changed her mind about Quentin's last document and decided to try out some fantastic hoo-doo of her own. The results speak for themselves. Just as in the case of Russ Leonard, Helen had to find a fall guy to take the blame for her mistake. Quentin was the obvious choice. And he deserved better than that, after two hard years of work. That's what I told him on Friday, and he knew that I was right. Why should he have shown any loyalty to a woman who had wrecked two years of work and then tried to fob the disaster off on him? Of course, he had a right to look for another job. A perfect right."

I began to wonder whether we were talking about the same man. But, of course, we were. I was just getting a different slant on him. Something, perhaps, closer to his own view of himself—or the view that he wanted his mother to take in. It was kind of interesting.

"The project he mentioned—you thought it was another TV deal?"

"That was my conclusion, yes. Quentin didn't say so specifically."

"Did he say anything, specifically? At lunch or when he called you that night?"

"Only what I have told you. That it was something new, something he found more exciting than 'Phoenix.' "

"He said that?"

"No. I said it for him, and he agreed."

"During the preceding week, do you know if he talked to anyone in the industry?"

"I believe he talked with Frank Glendora on Thursday. That was one of the reasons I assumed it was a TV project."

"United claims that they didn't offer him anything."

Connie Dover bit lightly at her lip. "It could have been with someone else, couldn't it? He had other friends in the business. Did you talk to Harris?"

I nodded. "He didn't know anything about any TV project outside of 'Phoenix.' "

"That's surprising," she admitted. "Quentin generally depended on Harris for all of his television contracts."

I looked at her and she looked at me.

"He didn't actually say it was a television project," she said guardedly. "It could have been something else."

"Like what?"

"A movie. A play. A novelization. There are many possibilities."

Too damn many, I thought. And too goddamn much secrecy.

"He said nothing about it on the phone when he called you from the Belle Vista?"

"It wasn't a long talk. Good Lord, it was past two in the morning. He just said what I told you—that he'd had a bumpy flight and that he would be out of touch for several days."

But Quentin Dover was already out of touch, although it took me a second to realize it. "He called you at two A.M. Cincinnati time?"

"Somewhere around then—yes," the woman said. "He often called me late at night from L.A. He knew I'd worry if he didn't. You know, there's a three-hour time difference on the coast."

"I know," I said. "Two in Cincinnati would have been eleven P.M. in L.A."

"Yes. He'd just gotten back to his hotel room after dinner."

"He said that?" I asked her.

She nodded. "Yes. What of it?"

"That wasn't the strict truth," I said.

She laughed peremptorily. "Don't be ridiculous."

"Quentin wasn't in his hotel room at eleven P.M. He checked into the Belle Vista early that afternoon, had supper in his room, made several phone calls—one of which I thought was to you—then drove off in a rented car at eight P.M. and didn't return to the Belle Vista until after midnight."

I left out what he'd done after that. The woman was already upset and there was no sense in making her feel any worse.

"Are you telling me that he lied to me?" she said weakly.

"I'm telling you that he wasn't in the hotel when he called."

"Maybe he didn't say he was in the hotel. Maybe I was

159

mistaken. Maybe it was just a manner of speaking—another way of saying that he was in L.A."

"Or of saying that he was working on a new TV project?"

"Take that back," she said angrily. "My son didn't lie to me. He had no reason to lie to me."

"Does it make a difference?" I said.

For a second I thought she was going to hit me. "Of course, it makes a difference," she said through her teeth.

I got up from the table. "I'm sorry, Connie. He just told so many different stories to so many different people."

She didn't say anything.

"I'll let you know when I find out what was really going on."

She nodded slightly. "Let me know."

23

I stopped at a phone booth on the way downtown and called Seymour Wattle in L.A. It was about nine in the morning on the coast, and Seymour sounded as if he'd had a rough night.

"No, I haven't got nothing yet," he said before I could say anything more than my name. "Chrissake, it's only been one day."

"That's not what I called about."

"Well, what *did* you want?"

"The phone call that Dover made to Cincinnati on Friday night—do you have a record of the number?"

"Yeah, it's right at my fingertips."

"Take it easy, Sy. Find it, and I'll call you back later in the day."

"Make it a lot later, man," Seymour said. "I don't need to use you for no wake-up service. Shit, do you have any idea how many television production companies there are in L.A.?"

"Keep at it," I said.

But after I hung up, I wondered if that was such a good idea. I was pretty sure that no matter how long he looked, Wattle wasn't going to come up with anything about Dover's mysterious TV project. I had the feeling that there wasn't anything to come up with. Connie Dover had had the same feeling—that Quentin had allowed her to believe something that wasn't true. It wouldn't have been the first time he'd done that, either.

He'd certainly lied to her about the document he'd said he was working on. He'd told Helen Rose the same lie at just about the same time. But then lie was a strong word for it. He'd told them what they wanted to hear. I had the feeling that he'd been doing that with his mother for a long time. Most children paint a brighter picture for their parents. And Quentin had played son to a lot of people. Son and father, like Connie had said.

I got to the Maisonette at twelve thirty-five and found that Frank Glendora had reserved one of the private rooms on the second floor. He was a careful man, no question about it. The maitre d' directed me upstairs to a small, paneled dining room, furnished with French provincial sideboards and chairs. A linen-covered table was set in the center of the room, sparkling with crystal and silver. Frank Glendora was sitting at it, his elbows on the tabletop.

"Hello, Harry," he said.

"Frank."

He pointed to the other chair at the table and I sat down.

"Charles," he said to the maitre d', "bring us some drinks and a menu."

Charles took our bar orders and left. Glendora didn't have to tell him to close the door. He did it on his own.

"You had a pleasant trip back?" Glendora asked.

"What I remember of it."

He gave me a perplexed look.

"I was drunk, Frank. I don't like airplanes."

"I don't blame you," he said. "I used to hate them myself, before I went to work for United. Then it became a contest of wills—mine and the company's." He laughed. "The company won out."

So Jack Moon had said.

"You have something to tell me?" Glendora asked.

I said, "Quentin went to L.A. on Friday night—three days before his usual meeting with the 'Phoenix' team."

"Yes," Glendora said. "I've been at some of their Monday meetings."

"At this point, I'm not really sure why he made the trip. He checked into the Belle Vista Hotel, then left again late on Friday night."

"He left the hotel?" Glendora said with surprise. "I thought he'd been there the whole weekend. That was the impression I got from the police."

"That was the impression he wanted to create. However, he wasn't in his room between sometime after one on Friday and sometime before he died early Sunday morning."

There was a knock at the door. Glendora's hand shot to his lips. It was an involuntary gesture—a reflex. It surprised me. And it rather surprised him, too. He dropped his hand from his mouth and rubbed his chin in perplexity.

"Now why the hell did I do that?" he said.

The door opened and Charles came in with our drinks. He served them and handed each of us a menu. After we'd ordered and Charles had departed, Glendora picked up his glass and the conversation. "You said he was out of his room between Friday and Sunday. Do you know where he was?"

I shook my head. "I was working on the theory that he was meeting with someone about a television project. That's what he implied to his mother. But it might not have been the truth."

"It was always a hard thing to know with Quentin," he said with a touch of sadness.

163

"I thought you liked him."

"Oh, I did," Glendora said. "I liked him enormously. But he was a complicated man—a troubled man. And not entirely an honest one."

"Are you basing that on the rumors you heard?"

Frank Glendora looked offended. "I'm not a fool, Harry. Contrary to general opinion, I do occasionally see things for myself."

"Sorry," I said.

He smiled. "Oh, it's all right. I'm quite used to being considered an ogre or an automaton. It's part of the job. I can't say that it's a part I enjoy. But every businessman has to make hard decisions. Otherwise there wouldn't be any business to run. I wouldn't have acted on the rumors I'd heard if I hadn't thought they were grounded in fact. Facts that I'd personally observed."

"What exactly did you hear?" I asked him. It was one of two questions that I'd wanted to ask for days.

"That Quentin wasn't doing the job he was hired to do," Glendora said. "That he was taking a lot of pills and drinking a great deal. That he was depressed, possibly suicidal. That he'd lost his way and grown desperate."

I asked the second question. "And who did you hear this from?"

Glendora took another sip of his drink. He put the glass back down on the table and folded his fingers beneath his chin. "I heard it from Quentin," he said.

I stared at him. "I beg your pardon? You heard it from Quentin?"

"Yes. Oh, I heard other things from other people, too." He tossed one hand out, as if the other things didn't matter. "From Walt and Helen and Jack. But then you always hear these sorts of things in this business. You get used to it after a time. The constant placing of blame. The scuttling after dollars. You get used to it." But he sounded as if he hadn't quite gotten used to it yet. "Walt called me three weeks ago. Helen sometime before that. And

Jack . . . well, I talk to Jack almost every day. Each of them had his own reasons for complaint—some better, some worse. Quentin had a reason, too, I suppose. In a way, I was hoping that you'd find out what it was. It's been bothering me since last Thursday."

"Quentin's mother said you had a meeting with him on Thursday."

"Yes. I saw him that afternoon. Here, as a matter of fact. In this room. We had lunch together."

"What was the purpose of the meeting?"

"Quentin wanted to talk to me."

"About what?"

"I thought he was going to talk about 'Phoenix,' about the problems he'd been having completing a document. That's what he'd said on the phone, when he arranged the meeting on Thursday morning. You know he'd promised Helen three weeks before that he and Walt would deliver a document by this Monday. Helen, Jack, and I discussed it in New York, and we'd agreed to give him one more week if he asked for it. But no longer than that. The show simply couldn't have survived any longer without a workable story line. To be frank, I don't know if it will survive anyway—a lot of damage has already been done. That was what I was going to tell him on Thursday—that he had one more week to deliver or his job was in serious jeopardy."

Glendora unlocked his hands and dropped them heavily on the table, as if he were done using them for the day. "As it worked out, I didn't have to say that to him. I didn't really do much talking at all. Neither did Quentin. It was a very odd meeting.

"When he arrived I could see that he was in a bad way. He'd been in a bad way for months; but that morning he looked like he was going to die. He kept taking pills. Pacing nervously around the room. Once he phoned his doctor. I was seriously afraid he was going to have an attack. I'd never seen him like that before. He'd always seemed so much in control. So unflappable. It was very upsetting. Jack, Walt, and Helen had said that he was in a decline, but this was worse than I'd thought. The first thing he said to me was that if he couldn't produce the document by Monday, he was going to resign. Under the circumstances, I was grateful that he'd said it."

"Better than leaving him in the room with a loaded gun," I said.

Glendora frowned. "I don't like kicking someone when he's down, Harry. You're quite wrong if you think I do."

"Sorry," I said.

"We had a few drinks. Quentin had more than a few. Then he told me a peculiar story—one that has stayed with me. He said that he'd spent most of that week visiting places from his past, just as if he knew he was going to die that weekend. I didn't know whether to believe him or not. But when he did die on Monday, I called one of the people he'd mentioned—a school teacher. And she told me that he had, in fact, come to see her on Wednesday. I asked her what they'd talked about, and she'd said that he'd wanted to know what he'd been like as a boy—what she'd thought of him."

Charles knocked on the door and rolled in a cart with our food on it. He served the meals and left, but neither of us touched our plates.

"He said other things," Glendora said. "About drugs and liquor. And then he told me if things kept going the way they were, he was going to take his own life. That's why, on Monday, when I heard he was dead, I thought . . ."

"That he'd killed himself," I said.

Glendora nodded. "I didn't know what to say to him at the time. You know, we liked each other but he'd never been intimate. He wasn't a warm man. I suppose I'm not either. I said something feeble—the sort of thing you always say in the face of an unexpected collapse. That it would be all right. That we would work with him. I think I even said that he could have more time to finish the document. But I don't think he was disappointed at my loss for words. In fact, before he left, he regained his composure and told me not to worry about him—that he'd be all right. Later on, after he died, I had the terrible feeling that I had been part of that tour he'd been making. Perhaps the last stop. That I was just one more person whom he had visited—to find out what we'd thought of him."

Glendora shook his head sadly. "Can you imagine that? A man like him, with that much experience and personal charm, coming to me—a virtual stranger—to find out who he was?"

I didn't say it out loud. But I wondered where else a man like Quentin Dover could have gone.

24

Talking about Quentin's last days didn't do much for our appetites. Glendora picked through his salad and I stared at mine without interest. What I really wanted was another drink. But since Charles seemed to come at discreet intervals, I had to make do with a glass of ice water.

When he'd finished toying with his food, Glendora put the silverware down gently beside the plate, as if he were setting the table again, and gave me one of his grave, sad-eyed looks. It was hard for me to tell what he was thinking since he always wore the same long-suffering expression. But what he'd said earlier, and the way that he'd said it, made me wonder if I'd misjudged him. Perhaps he really had hired me to find the truth about Quentin's death. There was no telling what might devil a man's conscience, even an executive of United American. And Quentin had clearly troubled Glendora. And moved him. It was strange, I thought, how many people had cared for Dover, in spite of himself.

"Do you think he *did* kill himself?" Glendora said as he pushed gently at his fork and knife.

"It's possible," I said.

"Do you think you could find out for sure?"

"For United?"

"For me," he said.

"I can try, Frank."

He nodded. "That's all I want—for someone to try."

"There's no need to feel guilty about him," I said. "He created most of the trouble he was in by himself."

"I'm aware of that." Glendora cleared his throat, as if to warn me off the subject of his possible guilts. "Did you want to talk to Seth?" he said.

"Quentin's lawyer?"

He nodded.

"Yes. This afternoon if possible."

There was a phone on one of the sideboards. Glendora picked it up and made the call.

Seth Murdock had an office in the Central Trust Building, a few blocks west of the Maisonette. I walked over to it, through the hot, sultry afternoon. I found Murdock's name in the lobby display case. He was high up—2015. A black bellman in a red cap showed me to the express elevator and a few seconds later I got out on the twentieth floor.

The hallway, like the lobby, was old-fashioned, all marble pilasters and plastered walls. But Murdock's office was surprisingly up to date. It had been rehabbed in a contemporary style—dry-wall and chrome fixtures, plush carpeting on the floors and Danish modern furniture in the waiting area. I gave the secretary my name and sat down beside a woman with a fat, padded brace on her neck.

After a moment, the secretary told me I could go in.

The inner office was as plush as the waiting area. Heavily carpeted, dry-walled, and furnished in a variety of dark glossy woods. The only things that hadn't been redone were the windows. They were tall, old-fashioned fans with round tops segmented like slices of orange.

Murdock was standing in front of one of the windows when I came in—his hands clasped behind his back. He had silvery white hair, slick with pomade. He turned around as I walked up to his desk.

"You Stoner?" he said in a raspy voice.

I nodded.

"Have a seat."

I sat down in front of a huge cherrywood desk, tiered and ornamented like a three-decked battleship. Murdock sat down behind it in a tall leather chair. In front his hair had been combed and chopped in a crew cut. He wore gold-rimmed spectacles, cleaned so immaculately that they flashed in the sunlight coming through the windows. His face was haggard, hollow at the cheeks, pallid, and spotted with age. He could have been in his late fifties, but his pallor made him seem much older.

Murdock coughed hoarsely and wiped his mouth with the back of his hand. "You're here to talk about Quentin?"

"Yes."

He tented his hands at his lips. "I really shouldn't be talking about him at all, you know. His estate is still in probate." He swiveled slightly in his chair and his glasses caught the sunlight again. "However, since you're a friend of Frank's, I'm willing to make an exception. With the understanding that I will not talk about the provisions of Quentin's will. Is that agreeable?"

"Yes."

"Then you may proceed."

I smiled at his locution. "I'm mainly interested in Quentin's financial situation."

"And what does that mean?"

"Whether he was having any serious financial problems prior to his death."

"I guess that depends on your definition of serious." Murdock pulled a silver case out of his pocket, flipped it open, and took out a cigarette. He tapped it several times on the case, then stuck it in his mouth. "He was having problems," he said as he lit the cigarette. "However with an income the size of his, such problems were only temporary, cash-flow things. Within a matter of months he would have straightened them out."

"Within a matter of days he might have lost his job," I said.

Murdock plucked the cigarette from his mouth and held it between his thumb and forefinger, letting the blue smoke crawl over his hand. "I was not aware of that," he said after a moment. "The last time I spoke to Quentin he was sanguine about his prospects."

"When was that?"

"On Friday morning," Murdock said. "He mentioned a new project he'd become involved in. I had the impression it was something lucrative."

"Did he tell you anything specifically about the project?"

"We were supposed to discuss it in detail when he came back to town on Wednesday. There were apparently some papers to sign."

"Were you in the habit of negotiating Quentin's contracts for him?"

"Those that didn't involve show business, yes."

"So you had the feeling that this wasn't a show business project?"

"That was my impression."

I laughed softly and Murdock gave me an odd look. He'd had a story for everyone—Quentin. I wondered if I'd ever find out which one had been true.

"What exactly was the nature of Quentin's financial problems?" I asked.

"He'd made some poor investments," Murdock said. "Against my judgment, he'd purchased a condominium for his mother. I don't suppose I need tell you that the condominium market is not the place to be buying at this time. Then Connie ran up quite a number of bills furnishing the place. And Marsha did the same with his estate

171

house. He also bought a ranch in New Mexico that gave him nothing but trouble. It was situated near a dry wash and every spring it was flooded out. Quentin spent a small fortune keeping it in repair."

"Why didn't he sell it?"

"Why, indeed?" Murdock said. "I urged him to on several occasions, but he claimed to be attached to the place. Why, I don't know. I saw no good reason why Connie had to have her own condo, either. That mansion house is far too big for two people."

"Perhaps the three of them couldn't get along."

Murdock looked at me as if that were balderdash. "With thirty-odd rooms they could have found a way."

I smiled at him. "How long have you known Quentin?"

"Since he was a boy. I used to be a friend of his father's."

"The mansion house belonged to his father?"

Murdock smiled. "Christ, no. Jim Dover was a chemical engineer. They lived in Mariemont. Quentin bought the house after he began to work in television. It was Connie's idea, I think. Few of Quentin's excesses were his own."

"He was run by his mother?"

"Not run," Murdock said. "But heavily influenced. And also influenced by his wife. That's not unusual in men who have grown up without a father."

"His father died when he was a boy?"

"Of heart disease. When Quentin was ten. It was a tragic thing and I'm sure it left its scar on Quentin. He was always haunted by a fear of premature death." Murdock stubbed his cigarette out in a glass ashtray. "It appears his fears were justified," he said.

"He seemed to be a very insecure man."

"That was his mother," Murdock said. "She's distantly related to the Swifts and she filled him full of stupid ideas—about who he should be and how he should live. It was a bad game plan for a kid of ten. He just couldn't ever live up to her ambitions for him."

"He had the house and the money," I said.

"Yes, but he wasn't the real thing. And he knew it. He'd had to work too hard to get what he wanted. He'd had to make too many compromises. It tainted everything. He told me that once, that by the time he'd gotten what he wanted, he didn't want it anymore. If he could have had it all at once—if he'd been born to it—maybe it would have been different. But . . ." Murdock waved his hand in the air.

I thought of Walt Mack, who had said virtually the same thing about his job.

"Quentin seemed to have told a lot of stories."

"You mean lies, don't you?" Murdock said.

"I guess I do."

"It was an affliction with him. It was also part of his charm. You know the story of the boy who cried 'Wolf!'" That was Quentin. Only in his case nobody ever disbelieved him. He kept crying and people kept paying attention. And before you knew it, it had become a mainstay of his personality. When in doubt, he lied. When not in doubt, he lied. He did it the way some people eat—obsessively. To comfort himself for whatever he lacked in natural charm or grace or breeding. One got used to it, after a time. I actually grew rather fond of it myself, but then I could generally tell when he was lying."

That was what his mother had thought, too. And Murdock sounded like an adoptive father—one of the many, from Harris Sugarman to Frank Glendora, that Quentin had cultivated.

"Was he lying about the new project?" I asked him.

"I don't think so. When it came down to it, Quentin could be pretty shrewd and pretty hard about money. All those years hustling a dollar on the West Coast hadn't been wasted. He needed money and I'm fairly sure he would have found a way to get it. He was ten thousand in the hole over the condo. And a hundred thousand in the hole over that damn house in New Mexico."

"A hundred grand?" I said.

"The last flood almost wiped it out. He had to sell off most of his stocks and bonds to get the cash. Of course, it was just like throwing it into a dry well. But I couldn't talk him out of it."

"This was recently?"

"Over the last couple of months," Murdock said.

"Then he really needed to score?"

"What he really needed was a few months of solitude. A few untroubled months to do his work. That would have been sufficient, at the salary he was making."

"If he could have kept making it," I said.

Murdock nodded.

I got up to go. Murdock stood up, too.

"One last question," I said from the door.

"Yes?"

"You knew him. Do you think he might have taken his own life?"

Murdock didn't say anything for a time. "What makes you ask that?" he finally said.

I told him the story that Frank Glendora had told me—about Quentin's odyssey through the past.

Murdock thought about it. "Yes," he said. "It's possible. If he saw no other way out."

25

It was close to five when I got to the big house on Camargo. I drove through a confetti of sunlight and shade, up the oak-lined drive to the garages. There was nobody mowing the lawn this time. No farrago of sounds. Just the squawking of cardinals hidden in the oaks and that green, placid, sunlit lawn, and that great house, half-hidden in its own shadow. I walked up to the door and knocked. A few minutes passed and Marsha Dover answered. She looked as if she'd been running from some-one—someone she hoped would catch her. Her beautiful face was ruddy and full of laughter. Her blonde hair was tangled about her forehead and cheeks, jeweled at the hairline with beads of sweat. She brushed the damp hair back and eyed me breathlessly.

"Hi, there," she said.

"Hi."

She was wearing a loose cotton blouse, unbuttoned at the top. I could see her beautiful breasts when she leaned over to roll up the cuffs on her shorts. Her breasts were beaded with sweat, too. She smelled strongly of sweat, alcohol, and musk. For the second time since I'd met her, I had trouble concentrating on anything but that face and body. She was that stunning.

She looked up at me, still bent over her shorts, and smiled. "I know you, don't I?"

"Stoner. Harry Stoner."

She straightened up. "Wanna play, Harry Stoner?"

I almost said yes. Instead, I asked, "What's the game?"

"Hide and seek."

Just as she said it, a tall shirtless kid with a brown, muscular chest sprang out from somewhere behind the door and grabbed Marsha around the waist. The girl shrieked with laughter and struggled wildly in his arms.

"I win," the boy said.

The girl stopped struggling and twisted her head around to face him. "What do you win?" she said huskily. I could almost see the kid weaken at the knees. I felt my own knees give a little. She couldn't have been more inviting if she'd been lying naked on the floor.

The boy stared at her a long moment. "Christ," he said heavily and rubbed her breasts through the shirt.

"Excuse me," I said.

He looked up. "Where the hell did you come from?"

"The name is Stoner."

"Fine," he said. "We don't want any."

The girl laughed and her boyfriend started to close the door in my face. I pushed it back at him, a little harder than I should have.

"Hey!" he said, catching the door in one palm. "What's the idea?"

"I want to talk to Marsha."

"Well, suppose she don't want to talk to you?"

"Why don't we ask her and see?"

"Marsha, what is this shit?" the boy said, turning to her.

She shrugged. "I dunno. He was there when I opened the door."

The boy turned back to me and flexed his arm menacingly. "Beat it."

Maybe it was the girl. Maybe it was Quentin Dover.

176

Maybe it was the heat and the jet lag. But I wasn't in the mood to play. I stepped through the doorway and jabbed the kid in the chest with my right hand. "You beat it," I said. "Go on out to the pool and cool off."

The girl laughed again and the boy rubbed his chest where I had poked him. I was a lot bigger than he was, and he was smart enough to know that I meant business.

"I'm gonna go out to the pool," he said to Marsha. "Call me if you need me."

The girl gave him a disappointed look as he walked away.

"You wanted to see a fight, didn't you?" I said to Marsha.

The girl nodded stupidly and giggled.

I felt like slapping her. I wondered how Dover had resisted the same impulse. I wondered how he'd dealt with her at all.

I stared at her for a moment, and she seemed to sober up a little. She fidgeted with a button on her shirt and dropped her eyes nervously to the floor. "What do you want?" she said.

"We met before, remember?"

"I remember," she said, although I wasn't sure she did.

"I'm the guy that's looking into your husband's death. Remember him? Quentin Dover?"

She made a sulky face. "Yeah, I remember Quentin."

"What's it been—six days now since he died?"

"And you figure I oughta be wearing crepe, right?" She stared at me with defiance. "What the fuck do you know about it, anyway? What do you know about anything?"

"I know that he's dead," I said. "I'd like to know why."

"Why don't you ask Connie why?" the girl said. "She's the big cheese, isn't she? The one with all the class? I'm just the slot that Quentin parked in at night."

"Quit feeling sorry for yourself," I said.

She sucked her breath in sharply, as if I'd slapped her.

"You think I'm feeling sorry for myself? O.K., Buster Brown. You wanna hear about ol' Quentin. I'll tell you. C'mon."

She led me down the hall to the back of the house. It was the first time I'd seen Quentin's home by daylight, and I was a little disappointed in what I saw. The house itself was beautiful—big, high-ceilinged rooms, with hardwood floors and Rookwood mantles and glossy mahogany trim around doors and windows. It was what was inside the rooms that was disappointing. All the furniture was new, and I mean brand new. The place looked as if Marsha or someone had gone on a shopping spree in Closson's or Pogue's, had them box up an entire floor of display items, and had the stuff delivered to the house. Individually the pieces were handsome but they were stacked in the rooms without rhyme or reason. Or if there was a reason, it was simply that all the junk was expensive.

We ended up in the same study that I'd taken Marsha to when she'd tried to drown herself on Tuesday, if she had tried to drown herself, if it hadn't been an ostentatious display like the furniture. Through the sliding glass doors I could see the sunlit terrace, the umbrella table, and the chaise beside the pool. The kid I'd chased off was lying on the chaise, holding the sun-reflector under his chin. There was a sideboard on the wall by the door, with whiskey decanters on it. Marsha went straight to it, as if she were being drawn on a string.

"Buster Brown," she said with a laugh. She pulled the crystal stopper out of one of the decanters, dropped the stopper on the sideboard, and splashed two fingers of bourbon into a cut-glass tumbler. She turned to me—the glass in her hand. "Well, Buster, what do you wanna know?"

"You have one of those for me?" I said, pointing to the glass.

"Help yourself."

I got up, walked over to the sideboard, and poured

myself a Scotch. The girl brushed against me as I stood beside her. I could feel her nipples through the thin fabric of her blouse, like pebbles in her shirtpockets.

"I got one of everything," she said, pivoting on a foot.

I looked at her, as she leaned against my arm.

"Why the hell did you marry him, Marsha?" I said.

She leaned back against the sideboard and took a long drink of whiskey. "For his money, why do you think?"

"You said something about love the last time I saw you."

"I always say something about love when I'm crocked."

I walked over to the couch and sat down. Marsha braced one arm on the sideboard and stared at me knowingly. "You think I'm a real cunt, don't you?"

I said, "Yeah."

Her face fell. "You're kind of nasty, aren't you, Buster? Are you that way in bed, too? Quentin wasn't." She took another long pull of bourbon. "I got news for you, friend. Cunts are made, not born. If I'm a tramp, Quentin made me that way. I was just a dumbass kid when I met him. Just a dumbass kid—"

"I've heard it, Marsha. I heard the part about your family, too."

She gave me a hurt look. "You think I was lying?"

"I think it takes two to tango."

"Sometimes it takes three," the girl said with a bitter laugh. "With Quentin, it took three."

"And what does that mean?"

"Put on your thinking cap, Buster. It'll come to you."

"Why don't you spell it out, instead?"

"He couldn't get it up. Is that plain enough for you?"

"After the heart surgery?"

"Before, during, and after," she said coldly. "Let's see if I can explain it so even an asshole like you will understand. See there was this dumb cunt . . . oh, but you heard that part, didn't you?"

"I'll hear it again."

"No. I'll skip over that crap and get to the hard-core.

179

She meets this guy one day, see? And he's really sweet. He doesn't even try to get into her pants, which she wouldn't mind, you know? But this one's different. He's smart. He knows things. He really makes this dumb little cunt feel like she's something. And he ain't even good-looking. He's just the best thing the cunt ever met. And he's loaded, to boot. Which doesn't hurt. And he treats her like a goddamn princess, like she's too good to fuck. He tells her that she's what he's always wanted. And the dumb cunt believes him, because that's what *she's* always wanted to hear from someone like that." The girl splashed some more whiskey into the tumbler. "So they live happily ever after. The end. Right?"

She raised the glass and smiled. "Not quite right," she said. "It turns out the prince has some funny ideas. It turns out the prince isn't a prince, after all. But the dumb cunt doesn't care. In fact, she wants to do anything she can for him, 'cause he's had such a hard time. He's had to do some bad things. He's had to suck and fuck and ream just about every wet asshole in Hollywood. And if the poor son-of-a-bitch can't fuck anymore, then there are other ways to get diddled." She laughed. "I guess I know. I've tried them all. But pretty soon that isn't enough. It isn't enough to sit and watch the cunt stick things up inside her, while the prince pulls his pud. Pretty soon, the prince wants some real hard-core action. And when the cunt doesn't want to go along with it, the prince tells her the facts. He tells her what a cunt she really is—what a fool she is to love him, because anything that would love him ain't worth two shits, because he ain't worth two shits, because nothing in the whole goddamn world is worth two shits. He really opens her eyes, you know? Only she still wants to make it with him. She thinks, maybe, if she does what he wants, he'll want to make it with her, too. So she starts fucking around. She goes out to a bar, while the prince waits in the car, and picks up some jerk—the cruder, the better. Then she and the prince take the jerk home. And they all get real loose. Then the prince says, 'Goodnight.' Only he doesn't go to bed. He goes to a hole in the wall or a closet and he watches. And sometimes the cunt forgets that he's watching. Sometimes she gets a little messed up, and she thinks there's nobody there. She thinks, 'There never was anybody there.' And after awhile, it's like there isn't. It's like it's just her and whatever she brings home. The kinkier, the better. The more it hurts, the better. Like she's trying to see just what it would take to make princey reappear. Only he never does. And now he never will."

She swallowed the rest of her drink and stared at me. "Is that what you wanted to hear?"

I didn't say anything.

The girl smiled. "Stop feeling sorry for me, Buster. Why the hell should you feel sorry? You're just snooping around for Connie. Trying to find out what I'm up to. Just like she used to do with Quentin. God, how he hated that bitch! Well, you can go on back and tell her that the cunt's doing fine. The cunt is mourning in her own way—the way Quentin would have liked it."

She started to cry. I got up and walked over to her.

"Stay away from me," she said through her tears. "I don't want you touching me. I'm no charity case, man."

I put my arm on her shoulder, and she threw the tumbler at me. It hit me in the chest and fell to the floor.

"Who do you think you are, man?" she said with a laugh. "Another prince? I don't fuck princes anymore."

She turned on her heel and walked out of the room.

26

I opened the sliding glass door and went out onto the terrace. The kid on the chaise looked up at me. He wanted to be pals, now. I could see it in his face. Now that I'd joined the Marsha Dover Club. He didn't realize it, but he'd picked the wrong moment to buddy up to me.

"She's really something, isn't she?" he said. "Really wild."

I kicked the chaise over, and the kid tumbled onto the tiles.

"Jesus," he said frantically. "Take it easy. What are you? Her old man or something? I thought he was dead. Honest to God, mister. She told me he was dead."

I felt the anger drain out of me. It had been a stupid thing to do. "I'm no relative," I said.

He nodded uncertainly—on all fours, on the terrace. "Just take it easy, O.K.?"

"Who are you?"

"Me?" He pointed to himself "Me—I'm nothing, man. Just the phone repairman."

I started to laugh.

He smiled weakly and got to his feet. "You ain't gonna report me, are you?"

I shook my head. "C'mon. You can relax. I'm not going to do anything to you."

"Sure?" he said.

"Yeah. I shouldn't have leaned on you in the first place."

" 'S'all right," he said, waving his hands. "No problem." He tipped the chaise back onto its feet, started to sit down, then looked at me. "Is it O.K.?"

"Christ, yes," I said. "I told you—forget it. What are you out here for, anyway?"

"One of the phones is fucked," he said. He sat down gingerly on the chaise. "Marsha put call-forwarding on it and forgot how to take it off. Marsha . . . she don't seem real bright about phones and shit. All she had to do was press a couple of buttons and hang up. I fixed it."

"I'll bet you did."

"Hey," the kid said. "What are you going to do when it's thrown in your face? I got a wife. I got kids. But, Christ, she's the most beautiful thing I've ever seen. You know? I mean I couldn't believe it."

"I guess not."

"She wanted to do some funky things. Backdoor, you know? It was O.K. with me. Plenty O.K. But I think I might have hurt her."

I stared at him.

He stood up suddenly, as if he figured he'd spent enough time humoring me. "I better get going," he said. "O.K.?"

"Yeah. You can go."

"Thanks." He walked slowly across the terrace, scooping up a workshirt where he'd dropped it on the tiles. When he got to the stairs, he picked up his pace. He was running by the time he got to the garden—past Cupid and the rosebushes and out to the lawn.

I sat down on the chaise and waited. The sun started to set over the garden, lighting up the oaks. After a time, she came back out onto the terrace. She had on a terry robe. There was another glass of booze in her hand.

"You still here?" she said.

"Still here."

She walked over to the edge of the terrace and looked down at the garden. The setting sun caught in her hair, making it glow.

"Why?" she said without looking at me.

"I wanted to say I was sorry."

She turned around, bracing her hands behind her on the balcony rail. The wind tossed her golden hair and the lapel of her robe.

"That's not why," she said.

"No," I said. "It isn't." I got up and walked over to where she was standing. She smiled—a little triumphantly. Enough to make me feel vaguely ashamed.

"You're not one of those reformer types, are you?" she said. "If so, you're years too late."

I pulled her to me. She didn't resist. She came into my arms almost involuntarily, as if it were a reflex with her, and laid her head on my chest.

"He wasn't bad," she said. "I didn't mean to make him sound bad. He was just scared, you know? All the time scared."

"I don't want to talk about Quentin," I said.

"That's funny," she said with a laugh. "I do."

I put my arms around her.

Marsha reached down and undid the belt of her robe, letting it fall open on either side. She was naked underneath it. She pulled my head close to her face and held it steady for a moment, like a mother looking searchingly at her child.

I wasn't sure what she was looking for, but her eyes glazed over suddenly, as if it didn't matter after all. She pulled my head to her and we kissed. She began to groan, grinding her naked pelvis into my groin.

184

"Do it babe," she whispered hoarsely. "Right out here. Do it."

When it was done, she got up, naked, and walked across the dark terrace to the study. She flipped a switch by the sliding glass door and the pool lights went on—a soft aqua glow. She came back out with two glasses of booze and sat down on the apron of the pool, paddling her feet in the water. I worked my way, bare-assed, across the cold tiles and sat down beside her.

She handed me a drink. "Well, that was different," she said. "I'd almost forgotten what straight sex was like."

I stared at her for a moment. The pool lights rippled across her body, making her look like she was underwater. "You're very beautiful," I said.

She laughed, glanced at me, and laughed again. "You go to too many movies, you know? You had me pegged right the first time. I'm a real cunt."

"It sounded like you had some help," I said, sipping the Scotch.

"Oh, don't go getting pissed off at Quentin," she said. "You don't have much right now, do you?"

I wondered for a second if that was why I'd taken her—to get back at him. I hoped she was wrong.

"Anyway, like you said, it takes two to tango. I didn't have to do it. I guess I wanted to. I guess, maybe, I wanted to all along." She pulled one leg out of the water, cocked it on the tiles, and planted her chin on her knee. "Toward the end, he wanted me to stop. The last two weeks, especially. But once you get locked into a game like that . . . you just can't go back again. No matter what. Like on Thursday, the day before he left, he just wanted it to be him and me again, you know? He was scared. He'd been having bad dreams. About his dad." The girl turned her head on her knee and stared at me. "He would have been all right if she'd have left him alone."

185

"Connie?"

Marsha nodded. "But she just wouldn't ever let him forget what a fuck-up his old man had been and how he had to watch out or he'd end up that way, too. Like everything he did had to be different or he'd croak like his dad."

"Of heart disease?" I said.

Marsha laughed. "Is that what she told you?"

"She didn't tell me anything. A man named Murdock told me that."

"Oh, yeah. Old man Murdock. He's a nice old coot. Quentin liked him because he acted like his dad—always making him toe the line and shit. Quentin liked that. I guess that's why he put up with Connie, too. All he ever wanted was for somebody to tell him what to do."

"What did Quentin's father die of?" I asked.

Marsha put a finger to her temple and pulled an imaginary trigger. "He blew his head off. Quentin was there, you know?" The girl shuddered. "The poor fucker. He used to have dreams about it all the time. Real screaming nightmares."

"His father didn't have heart disease?"

"Yeah, he had that, too. That's why he killed himself. He just couldn't take it—waiting to die. Then I guess living with Connie didn't help any. You know, sometimes I think that's what she wants me to do. Sometimes I think I want to do it myself."

"Don't talk like that."

"Why?" she said. "Not talking about it ain't gonna change anything. My life's fucked. Quentin was all I had left."

"Then I feel sorry for you," I said.

"Well, don't," she snapped. "We understood each other. In spite of all the shit. It might not have been love anymore, but it was better than nothing. Better than this."

She looked at me, and I blushed.

"The only thing I wish is that I'd spent that last night

with him, like he wanted. It wouldn't have been any skin off my nose. And it would have meant a lot to him."

"That was the last time you saw him—Thursday night?"

"Yeah. Right before I went out."

"He didn't say anything to you, did he? About where he would be or what he'd be doing?"

"No. He didn't even say goodbye." Her eyes got hazy. "The poor son-of-a-bitch. He was so alone."

I put my arm around her shoulder. "Do you want to go out?" I said after a time. "Get something to eat?"

She laughed. "I don't eat. I drink. No thanks, Harry. That is your name, isn't it?"

"Yeah," I said. "Harry."

"You can go if you want."

"I don't feel right about leaving you here," I said.

She pressed my hand against her shoulder. "Don't be a jerk. It isn't gonna make a difference."

She dropped her hand from mine and I stood up.

"Maybe I'll stop by again tomorrow," I said.

"Any time," she said. "We're always open."

I bent over and kissed her. "Goodbye, Marsha."

"Goodbye, Harry."

I slipped into my clothes and left her sitting by the pool.

27

I grabbed a bite to eat at a hamburger joint in Kenwood, then drove back home. It was almost ten when I stepped into the apartment. I took a hot shower, towelled off, and went into the bedroom to lie down. I tried to go to sleep, but I couldn't relax. I kept thinking about the girl. I shouldn't have screwed her, I knew that. But I'd gone ahead and done it anyway, because she was so beautiful and so hurt. And so easy. What are you going to do when it's thrown at you? That's what the phone guy had said. Lying there in the darkness, I couldn't see much difference between him and me. Or between me and all the others.

The thought bothered me so much that I got up. I decided to call Wattle in L.A. It was only about eight-thirty on the coast. He answered on the second ring.

"Yeah?" he said.

"It's me."

"Oh, yeah. Stoner. I tried to call you earlier tonight."

"I went out," I said.

"I've got that phone number you wanted."

He read it off to me.

"Do you know whose it is?" I asked.

"Dover's," he said. "It's his private phone. The wife told

us on Monday. It just slipped my mind."

"He called Marsha on Friday night?"

"That's the way it looks."

"She didn't say anything about it to me."

"Take it up with the lady," Wattle said. "Oh, by the way, I got some news for you. You know the Mex maid, the one who found Dover's body?"

"Maria Sanchez?"

"That's the one," he said. "Well, somebody offed her last night."

"No," I said.

"Yeah. Her and her kid both."

"Jesus. How?"

"Some psycho broke into her house and cut them up. I don't know all the details. The Pacoima police are handling it."

"You got their number?"

"Just a sec." He went off the line. When he came back on, he gave me a number in L.A. county. "Look, Harry, if there's some connection here, I want to hear about it. This is murder, man. Can't play footsie on the big Number One."

"I talked to the girl," I said. "On Thursday night. She told me a few things about Dover. I can't see how it would have gotten her killed."

"Why not let me be the judge of that?"

I told him what Maria had told me—that Dover hadn't been in his room on Friday night or on Saturday.

"Well, where was he, then?" Wattle asked.

"I don't know," I said.

"I thought he was working on some TV thing."

"That was a lie."

"Thanks for letting me know."

"I just found out about it myself, Sy. I was going to tell you. You can forget about TV. At least, I think you can."

"How 'bout my two hundred bucks?"

"I'll get it to you through Jack."

189

"Don't *you* forget, man," he said. "And if you find out where Dover went, let me know."

He rang off. I put the phone down, laid back on the bed, and thought about that candlelit room and the little boy, hiding in his mother's skirt. I took a cigarette from the pack lying on the nightstand. When I went to light it, I could see my hand shaking in the matchlight. I blew the match out and smoked for awhile in the darkness. Then I made the call to the Pacoima police.

I got a duty sergeant named Jackson—a black man by the sound of his voice. He was cautious but fairly cooperative.

"What can you tell me about the Sanchez killings," I asked, after I'd given him my name, address, phone number, social security number, and Sy Goldblum's name and address, to boot.

"I can read you the official bulletin: 'Maria Sanchez, female, Hispanic, 24, was found dead in her home, 4420 Coronado Avenue, at seven A.M. on Saturday morning. Her son, Rafael, 6, was found dead with her. Homicide is suspected.'"

"Can you tell me how she died?"

"We don't usually give out that information."

"Make an exception," I said. "Call Goldblum if you want to verify my credentials."

Jackson sighed. Either it was a busy night or I'd made a convincing case for myself, because he relented. "All right. She died from burns and stab wounds."

I was sorry I'd asked.

"She was stabbed thirty-two times with a short-bladed knife. Parts of her body had been painted with plastic glue—you know, the kind that kids use on model airplanes. The glue patches had been set on fire. It burns for a long time, man. Like napalm."

"Jesus," I said, feeling sick. "The boy, too?"

"The boy first, near as we can tell."

"He was tortured, too?"

190

"That's the way it looks."

"Do you have any suspects?"

"You get Goldblum to call us," he said.

I took that as a yes. But I didn't press him on it. He was right. I should have been letting Wattle do the work. I thanked Jackson for his help and hung up. Then I called Wattle back and told him I wanted everything he could get on the Sanchez murders.

"What's the big deal?" he said. "Like you said, I don't see the connection."

"I didn't know how she died before. She was tortured, Sy. Her kid was tortured to death in front of her eyes."

"This ain't Cincinnati," Wattle said.

"There has to be a reason why she and the boy were tortured."

"Why?" he said coldly. "Maybe somebody just wanted to see them suffer. They come like that out here, man. Or maybe she got on the wrong side of the Mex maf'. Those greasers like to make lasting examples of folks they don't like. You don't really think this has anything to do with you, do you? Because I hate to be the one to tell you this, but you're not that big a deal. This is L.A., man. Nobody gives a shit about you."

I said, "Maybe Dover was the big deal."

"Dover died in the shower," Wattle said. "Why don't you make yourself useful and find out why his wifey forgot to tell you about the phone call?"

"I still want to know about the killings."

"All right. But it's gonna cost—"

"Put it on my tab," I told him.

After I hung up, I went for a drive—to cool out completely. I thought I'd end up closing some bar, seeing what a few double Scotches would do for the ache in my small-town gut. But I was northbound on 71 before I knew it. And then I was off it, on the oak-lined boulevard that led to her house—to Quentin's house.

I pulled into the driveway, flipped off my lights, and coasted to a stop in front of the garage. There was moonlight on the lawn and in the dark, broad-limbed oaks. It was shining on the rooftops and reflecting off the dormers and leaded casements. I sat in the car and studied the house, wondering what I was doing there. It wasn't just Quentin's phone call—that would have waited until morning. It wasn't just Maria Sanchez and her little boy. I wasn't sure I wanted to give myself a reason for being at that house. It might have been a good reason to leave, as well. It was enough that it was late and that I was low and that I was already there.

That's what I told myself, anyway, as I got out of the car. But halfway up the walk to the front stoop, I started to feel foolish. I glanced at my watch—it was past two—and asked myself again, "What are you doing?" It felt too much like high school, standing there in the moonlight at two in the morning on that broad, empty lawn.

I looked up at the second story. A lamp clicked on behind a moonlit window. The moon disappeared and I could see a curtain and the shadow of a woman. There was another shadow beside her. I walked back to the car and got in. As I was backing out of the driveway, the light went off and the moon reappeared, reflected off the windowpanes.

28

I called the girl the next morning about eleven and asked if I could come out to talk. She sounded sleepy and hung-over. She also sounded as if she weren't alone.

"Give me an hour, O.K.?" Marsha said.

Around noon, I drove out to the Dover house. The boy on the mower was back at it, cutting long parallel lines on the huge lawn. Sprinklers were on, buzzing and whisking like wasps beneath the oaks. I walked up to the stoop and tried the doorbell. When no one answered, I walked around the house, through the topiary garden, to the terrace stairs. Someone had hung a Dixie cup on Cupid's foot. I gave it a spin and went up to the pool.

Marsha was sitting on the chaise—a glass of tomato juice in her right hand. She was wearing those aviator glasses and a string bikini. I watched myself in the sunglasses as I walked up to her—a big, sandy-haired man in a short-sleeved shirt and slacks.

"Hi," I said.

"Hi," she said back. "Why didn't you stay last night? That *was* you wasn't it?"

I looked at her for a moment. "I don't like to watch."

"Oh, hell, I would have gotten rid of him. It didn't mean anything, anyway."

"What does, Marsha?" I said it before I could think about it.

"Lighten up, Harry, will you? That asshole was kinda hard on me last night, and I got a bad headache. I told you you were welcome. What more do you want me to say?"

I sat down on the diving board and stared into the blue, sun-streaked pool. Another Dixie cup was bobbing in the water, like a small white buoy.

"Quentin called you last Friday."

The girl took her sunglasses off, dangling them in her free hand. Her eyes looked bruised and puffy, as if she hadn't slept at all.

"So this is a business visit, right?"

"I guess it is," I said.

She stared at me for a brief second, then flipped the glasses back on her nose. "I didn't get any phone call on Friday."

"Don't fuck with me, Marsha. Please? The hotel has a record of it. So do the cops."

"I don't give a shit what the cops have a record of," she said. "I didn't get any goddamn phone call."

"Were you out?"

"Yeah," she said sharply. "As a matter of fact, I was." She pursed her lips and sighed. "I didn't get the phone call because Quentin left call-forwarding on his phone— not because I was out. The phone didn't even ring here. It rang wherever he forwarded the call to. O.K.? I didn't even know about it until Monday night."

"You mean you didn't use the phone until Monday?" I asked.

"I don't use that phone at all—the one in Quentin's study. That's Quentin's phone. It took the phone company a whole week to get around to fixing it." She giggled. "I guess you know that, don't you?"

"I guess I do," I said. "How'd you find out about the call-forwarding?"

"Quentin's cardiologist, Phil Feldman, called me on

194

Monday evening, after I got back from L.A. Quentin always left Feldman a number where he could be reached when he went out of town—it made him feel safer. This time he left him the number of his study phone. Feldman had been trying to get hold of Quentin since Saturday and kept getting no answer. So he called me on my line. Eventually we figured out what was wrong. The phone repairman explained it to me. Quentin had forwarded his calls, so that the phone was ringing out on the coast. Somewhere in L.A., I guess."

"Yeah, but why would Quentin call his own phone on Friday if he was trying to reach someone in L.A.?"

"I don't know," she said.

"And you don't know exactly where Quentin forwarded his calls to?"

"No," Marsha said. "Maybe Feldman does. I think he talked to Quentin on Saturday morning. What difference does it make at this point?"

It made a big difference to me. Those calls might have been going to wherever Dover had been staying on Friday night and Saturday, although it was damn odd that he would have used call-forwarding to reach somebody in L.A. when he could have dialed directly from the Belle Vista phone.

"I guess I'll have to talk to Feldman," I said. "Do you know his address?"

"Quentin made me memorize it," she said. She gave me an address on Burnett, a couple of blocks from the Delores.

"Is that it with the business?" Marsha said, getting up off the chaise. She walked over to where I was sitting and kissed me hungrily on the mouth.

"Don't you ever get enough?" I said, when she came up for air.

"Aw, don't be shitty, Harry. Please?"

She stared at me for a moment. "Why'd you come out here last night?"

"I heard some bad news," I said. "I wanted some company."

"Yeah, but why me?"

"I don't know why."

"Sure you do." She stretched her arms above her head and her breasts rose beneath the light bikini halter. "Just like me. You wanted some more."

"I guess I did," I admitted.

"So why don't we do it?"

" 'Cause I gotta go talk to Dr. Feldman."

"Oh, don't go," she said. "Please? I'm sorry about last night. I didn't know you were going to come back."

"I'll come out later."

"I don't need you later," she said. "I need you now. I don't feel good. I can't sleep. Just stick around until I fall asleep, O.K.?"

I couldn't help thinking about the night she'd asked Connie to stay with her—to keep her from having bad dreams. As beautiful as she was, I didn't want to be her babysitter. I didn't know what I wanted to be to Marsha Dover. But I didn't want to leave her alone, either.

We ended up making love—that was almost a given with Marsha—in a big bed with bolster pillows and pale blue silk sheets. I watched her face as I screwed her—that beautiful, blonde child's face. She kept her eyes squeezed shut while we made love—not fluttering shut as if she were fantasizing, but shut tight as if she were afraid to open them. When she came, she turned her head back and forth on the pillow and pushed me away from her with the palms of her hands, as if she needed room to breath. Her hips never stopped moving. I came immediately after she did.

Afterward, she curled up against me beneath the cold sheets, burying her head in my chest and draping her arms around my neck. She stayed huddled against me for a long while—not saying a word, sheltering herself against my body. I looked around the dim room at the shuttered, off-white closets and the creamy enameled furniture, and knew that she was thinking of Quentin—that she'd been thinking of him all along, as if he were still with us, hidden somewhere in that shuttered room. It was an unsettling thought—enough to make me close my eyes, too.

"You've got to get out of here, Marsha," I said. "Take a couple of weeks and go somewhere."

She didn't say anything for a moment. "I don't know if I could leave."

"Sure you could."

"Sure," she said weakly. "It isn't that simple. If it was that simple . . . I would have gone." She raised her head and peeked out at the room. "You know, sometimes I still think he's out there. Sitting like he used to sit."

She swallowed hard and dropped her head back on my chest.

"The only way to get away from him is to get away from this room. You know that. Away from this room and everything else that reminds you of him."

"Fucking reminds me of him," she whispered.

I guess so, I said to myself. I stroked her hair and she looked up at me.

"You're very beautiful," I said.

She bit her lip. "You still think so."

"I know so."

She started to smile.

"You think you're going to be able to get some sleep now?"

"I can try," she said. "There are some Nembutols in the medicine chest."

"You take a lot of them?"

"Only when I'm worn out and can't sleep. It's them or booze or fucking."

"Stick to booze and fucking," I said.

She pulled herself up to my face and kissed me. "I like you," she said. "You're like him—only different."

197

"I'm not like him at all," I said.

"I know one way you're not like him."

She ran her hand down my belly.

"Marsha," I said with a laugh. "I gotta go."

"I just want to hold it for a minute," she said.

We ended up fucking again. I didn't watch her this time. This time, I kept my eyes shut, too.

29

By the time I'd tucked Marsha in for the afternoon, it was three-thirty. She promised to stay in bed until I came back later that night. But I had my doubts whether she'd be able to keep that promise. She didn't look too confident herself about braving the day alone, in that house, without booze or drugs or a man to protect her from her bad dreams. As I was leaving the bedroom, I could feel her watching me—clinging to me with her eyes. It wasn't a feeling I liked.

I found myself hurrying down the stairs and out into the sunlight, where the smell of freshly cut grass smacked me like a sea breeze. It felt good to be outside. I walked quickly to the car and drove off.

It took me about fifteen minutes to get back to Clifton on 71. I exited on Taft Road and coasted up to Burnett. Philip Feldman's office was located at the corner in a converted brownstone—one block north of the Delores. I'd passed it a thousand times without giving it a second look.

There was a tar lot on the south side of the building. I parked in it and walked up a short flight of concrete stairs, past a big bed of peonies, to the front door. A sign on the door said "Ring Before Entering." I pressed the doorbell and went in. A pretty nurse with teased brown hair was sitting behind a white counter to the right of the door. There was a waiting room to the left, half-filled with patients.

"Can I help you?" the nurse said.

"I'd like to speak to Dr. Feldman. About Quentin Dover."

The nurse gave me a funny look. "I thought Mr. Dover had died?"

"He did. I'm a private investigator, looking into his death. I don't need much of the doctor's time. Just a few minutes."

"I'll see if I can fit you in," she said.

I went into the waiting room and sat down. It was not a happy place—most of the people waiting with me looked very ill. I sat there for about fifteen minutes, then the nurse came out from behind the counter and called my name.

"This way," she said.

She directed me down a tiled corridor, lined with examination rooms, to a small, paneled office at the back of the building. It was an unprepossessing place compared to some of the doctors' offices I'd visited—a tiny desk in one corner, a desk chair behind it, a green vinyl couch on the opposite wall, and a few bookshelves above the couch filled with numbers of the Journal of the American Surgical Society.

I sat down on the couch and waited about ten more minutes. I wanted to smoke, but there weren't any ashtrays in the room. There was nothing to do, except to read Phil Feldman's diplomas. He had an impressive array of them on the walls. I was examining one of them—an honorary certificate from a surgical association—when he stepped into the room.

He was a tall, burly, rugged-looking man in his midforties, with crinkly brown hair, receding in narrow horns at either temple, and five o'clock shadow on his cheeks.

He had on a shirt and tie, but the shirt sleeves were rolled and the collar unbuttoned and the tie had been pulled loose at the knot. Perhaps it was his size and rugged face, but Feldman didn't look like a doctor.

"I'm Phil Feldman," he said, sitting down behind his small desk.

"Harry Stoner."

He reached into his pocket and pulled out a pair of hornrim glasses. "I've never met a private detective," he said, slipping the glasses on his nose. They made him look a lot more professional. "What can I do for you, Mr. Stoner?"

"Quentin Dover was a patient of yours, wasn't he?"

"Of mine and of half a dozen other specialists. I was his cardiologist, yes. I was also his friend."

"You knew him a long time?"

Feldman took his glasses off and tucked them back in his pocket, as if he'd seen all of me that he'd wanted to see. "For ten years."

"You were close, then?"

"As close as Quentin ever let anyone get." Feldman leaned back in his chair. "Why all the questions?"

"I've been looking into his death."

"I was told that it was accidental," Feldman said.

"I think it might have been a suicide."

He looked sadly off into space. "I guess that doesn't surprise me. His father killed himself, you know."

"I know," I said.

"Quentin was always afraid that he'd end up doing the same thing. All the pills in the world couldn't protect him from that fear."

I thought of the coroner's verdict of death by natural causes and of all those pills. Fourteen a day, Jack had said. "Were any of the medications he took for his heart potentially lethal?"

"Almost all medications are potentially lethal," Feldman said, "if taken in sufficient quantity."

"If he'd overdosed himself with some of them, wouldn't it have shown up in the autopsy?"

"It depends on the condition of his body," Feldman said. "He took so many different potent drugs that there would have been large traces of a number of them. That makes a confusing picture for a coroner, especially if the body has decomposed."

"But he could have poisoned himself with the medicines that he carried with him?"

"Easily," Feldman said.

I turned to the phone call. "When was the last time you talked to Dover?"

"On Saturday morning."

I edged forward on the couch. "And do you know where he was when you talked to him?"

Feldman smiled. "I'm not sure. I thought he was in Cincinnati, but that apparently wasn't the case. You see, he always left a number with my answering service where he could be reached, especially when he went out of town. It was a habit with him—more than a habit, an obsession. He wanted me to know where he was in case he needed emergency medical attention. This past Friday he left his private home phone number."

"Had he ever done that before when he went out of the city?"

Feldman shook his head. "No. Usually he left me the number of the Belle Vista in Los Angeles or of the Plaza in New York—his regular stops. That's why I assumed he was still in town when I talked to him on Saturday. He'd told me on Thursday morning that he was going to the coast for some new project."

"Did he happen to mention what the project was?"

"No," Feldman said. "But I had the feeling that he wasn't looking forward to the trip. He seemed rather melancholy about it. When I got the number that he'd left with the answering service, I assumed he'd changed his mind about going. So I called to find out what had happened. It wasn't a professional call."

"What did he say?"

"He said that he was feeling fine and that he hadn't changed his mind about the project, he'd just postponed it. I thought I was talking to him at his home in Indian Hill."

"He gave you no indication of where he really was?"

"No," Feldman said. "Quentin didn't always tell the truth, Mr. Stoner."

"So I've learned," I said.

"He sounded a little edgy. That's why I tried calling him again on Saturday night at the same number. But there wasn't any answer. I tried several times on Sunday. On Monday morning I finally got through to someone. But it was a weird conversation."

"How so?"

"The man I talked to spoke with a Spanish accent and hung up on me abruptly when I mentioned Quentin's name. So I decided to call Marsha to find out what was going on—whether they'd hired a Mexican houseman, or what. Of course, she wasn't home either. She was in L.A., identifying the body. I didn't get through to her until late that night. That's when she told me that Quentin had died in L.A. and that he'd been there the entire weekend. It was only then that I realized that that was where I must have been talking to him on Saturday. With some help from the phone company, we eventually figured out that he'd forwarded his calls from the number here in Cincinnati out to the coast."

"Yeah, but to where exactly in L.A.?"

"You're asking the wrong man," Feldman said. "It's pretty clear that Quentin didn't want me to know where he was. I wish I knew why."

It was pretty clear that Quentin hadn't wanted anyone to know where he was. And if Feldman hadn't acted like a friend on Saturday morning, no one probably ever would have known.

Feldman looked at me for a moment. "I can accept the

fact that Quentin killed himself. But I'd like to know why. I mean, why on Sunday rather than on some other day."

"He was in deep trouble in just about every aspect of his life. I guess you're aware of that."

He shook his head. "For a frightened man, Quentin had a lot of courage. He put up a brave front, most of the time. The only trouble I knew about was his medical problems. And, of course, Marsha's problems. I've had to make several late-night trips to their home."

"She's tried to kill herself?" I said.

He nodded. "I wonder what she's going to do without him. They were suited to each other in a way."

"What makes you say that?"

"They were both pretty badly wounded by their childhoods. Quentin by his father's suicide. Marsha by her fundamentalist upbringing. Being as pretty as she is was not an advantage in her family. Her parents gave her a hard time, and she's never gotten over it. Quentin protected her from her fears to a degree—mostly by allowing her to indulge herself. With him gone . . . " He sighed. "I don't know what's going to happen to her."

"I don't think her marriage was as healthy as you think."

"I didn't say it was healthy. I just said they suited each other. Marsha's problems predate her marriage, anyway. She was institutionalized rightly or wrongly by her family several times before she met Quentin."

"For what?"

"For being herself, I think. For being promiscuous. They claimed she was mentally ill. By the time they'd finished with her, she undoubtedly was. I think that's partly why Quentin was attracted to her—not just because she was so beautiful but because she was so unhappy with her life, like him."

"Is that what he said?"

Feldman nodded. "He said they might have been made for each other."

30

After leaving Feldman's office, I pulled the car down one block and parked in front of the Delores. Then I went upstairs and called Frank Glendora from the bedroom phone. It was Sunday, so I called him at home.

"I need some help," I said to him. "Who do you know at the phone company?"

"I know the vice-president," Glendora said. "We play racquet ball together."

"Do you feel up to pulling a few more strings? I think I've got a lead on where Quentin was last weekend, but I need someone with access to phone company records in order to confirm it."

"It *is* Sunday," Glendora said.

"It's up to you, Frank," I said. "You can call him now or you can call him in the morning."

He thought about it for a moment. "What exactly do you need to know?"

"I need a record of any long-distance calls made on Dover's private phone this past weekend."

"On his private phone here in town?"

"Yeah." I gave him the number.

"I'll see what I can do," he said. "Where will you be?"

I glanced at the clock on the nightstand. It was half-past

five. "I'll be here for another couple of hours. After that you can get me at the Dover home."

"Marsha's or Connie's?"

"Marsha's," I said.

He didn't say anything.

"I'll talk to you later, Frank," I said and hung up.

Glendora wasn't a fool. I figured he'd guessed why I was going out to the Dover house. It wasn't a tough thing to guess at. All you had to do was know Marsha. Or know me. Either way, it wasn't a flattering deduction.

At half-past six, Glendora called back.

"I've got what you wanted," he said. "Do you have a pencil handy?"

I took one out of the nightstand drawer and tore off a piece of the phone book to write on.

"Quentin made five long-distance calls last weekend on his private line—all to the same number. One on Friday night. Three on Saturday. And one that I don't understand on Monday afternoon."

"Quentin didn't make the last few calls—his doctor did."

"I see," Glendora said. "Well, I don't really see. But I'll take your word for it. The number called was 505-889-9206."

"That's not L.A.'s area code—505," I said with surprise.

"No. It's New Mexico," Glendora said. "I had it checked. It was Quentin's ranch in New Mexico."

"Well, I'll be goddamned," I said. "Then he wasn't in L.A. on Friday night and on Saturday after all."

"Why do you say that?" Glendora said with alarm.

"Because his cardiologist talked to him at the 505 number on Saturday morning."

There were other reasons—the timing of the phone call to his mother on Friday night, the man with the Mexican accent whom Feldman had talked to on Monday, above all the phone call Quentin himself had made to his private phone in Cincinnati. It hadn't made much sense for him to call-forward if he were trying to reach someone in L.A., which is what I'd assumed. He could have dialed directly from the Belle Vista and no one would have known whom he'd talked to. But if he'd been calling someone at his ranch in New Mexico—the man with the Mexican accent—then he would have had to have made a long-distance call from the Belle Vista and he must have known that the hotel kept a record of long-distance calls. So he'd put call-forwarding on his own phone to disguise the destination of the call. All of Quentin's behavior pointed to the fact that he hadn't wanted anyone to know about, much less have a record of, his New Mexican sidetrip. I didn't go into it with Glendora. He sounded too confused already.

"How did he manage it?" he said with a touch of awe. "Getting out of the hotel? Flying to Las Cruces? Coming back again without anybody knowing that he'd gone?"

The answer was that he'd had some help—there was no other way to explain how the rental car had gotten back to the Belle Vista lot while Quentin was on his way to Las Cruces. Or how Quentin had gotten back to the hotel on Sunday. "I'm more interested in knowing what he was doing at that ranch," I said. "And I won't be able to figure that out from here. Is Jack still on the coast?"

"Yes."

"Call him and tell him to meet me at LAX tonight. I'll come in on the red-eye, about twelve-thirty A.M. his time. Tell him to get in touch with Sy Goldblum, too. I'd like to have him at the airport when I come in."

"I'll see to it," Glendora said. "This is very confusing to me."

"To me, too."

He sighed. "It appears to have been a deliberate confusion, doesn't it?"

"I'm afraid so, Frank. Whatever Quentin was up to, it looks as if it was unethical at best and illegal at worst.

There's no other way to explain the coverup. The whole thing was clearly planned in advance—the call-forwarding tells us that."

"But why?" Glendora said.

"He apparently thought that he needed an alibi to cover his trip to Las Cruces. Draw your own conclusions."

"Lord, Quentin," Glendora said unhappily and rang off.

I packed my overnighter and my Dopp kit again and called Cincinnati International to make a reservation on the red-eye to the coast. While I had the ticket agent on the line, I decided to do a little digging. I had a fairly good idea of when Dover had left L.A.—sometime after he'd picked up the rental car at eight P.M. Pacific time. He'd called his mother at two A.M. Eastern time, which was eleven Pacific time. Unless he'd stopped some place in L.A. for the night and then gone on to Las Cruces in the morning, he was probably at his ranch when he made that call to Connie. Assuming my timetable was correct, he'd had three hours to get from L.A. to Las Cruces—between eight and eleven P.M. What I needed to know from the ticket agent was whether that could be done on a commercial flight or whether, as I suspected on the basis of all the other diversions, Quentin had found some other, less public way of getting to New Mexico.

"I may need to catch a flight to Las Cruces, New Mexico, next Friday," I said to her.

"From L.A.?"

"Yes. I want to leave between, say, eight-thirty and nine-thirty in the evening, if possible. Can you set that up for me?"

I could hear her punching buttons on her computer terminal. "There are no direct commercial flights to Las Cruces," she said. "The nearest I can get you is El Paso, leaving at six-thirty, arriving at nine-thirty Mountain Time. There's nothing flying later than that on Friday night."

208

"So I'll have to charter something?"

"Yes," she said.

I thanked her and made a mental note to have Wattle check the L.A. charter flights. Then I dialed the New Mexican number. I let the phone ring ten or twelve times, but no one picked it up. It would have been too easy, anyway. The only things I could recall being told about the ranch were that Quentin had sunk a bundle of money into it and that it was run by an overseer named Ramirez, who had visited Dover the week before he went on his trip. Connie Dover had been the one who'd mentioned Ramirez. If anyone would know his number, it was probably her. I called her up.

"This is Stoner," I said.

"Yes?" Her voice sounded more bitter than usual. For a second I thought she'd found out about me and Marsha. Then I remembered the way our last conversation had gone and decided I was merely feeling guilty.

"I have some news for you," I told her.

"About Quentin?" she said anxiously.

"Yes. He left L.A. on Friday night and went to his ranch in Las Cruces."

"On Friday night?"

"That's where he was calling you from—not from the Belle Vista."

"I don't believe it," she said flatly. "He wouldn't have lied to me like that. You must be mistaken. He was in Los Angeles, preparing for a meeting."

Whatever he'd been preparing for, it wasn't in Los Angeles. But I saw no point in trying to convince Connie of that. After what Murdock and Marsha had told me, I didn't see much point in talking to her about her son at all. She'd hardly known him.

"You mentioned Quentin's overseer on Saturday."

"Jorge Ramirez?"

"Yes. He visited Quentin a week ago last Wednesday?"

"So what?" Her voice sounded downright hostile. She'd

209

written me off. I could hear it. We had nothing more to talk about.

I went ahead anyway, even though I knew she wasn't going to cooperate. "Do you know what that meeting was about?"

"The ranch. I already told you that. There had been flood damage."

"What was Quentin's plan?"

"To repair it."

"That's right. Quentin's lawyer told me that he'd spent a fortune on it in the last two months. Over a hundred thousand dollars."

I could hear her suck in her breath. "If you knew that, why did you ask?"

"You wouldn't know Ramirez's phone number?"

"Find it somewhere else," she snapped. "I don't think we have anything more to discuss. And let me assure you, Stoner, that I know what you're up to. You may be able to dishonor my son's memory with his tramp of a wife, but don't try it publicly."

I'd been wrong. She did know about me and Marsha. But then she had a lot of practice prying into her son's life.

"If you proceed in smearing Quentin's name and memory," she went on, "I will sue you. That is a promise. You and United American and Frank Glendora. I wonder how happy they would be about having the Russ Leonard story come out in open court? I have enough materials at my disposal to create quite a stink. About that and about any number of little incidents. And I won't hesitate to use them, if it takes every penny I can raise. Leave this thing alone, I'm warning you. And leave that whore alone, too."

"You'd like to see her dead, wouldn't you, Connie?"

"Yes," she said.

Suddenly I was as sick of her as she was of me. "How about Quentin?" I said. "Aren't you a little glad that he's dead, too?"

"That's a horrible thing to say to me!" she screamed. "An unforgivable thing!"

"No more pretending everything's swell when it's not. No more lies to cover up. Nice and safe in the ground, like his father."

"Shut up!" she shouted. "You son-of-a-bitch!"

She slammed the receiver down in my ear.

31

At eight-thirty I drove out to the Dover house to say goodbye to Marsha. But she wasn't there. I guess I hadn't really expected her to be. The house was dark. After trying the front door, I walked around to the garden and up to the terrace. I sat there for a while on the chaise, listening to the wind in the oaks and staring at the Dixie cup in the pool. Maybe it was better that she was gone, I thought. At least she wouldn't be alone that night. The reflector was lying on the tiles by the chaise. I picked it up and put it on the liquor cart. Then I walked back to the car and drove to the airport.

I thought about her on the flight out. Most of the people on the plane were asleep. All the lights were dimmed, except for a few reading lamps overhead. There wasn't any sound but the engines and the rush of the wind. It was more like a Pullman than an airplane—that late at night. I had my usual complement of Scotches, smoked a pack of cigarettes, and thought about Marsha.

I thought about Quentin, too. About him and the girl, when I should have been thinking about how he'd gotten to New Mexico and how that rented car had gotten back to the Belle Vista lot and why he'd gone so far away to die.

I should have been thinking about his project—the one he'd been so happy and sad and noncommittal about, the one he'd told his lawyer he might need his help on. Instead, I thought about what Maria Sanchez had told me, about how Quentin had said that he'd loved Marsha. Maria hadn't believed him. But I wasn't so sure. At first Marsha had told me that he'd made her sleep with other men. But later on, she'd said it had been her idea. I wasn't so sure that it made a difference—whose idea it had been. Like Quentin had told Feldman, they'd suited each other in some sad, indelible way. That's what had made the difference.

The plane touched down at LAX at one A.M. L.A. time. It was four by my watch and I was fagged out—rotten with booze and cigarettes and fatigue. Jack met me at the arrival gate. He was wearing a Hawaiian shirt and khaki pants. He looked as if I should have been meeting him. Sy Goldblum wasn't there.

Moon smiled at me affectionately and I smiled weakly back at him.

"Tired, huh?" he said.

I nodded.

He picked up my bag and carried it down the long, empty corridor to the taxi stands in front of the terminal. We caught a cab and Jack told the cabbie to take us to the Marquis.

"You can bunk with me," he said. "Goldblum's going to meet us tomorrow morning for coffee. He couldn't get away tonight. He said to tell you it was something about the Sanchez killings. Christ, that made a splash out here. They love their psychopaths."

"More homegrown fruit," I said.

He laughed.

"How's 'Phoenix'?" I asked him.

"Well, we made it through the weekend without any major losses. That's something."

"You haven't been home in a while, have you?"

"Five days," he said. "I would have left tomorrow, if you hadn't needed me."

"I'm sorry, Jack."

"It's all right," he said. "They won't forget me. I won't let 'em."

I fell asleep, fully clothed, on the daybed in Jack's suite at the Marquis and woke up eight hours later. It was ten A.M. by the digital clock built into the huge television set. I stood up and wandered into the john to shower and shave. As I was stepping out of the tub, the phone rang. I picked up the one by the toilet.

"Hi." It was Jack. "I'm downstairs at the bar with Sy."

"I'm up here in the john with the telephone."

"You think you can make it down here in the next half hour?"

"Give me ten minutes," I said.

I dug a sports shirt out of my overnighter and slipped it on with a pair of jeans. When in Rome, as Jack had said. This time, I'd come prepared. After stepping into a pair of socks and shoes, I took the elevator down to the lobby and walked into the Marquis bar. It was virtually empty at a quarter of eleven in the morning—just a few tourists, sipping Tequilla Sunrises out of brandy snifters, and Jack and Sy.

I went over to their table and sat down.

"Sy," I said.

"Harry." He gave me a Boy Scout salute. I still had trouble picturing him in blue serge. That Monday he was wearing a muscle T-shirt and white boat pants. Big tufts of brown hair stuck out of the T-shirt from his chest, his armpits, his shoulders, and his back. He looked like Bel-Air's version of a lycanthrope.

Jack looked very uncomfortable. He didn't like Wattle; he didn't have any reason to, after their last encounter. Seymour stared at him with amusement—one arm

214

draped over the back of his chair. Jack stared at the table or at his Bloody Mary or at me.

"So what do we got?" Wattle said.

I laid it out for him and Jack. "Quentin wasn't in L.A. on Friday or Saturday. Actually I'm not sure about Friday night—there's just a likely guess. But I am sure that on Saturday he was in Las Cruces, New Mexico."

Jack looked surprised. "He had a ranch there, didn't he?"

"That's where he was—at the ranch. Possibly with his overseer, a man named Ramirez." I looked at Wattle. "That name doesn't ring any bells, does it? Jorge Ramirez?"

He shook his head.

"I figured. But it was worth a shot."

"How in the world did he manage it?" Jack said with wonder.

"I don't know the details. All I can do is make guesses at this point. Guesses that fit the facts as we know them."

"Let's hear 'em," Wattle said.

"First of all, it looks as if Quentin checked into the Belle Vista on Friday not to prepare for a secret meeting about a TV project like we originally thought, but to establish an alibi. He wanted the world to think that he was at the Belle Vista the whole weekend."

"Then he wasn't looking for another job?" Jack said.

"Not in TV. Not at all, as far as I can see."

"Then what was his new project?"

I shrugged. "Your guess is as good as mine. He was badly in debt and he needed a good deal of money to make everything right again. The project was probably something that would make him money. Exactly what, I don't know. I do know that he wasn't counting on 'Phoenix' any more because he told Glendora that he was going to quit the show if he didn't finish the document by this past Monday."

"He said that?" Jack said. "Quentin said he was going to quit?"

"He said more than that. He told Glendora he was thinking of killing himself."

"Christ," Moon said. "What shit! He was just trying to buy more time on the show with a new lie."

"Possibly. But the part about killing himself was no joke. Dover's father killed himself. And Marsha, his wife, told me that he'd always been afraid that he'd end up a suicide, too. Phil Feldman, Dover's cardiologist, confirmed that."

"Are you saying that he killed himself?" Wattle asked.

I shrugged. "Dover had painted himself into a corner by last Friday. He was worried, depressed, talking about suicide, on the one hand. And on the other, he was promising people like his mother and his lawyer that everything was going to be O.K.—that he had a new project in the works that was going to get him off the hook on 'Phoenix' and put him in the black again financially. If he couldn't come up with a document or something just as good as a document, then, yes, I think he might have committed suicide."

"He hadn't been able to write a word in six months," Jack said. "What makes you think he could do it in two days?"

"I don't think he could. I think he was counting on something else."

"Like what?" Wattle said.

"Like I said, my guess is money. Money from some source other than his job. Money that he didn't want anyone to ask questions about. Money that he had to go secretly to New Mexico to get. I think that's why he concocted the project story and the L.A. trip—to cover his tracks while he was getting the money. As far as his mother, his lawyer, and his doctor knew, it would have been money from some kind of special project. Money from a TV deal, money from a business deal. If it was enough money, he could have quit 'Phoenix,' like he'd told Glendora he was going to do, and still have saved face with Mom, paid off his creditors, and kept his wife and his house and what was left of his way of life."

"I didn't like Quentin," Jack said. "But . . . I mean, what are you saying? That Dover was a smuggler or a gambler or a thief or what?"

"That's what we have to find out," I said. "Whatever he was up to had him scared to death. Scared enough to take the extraordinary precautions that he took to disguise what he was really doing over the weekend."

Jack shook his head. "He was always scared, Harry. What makes you think that this was any different? What makes you think that he wasn't lying to himself, as well? Maybe the trip to New Mexico was just a piece of wishful thinking. Maybe there was no pot of gold at the end of it—just Quentin face to face with his own demise."

"It's possible," I conceded. "He did spend a good deal of time last week visiting people and places from his past—like a man saying goodbye. But if the New Mexican trip was just a pipe dream, then it's hard to explain all the stories he told—all of the secrecy and lies."

Jack laughed. "That's always been hard to explain, hasn't it?"

He had a point.

"And don't forget," Moon went on. "Quentin was a physical coward—a hypochondriac, a lush, a sick man. I can't see him going into some . . . dangerous situation all by himself."

"He wasn't by himself," I said. "That I'm sure of."

"Spell it out," Wattle said.

"Quentin had at least one accomplice. He had to have someone to help him here in L.A. or he'd have had no way to get to the airport and back without tipping off the fact that he'd left the hotel."

"How'd he get out of the hotel?" Wattle asked.

"Well, I'm guessing," I said. "But I figure he had a key to one of the gates in the hotel wall. I originally thought that he'd used that key late on Friday night, after he'd gotten back with the rented car. I'd thought he had another car or a taxi waiting for him on Green Canyon Road. Now I don't think he came back to the Belle Vista at all on Friday. After he rented the car, I think he drove around to the gate in the south quadrangle, unlocked it, went to his room, took out his luggage, loaded it in the car, and drove to the airport. There was virtually nobody else staying on the south quadrangle that weekend and it's so goddamn dark back there that it probably wouldn't have made a difference anyway. So he was in little danger of being spotted. By the way, the airport is some thirty miles from the Belle Vista—which would account for the sixty miles on his odometer, if you figure on a round-trip."

"If he drove out there, how did the car get back in the lot?" Jack asked.

"He met someone at the airport," I said. "Or he picked someone up. Or someone followed him. I don't know. I really don't know for sure about any of this. But if I'm close to being right, then there had to have been an accomplice, who drove the car to the Belle Vista lot and then picked Dover up early Sunday morning at the airport and drove him back to the hotel gate."

"That's an awful lot of 'ifs,'" Wattle said. "How did Dover get to Las Cruces and back?"

"By charter or by private plane, I think. I did some checking and there aren't any commercial flights to Las Cruces on Friday night, so it had to be noncommercial. I was hoping you'd look into that, Sy."

He grunted. "It'll cost you."

"While you're doing that, I'm going to go to Las Cruces and see if I can find out what was happening on that end."

"You want me to come with you?' Jack said.

"I don't think so. You stay in L.A. and coordinate things with Sy and Frank. I'll keep in touch with you."

Jack sighed. "Executive producer again, huh?"

I smiled at him.

218

32

We ordered some drinks and nursed them in silence for a while. Jack, in particular, looked lost in thought. I had the feeling that a tiny, unregenerate part of him had still been hoping for the best from Quentin Dover. The best or the worst—something that would finally take him off the hook, absolve him of the guilt he felt for having recommended Dover in the first place. Wattle looked as if he were ruminating, too. With him it took a physical effort, brow knurled, eyes shut, jaw working as if he were chewing on something caught in his teeth.

He finally came out with it. "So how come he's dead?"

It was a good question. "I guess that depends on how things went in Las Cruces. If they didn't go the way Quentin hoped they would—and I have a gut feeling that they didn't—then I think he came back to the Belle Vista early Sunday morning and killed himself."

Nobody said anything for a moment.

"How come the coroner said he died of natural causes?" Wattle asked.

"He may have taken an overdose of one or more of his own medications. Given the condition of his body, that wouldn't have shown up clearly in a preliminary autopsy.

And remember, there must have been some confusion about what killed him because your forensic specialists are still running tests."

"He didn't die of drugs," Jack said. "He poisoned himself with lies. He poisoned all of us with lies."

"There is that," I admitted.

"About the Sanchez killings," Wattle said. "I went up to Pacoima last night and talked to their homicide man."

"And?"

"Now don't get all excited. But there is a link with Dover."

"For chrissake!" I said. "Why didn't you say so to begin with?"

"Because it isn't much. I don't think it means anything and neither does the Pacoima guy."

"What is it?"

"They found one of Dover's prescription bottles in the Sanchez house—some amyl nitrate. An old bottle with a coupla pills left in it. You know you can get high on amyl. We figure she swiped it from his room months ago. She had other bottles, too, belonging to parties who'd stayed at the Belle Vista. Some dex, some soapers, some 'ludes. The usual pharmacy."

I hated to say it, but it didn't sound like much to me, either. "Do they have any idea why she was murdered?"

"They think it's a gang thing. Drug-related, probably. They found a bag of cocaine taped inside her toilet. It was probably a gang thing."

"Well, keep on top of it," I said.

"I better get going." Wattle stood up. "I'll check out at the airport this afternoon. See what I can dig up."

He gave me a meaningful look.

"Will two bills cover it?" I said.

"Check."

"I'm probably going to go to Las Cruces this afternoon. So if you find anything, let Jack know and he'll pass it on."

He gave us another salute and lumbered out of the bar.

"You want me to go with you to the airport?" Jack said.

"No. First I want to go over the Belle Vista. There's a guy I want to talk to there."

"Let's go," Jack said.

We walked out to the taxi stand in front of the hotel. When the black doorman spotted me, he did a double-take.

"Is there two of you?" he said. "You just left a coupla days ago."

I laughed. "I got back last night."

"Must've been real late," he said. "Cause I didn't see none of you."

"Shades of Quentin," Jack said over my shoulder.

We caught a cab to the Belle Vista. The cabbie let us out in the parking lot. I looked for Jerry, but he wasn't at his usual post by the canopied bridge. The other kid—the one I'd talked to on Friday afternoon—was standing there. I walked over to him, with Jack trailing behind me.

"Where's Jerry?" I asked.

He shaded his eyes with one hand. "Who?"

I dug a five out of my wallet.

"Oh, Jerry!" he said. "You mean Jerry Ruiz. Haven't seen Jerry in a long time, man."

"How long?"

"Not since the last time you asked about him. He quit."

"Did he give a reason why?"

The kid laughed. "You gotta be joking. You ever park cars twelve, fourteen hours a day?"

"You don't know where he lives, do you?"

"Nope. He used to hang out at a bar on Sunset, but I haven't seen him around there since Friday."

"O.K. Thanks."

We walked across the bridge to the lobby, where the woman with the prim, pretty face was stationed at the front desk. She smiled familiarly at Jack.

221

"Good afternoon, Mr. Moon. Should I ring Miss Rose's room?"

Jack looked at me. "Do you want to talk to her?"

I thought about it. It was possible she knew something useful about Quentin's ranch. And since Connie Dover was threatening blackmail, I figured there'd be no harm in checking the story that she'd told me—about Helen supplying Russ Leonard with cocaine. If it was true, and it wouldn't have surprised me if it was, the Dover woman could make Glendora and United think twice about the investigation. There was one other reason, as well. Cocaine was a profitable business—a quick-kill business. Just the sort of thing to put a desperate man back on his feet.

"Yeah," I said. "You go on down to her room, and I'll be down in a minute."

Jack told the desk clerk to tell Helen he was coming, then went through the French doors into the garden. After the clerk had given Helen the message, I walked up to her. She forced a polite smile. I could see from her face that she was tired of me. She hadn't been cooperative the last time I'd questioned her. And I had the feeling that I wasn't going to get anywhere with her this time, either. She was clearly a job for Wattle.

"The boy who was working in your parking lot—Jerry Ruiz? I'd like to talk to him."

"Jerry is no longer with us. He failed to show up for work for three consecutive days."

"You wouldn't know where I could get in touch with him, would you?"

"Do you mean by that, would I give you his address or phone number?"

I nodded.

"We don't give out that information, sir," she said sternly.

I thought about trying to bribe her—everyone else in L.A. seemed to wear his price on his sleeve—right where his heart should have been. But while this one might have taken a bribe from the right sort of person, I didn't think I qualified. I wasn't Bel-Air enough for her.

"O.K.," I said. "Thanks."

"Don't mention it," she said coolly.

I stepped through the French doors into the courtyard and walked down to the south quadrangle. The fact that Jerry Ruiz had dropped out of sight bothered me a little. The first time I'd talked to Maria Sanchez, it had been Jerry Ruiz who had pointed me in her direction. At the time I'd had the feeling that they were working together. Cabbies and bar girls run the same kind of scam all the time. The cabbie steers the john to the hooker, for which he gets a small percentage of the action. Whether they were running a game or not, I had the feeling that they were connected. And the last time I'd talked to Jerry, he'd gotten very nervous when he thought that Maria had told me that he'd given Quentin a key to the Belle Vista gate. That was hardly a reason to murder anyone, but Maria *had* died the next day and Jerry had dropped out of sight. I figured it was worth looking into. Wattle would be the one to do it—for a price.

When I got to the south quadrangle, I found Jack Moon sitting on a bench by the bowl-shaped fountain. He had a dark look on his face. I sat down beside him.

"Someday I'm going to bust that bitch in the chops," he said, scowling at me.

"What now?"

"What else? The breakdowns aren't right. Walt is fucking up the blocking. He won't cooperate. And it's *my* fault." He shook his head. "It's Quentin all over again, I'm telling you."

"Russ Leonard, too," I said.

Jack looked up at me. "There are only so many story lines in daytime, Harry. And we've just about run the gamut—from A to B. Like she said, we don't merely write 'em, we live 'em. It's all going to start up again. I can see the handwriting on the chalkboard. The same endless round of recrimination and buck passing." He pressed his brow with the back of his hand, as if he was checking to see if he was running a fever. "I've got to get out of this racket. I'm not kidding. I'm a desperate man."

For a second I believed him. Then he dropped his hand with a sigh and slapped himself encouragingly on the knee. "C'mon, Jack," he said to himself. "Buck up. It's only a job."

"I'm afraid I've got some more bad news," I said.

He curled his hands and made a coaxing gesture at me, like a fighter baiting his opponent. "C'mon, lay it on me. I'm made of steel."

"Connie Dover told me that Helen was Russ Leonard's connection, that she had supplied him with coke."

Moon's face turned as white as milk. "Good God," he said softly. "You're not going to go in there and ask her about that, are you?"

"I'm going to ask you first."

Jack started wiping his beard nervously. I thought he might wipe it off. "Where the hell did Connie come up with that story?"

"From Quentin, I guess."

Jack laughed feebly. "From Quentin."

"She claimed she could document it."

"Oh, my God," Jack grabbed his stomach as if he were shot.

"Take it easy, Jack."

"Take it easy," he said manically. "The man says take it easy. Why the hell do you care what Helen may or may not have done for Russ Leonard?"

"I don't care, but United might. Connie conceded that Helen was probably feeding it to him to keep him from hustling it on the street."

"Then drop it, for chrissake. For *my* sake."

I stared at him for a second. "Why, Jack?"

"Because we don't need it," he said. "Can't you see that? Isn't the situation bad enough as it is?" He took a

224

deep breath and tried to pull himself together. "You don't understand, Harry. That stuff—it's commonplace out here. It comes with the table setting, to the left of the spoons."

"So?"

"So everybody does it. Do you hear what I'm saying? Do you have any idea how many people—I mean, famous people, people whose names you'd know in a second—have had their noses rebuilt and their blood washed? Some of them on a monthly basis. It's big business. It's perks. It's Hollywood beer. It's what they hand out now the way they used to hand out hookers and studs. You can't go in there and ask that woman whether she's a cocaine pusher. You don't ask that question out here—of anyone. You're looking for trouble if you do."

"From whom?"

"From everybody," he said. "It's like breaking the law of silence in the Mafia. It's just not done."

Jack fumbled with his hands as if he'd run out of rope. "Harry, please," he said. "Don't open this can of worms. Not today. Not this week."

"I'm sorry, Jack."

I got up and walked over to the room.

33

The door was open so I walked in. Helen wasn't in the living room, but I could hear her rummaging around the bedroom.

"If that's you, Jack, I apologize. If it isn't you, I still apologize."

"It's Harry Stoner," I called out.

"Harry!" she said, as if she were saying 'Dar-ling!' "I'll be out in a moment. I'm stopping a clock with my face. Make yourself comfortable."

I went over to the white couches and sat down in front of the fireplace. A cedar log was burning on the andirons. The room air conditioner was on, too, full blast. With the door open, it made for interesting weather, as if the room couldn't make up its mind what season it was. I stared out the door at the sunlit courtyard. Jack Moon was still sitting on the bench—hands clasped together, head bent.

Helen walked into the room and sat down across from me on the other couch. She had her head wrapped in a silk scarf, with the fringe of her curly bangs peeking out in front. Her face looked the same as it had on Wednesday—childish, bruised, full of worry.

"How's the scandal business?" she said hoarsely.

"Keeping me busy."

226

"Yes? Did Jack tell you about *our* latest misadventure?"

"You mean Walt's document?"

She nodded. "Isn't that something? Quentin would die again, if he knew."

I stared at her for a moment. "I don't understand. You would have fired Quentin if he had presented that document to you, wouldn't you?"

"Oh, course," she said. "The way things had been going, we wouldn't have had any other choice."

"Then why didn't you fire Walt?"

"Harry, sweetie," she said. "Stick to the detective biz. It's a lot more logical."

She glanced over her shoulder at Jack.

"That's his trouble," she said. "He keeps looking for reasons where there aren't any reasons. He keeps trying to figure things out. I tell him, 'Jack, as soon as you figure them out, they're going to change on you. You can't count on anything or anyone but yourself.'" She shook her head. "Look at him, sitting there. He looks like a penguin on a rock." She turned her head back to me. "I guess I hurt his feelings."

"He'll get over it."

"I don't know," she said. "He's going to have to grow up one of these days. Either that or he's going to have to quit the business. He doesn't have the right temperament for this kind of work."

"I guess so, Helen," I said. "He keeps feeling sorry for people like you."

She gave me a sharp look "Jack's no angel, sweetie. He's as hungry as the rest of us. He just hasn't learned how to use his knife and fork, yet."

"As long as we're on the subject, let's talk about spoons."

"What do you mean?" she said with a nervous laugh.

"Little silver spoons. The kind you use to snort coke with."

"Let's not," she said coldly.

227

"Quentin's mom told me about Russ Leonard," I said.

"Told you what?"

"That you were feeding his habit."

Helen stood up suddenly and turned to the open door. "Jack!" she shouted. "Get your ass in here!"

Moon didn't move.

"Jack, goddamnit!"

"Sit down, Helen," I said.

She whirled around. "What did you tell me to do?" she said. "When did you start giving me orders in my own hotel room?"

"Call a cop," I said. "You need a quarter?" I fished one out of my pocket and held it up to her. "Here."

She sat down slowly on the couch. "I think you must have lost your mind, Harry. Do you know who I am?"

I said, "Cut the crap, Helen. I'm not the police. But if you want to talk to them, I can arrange it."

"You'd tell the police about this?" she said with alarm.

I said, "All I want to know is whether or not it's true."

She looked hurt—the way she had when Jack had raised his voice to her. "Russ was a sick man. A desperate man. I couldn't just let him wander around the streets, could I? He would have gotten himself killed that way."

"And you would have lost the head writer on your show."

"That, too," she admitted. "This *is* a business, Harry. And I'm responsible for seeing that it's run efficiently."

Unless something or someone goes amok, I said to myself, in which case there would always be another fall guy. I had the feeling that Walt was the next one on the list. Or maybe it would be Jack Moon—who hadn't come running when she'd shouted for him.

"Then you did get the coke for Russ?"

Helen looked down at the floor, at the plush white carpeting. "I didn't," she said after a time. "Walt did."

"You know I'm going to ask him, don't you?"

228

"Walt got the stuff for him," she persisted. "I knew about it. I just . . . I looked the other way."

"Who paid for it?"

Helen squirmed on the couch. "What difference does it make?"

"You did?"

"All right," she said, looking up at me. "I paid for it. So what? It was Walt who kept feeding him more and more of it. He was supposed to keep him on a maintenance dose—until we could get Russ some professional help. But Walt had other ideas. Russ's habit went from two-fifty to a thousand dollars a day in less than six months. I simply couldn't afford it at that point. When I cut him off, Russ threatened to kill me. He actually came to my home in Long Island and threatened my life."

"Did Quentin know about this?"

She nodded. "That's when I brought him on the show, when Russ's drug habit started to get out of hand."

"Was Quentin ever involved in buying the stuff for Russ?"

"Walt supplied it. He was the one with the connection."

"All right," I said and stood up. It was too late in the day to ask her about the ranch.

Helen looked at me disgustedly. "I was wrong about you, Harry. You're not a heavy, you're too naive. You're Lenny with his rabbits."

"If you say so, Helen."

"You think Russ Leonard was a special case? You think you're going to raise any eyebrows with this story?" She laughed bitterly. " 'Phoenix' is my show. It's my life. And I'm willing to do anything in order to keep it going. Anything. I don't have to apologize for that—not to you or to Frank Glendora or to anyone else. But if you do tell Glendora about this, just remember that it's your boy Jack's ass, too."

"I thought he didn't come on the show until after Leonard was out."

"There was a transition period. He was around for the end of it."

"And he was involved in the drug transactions?"

"Why don't you ask him, Sweetie," she said. "He always tells the truth, doesn't he?"

I walked out of the room to the courtyard. Moon looked up at me, squinting into the sunshine.

"I heard her shouting," he said.

I sat down beside him on the bench. "Jack, did you have anything to do with this cocaine thing?"

He laughed half-heartedly. "Did she tell you that I did?"

I nodded.

Jack shut his eyes. "When I first came on 'Phoenix,' " he said, "one of my jobs was to act as errand boy for Helen. I used to carry documents and breakdowns back and forth between New York and L.A. Once in awhile the documents were sealed in manila envelopes." He opened his eyes and stared at me. "I wasn't supposed to know what was inside them."

"Did you know?"

He nodded. "It was an open secret. Sometimes it was money that Helen sent to Russ. Sometimes . . ." His voice died away. "I knew what I was doing and I did it, anyway. I was just too damn eager to please."

I looked away from him. "How about Quentin? Was he involved?"

"He knew about it. I'm pretty sure of that. But he wasn't involved."

"O.K.," I said. "Let's forget it came up."

"I tried to tell you the other night," Jack said. "It's my kind of sin—going along for the ride."

"Not that bad, Jack," I said.

Not a sin. More like an accident, I thought. Like grabbing a live wire and not being able to let go. The mistake was in the grabbing, not in holding on.

"You going to tell Frank?" he asked.

"No."

"It's O.K., Harry. I've had it with this business, anyway."

"We'll talk about it when I get back from Las Cruces." I patted him on the shoulder. "Don't be so hard on yourself, Jack. Life's too short."

"At this moment," he said, "it seems endless."

I got up. "I'm going to pay a call on Walt Mack, then catch a plane to Las Cruces. I want you to do something for me while I'm gone."

"What?"

"Get in touch with Goldblum—this afternoon, if possible. Tell him to locate a kid named Jerry Ruiz. He's Mexican American, about twenty-two, good-looking. He used to work as a carhop here at the Belle Vista. Tell Goldblum to contact the desk clerk—she has his address. And if Sy does find him, tell him to hang on to him until I get back."

"Why?" Jack said.

"Ruiz is connected to the Sanchez girl and to Quentin Dover. I'm pretty sure he's the one who got Quentin the key to the gate."

Jack got a small notepad out of his back pocket and wrote down Jerry's name. "Anything else?"

"Keep yourself available," I said. "I'll let you know where I am in Las Cruces as soon as I can." I looked at him. "You're no worse than anyone else in the world, Jack. In most ways, you're a lot better."

He frowned at me. "If you say so."

34

I caught a cab to Mack's house and told the cabbie to wait for me in the little turnoff above the beach. He parked at the foot of the stairs, and I got out and walked up to the fenced compound. There was a row of buzzers and a two-way intercom built into the wall. I pressed the button with Mack's name on it. After a moment I heard the intercom click on and someone said, "Yeah?"

"It's Harry Stoner, Walt. I need to talk to you."

There was a silence, then another buzzer went off. I pushed the gate and it opened at my touch. I let it fall shut behind me and walked over to Mack's stoop. I could hear the surf booming behind me. The wind was up that day; it whipped at my hair and my shirt collar.

Walt didn't look pleased to see me when he opened the door. "You'll have to make this quick," he said. " 'Days' is running a new story line this week, and I want to catch it."

"To pick up some fresh, new ideas?"

He curled his lip. "What do you want?"

"It's about Russ."

Mack shook his head. "I don't want to talk about that anymore. It took me a whole day to get over our last little chat. Russ Leonard is ancient history."

"Quentin isn't," I said. "Did he know that you were feeding Leonard cocaine?"

Mack gasped, then made a coughing noise that sounded a bit like laughter. "What are you talking about?"

"You know what I'm talking about. Helen Rose gave you money to keep your boyfriend in coke."

"She said that?" Mack said furiously. "She told you that?"

"Yes. She also told me that you kept feeding him more and more of it, until he fried his brains out."

Mack turned to the wall with the mirror on it and pounded it with his fist. He hit it so hard that he dented the drywall. "That fucking bitch!" he screamed. Then he winced and grabbed his hand. He'd hurt himself and it made him even madder to have to show it. "Get out of here. I've got nothing to say to you."

"Don't make me go to the cops," I said.

"You can go to hell," Mack said. "Talk to my lawyer."

I stared into that boyish face. "You're a real sweetheart, aren't you, Walt? Did you think that getting Russ high would land you his job?"

I thought he was going to throw another punch—this time, at me. I was kind of hoping he would try. But he thought better of it in a second. "Did you ever live with a man with a nose jones?" he said between his teeth. "Until you do, don't tell me why I did what I did, you stupid son-of-a-bitch. Now get the fuck out of my yard."

He slammed the door in my face.

I had the cabbie drive back to the Marquis. I hadn't accomplished much with Helen and Walt, except to confirm what Connie Dover had told me. If she had the proof she said she had, there wasn't anything I could do about it. As far as Quentin's possible connection with the cocaine trade went . . . it was just one possibility among many, and the only way I could narrow the field was to go to Las Cruces and pick up Dover's trail.

233

Once I got back to the hotel, I packed my overnighter and called LAX. There were no flights out to El Paso until Tuesday morning, but the ticket agent told me she could get me to Albuquerque that afternoon. I booked the flight and arranged to rent a car at the Albuquerque terminal. The drive to Las Cruces would take two or three hours. I figured I could find a motel room once I got there. Before I left for the airport, I called Marsha Dover. I wanted to get Jorge Ramirez's phone number and address. I also wanted to see if she was all right. I let the phone ring ten times. On the tenth ring, I told myself I'd have to find Ramirez on my own.

I took another cab to LAX and spent a half hour in one of the little bars scattered around the terminal. About four-thirty I made my way to the boarding gates. There weren't as many people going to Albuquerque as had been going to Cincinnati. I couldn't make up my mind whether that was a good omen or not. I handed my pass to the stewardess and experienced a moment of panic as I stepped into the plane. I felt like I was stepping into a well. But once I settled down in one of the seats, the panicky feeling went away. Ten minutes later, we were airborne. And an hour and a half after that, we were landing in the New Mexico desert.

It was about eight, Mountain time, when I got off the plane. I wandered down to the Hertz stand in the Albuquerque airport and picked up the keys to a Mustang. Then I went outside and waited for one of the parking attendants to drive the car around to the front of the terminal. It was a beautiful desert evening. The sun was setting in bands of violet and orange light, and overhead the stars were beginning to shine—the ones that you don't get to see through the haze of pollution and city lights. Albuquerque is high up in the Sangre de Cristo Mountains. The ride to Las Cruces would take me down, due south along the Rio Grande, through Socorro, Sierra, and Dona Ana counties to the Mexican border. I was looking forward to the drive. The desert would be cool at night, as sculpted and placid as the bed of the ocean it once was.

Half an hour out of Albuquerque and I was the only car on the road. For miles and miles around me, the desert glistened in the moonlight. Solitary buttes and flat-topped mesas grew out of the vacant earth, like great stone plants.

Around eleven I reached the outskirts of Las Cruces. I drove through a notch in the El Capitan mountains and there it was—a little cluster of lights on the black desert floor. I took the first exit off the expressway and pulled up at a Holiday Inn. I parked the Mustang in the large lot, took my overnighter out of the trunk, and went into the lobby. A pretty, black-eyed Mexican girl sitting behind the front desk smiled at me as I walked up to her.

"Can I help you?" she said.

"I need a room. For at least one night. Possibly longer."

I gave her a credit card and while she was making out the bill, I took a look around. The lobby was large and crowded. There was an indoor pool on one side of it, with a passel of kids splashing around in the water. On the other side, a little restaurant was set up like an outdoor cafe. The lobby formed a kind of courtyard, with the hotel rooms opening onto it on each side through handsome French doors built into the walls. A balconied second floor looked down on the pool and cafe; it, too, was lined with French doors. It was a pretty ritzy little place for Las Cruces.

The girl came back with my charge slip and I signed it. She gave me a key.

"You're in 'Maximilian,' " she said, pointing to a mahogany staircase leading up to the balcony.

"Where's 'Carlotta'?" I asked.

She grinned. "Right beside you. Where else?"

I grinned back at her, took my key, and walked upstairs to "Maximilian." It was a nice room—motel Spanish traditional, with heavy carved chairs and a stout four-poster and a TV in an elaborate stained cabinet. I flopped down on the mattress and reached for the phone book, sitting on a nightstand by the bed. The nightstand looked like a melted black candle; but then most Spanish traditional furniture looked that way to me. I flipped the phone book open and searched for Jorge Ramirez's name. I found it in the Mesilla section. According to the Chamber of Commerce brochure tucked in the front of the phone book, Mesilla was the old Spanish mission town—the original settlement from which Las Cruces had been born.

I pulled the phone onto the bed and dialed Ramirez's number. Someone picked up on the fourth ring.

"Yes?" a man with a Mexican accent said.

"Jorge Ramirez?" I said.

"Yes?"

"Mr. Ramirez, my name is Stoner. I've just got in from L.A. and I was hoping we could get together. I have some questions I'd like to ask you about Quentin Dover."

"You are a friend of Señor Dover?" he said.

"Not exactly. I've been hired by the company he worked for to look into his death."

"It was an accident, no?"

"That's what I'm trying to find out."

"Señor Dover was a good friend," Ramirez said. "I woul' be happy to help you. When woul' you like to talk?"

"Tomorrow morning, I guess. I just drove in from Albuquerque and I'm a little tired."

"Tomorrow woul' be O.K. Where are you staying at?"

"The Holiday Inn. But I have a car. I can meet you."

"You can find the town square in Mesilla?"

"I'm sure I can."

"Good. I meet you there tomorrow morning at nine. In front of the church."

I told him that would be fine.

236

35

I ordered a Scotch from room service, then phoned Jack Moon at the Marquis.

"I'm glad you called," he said. "Where are you staying in Las Cruces?"

I gave him the number of the hotel and of my room. I could hear him writing them down.

"Now what have you got for me?" I said.

"Goldblum called me early this afternoon, right after you left. He found the charter service that flew Quentin to Las Cruces. Apparently Quentin didn't use his real name, but the charter guy recognized him from Sy's description. Dover left L.A. at eight thirty-five P.M. on Friday night and got into Las Cruces at eleven forty Mountain time. He came back to L.A. at two-thirty A.M. on Sunday morning. By the way, Dover left his car in the charter service's lot."

"Did anyone notice who picked it up? Or who picked up Dover on Sunday morning?"

"There was nobody on duty when Quentin got back from Las Cruces. But someone did see a kid pick up the rental car at around twelve-fifteen A.M. on Saturday morning. The kid was driving a jalopy and he had a girl with him. Dover had left word that the car was going to be picked up, so nobody gave the kid any trouble."

"Did Sy get his description?"

"Goldblum thinks it was Jerry Ruiz," Jack said.

"I'll be damned," I said.

It was certainly possible. Jerry himself had told me that he'd gotten off duty at eleven-thirty or a quarter of twelve. That would have allowed him more than enough time to make it out to the airport by twelve-fifteen. It would also have given him a better reason to be nervous about Quentin's key. He'd apparently played a larger part in Dover's plans than I'd thought. It made me that much more certain that Quentin was desperate to score. Otherwise he wouldn't have taken a chance on a venal kid like Jerry.

"How about the girl in the car with Ruiz?" I said. "Any I.D. on her?"

"Goldblum thinks it was Maria Sanchez," Jack said. "She was seen leaving the hotel with the Ruiz boy late Friday night. And when Goldblum got in touch with the Pacoima police about him, it turned out that they were interested in Jerry for their own reasons."

"In connection with the murders?"

"I'm not sure. I do know that Jerry is a bad boy. Goldblum told me to tell you that. He'd been charged with several unsavory crimes, although he hadn't been convicted on any charges."

"Was Ruiz ever busted for pushing drugs?"

Jack sighed. "Yeah. But that doesn't necessarily mean that Quentin was involved in drug pushing."

"If you say so, Jack. Do the Pacoima police have any idea where Jerry is holed up?"

"Somewhere outside of Pacoima," Moon said. "That's where he lived, by the way. Goldblum found out through the Belle Vista desk clerk. Ruiz hasn't been in his room since Friday. In fact, no one seems to have seen him since he quit his job." Jack paused for a second. "I've got one more thing to tell you. It may make all the rest of this unimportant."

"What's that?" I asked.

"Frank wants to talk to you," he said. "He spoke to Connie this afternoon. She told him about the Leonard thing."

"All of it?"

"Enough to make Frank nervous," Jack said.

"What do you think Glendora wants to talk to me about, Jack?"

"Can't you guess?" he said. "Frank doesn't want trouble. United is his religion."

"Do me a favor, then," I said. "Don't tell him I was in touch with you. Tear up that piece of paper with the phone numbers on it, and, if he asks, say that I haven't contacted you yet."

"How can I stall him, Harry? He knows you're in Las Cruces and he's been calling me every hour."

"You can do it, Jack," I said. "All I need's another day or two."

"For what?" Jack said. "What's it going to amount to, anyway? It's ass-covering time, Harry. And you might as well face the fact that the truth about Quentin Dover is going to get lost in the shuffle."

"I still want that day," I said.

"I'll do my best," he said. But from the sound of his voice, I figured that Jack Moon would have been just as happy if the Quentin Dover case had ended that night.

I fell asleep after I drank the Scotch. When I woke up it was daylight outside. I opened the curtains and took a look at Las Cruces. There wasn't much to see. No buildings of more than two or three stories. A few concrete ramps leading to the expressway. The usual number of fast-food joints, their lots empty in the dawn light. And the desert, of course. Brown and scintillant in the white morning sun.

239

It wasn't the naked kind of desert—the sandy, Sahara kind. This one was clinging to life—or life was clinging to it. Sage grass, sprouting in rows like lettuce patches. Agave, like fat monstrous flowers. And barbed octillio. I looked for the twisted crosses of saguaro, but I didn't see any. No barrel cactus, either, although there was lobed prickly pear growing in the dirt beneath my window. In the distance were the mountains—always in the distance, nearer or farther, in the desert. They turned colors as the sun rose. At that early hour of the morning they were a bleached-out yellow—the same color as the sky. But in the evening, they'd purple like ripening fruit.

I showered and put on some fresh clothes—jeans and a workshirt. Then I went down to the lobby to get something to eat. It was seven-thirty by the clock above the front desk and the lobby was just coming to life. The pool area was roped off and deserted, but the smell of chlorine lingered in the air. A few travelers were sitting sleepy-eyed at the little tables of the cafe. I joined them, sitting by myself, drinking coffee and eating Rancher eggs with chilis and mangos in them. They were good. So was the coffee.

Around eight-thirty, I walked over to the front desk and asked the clerk how to get to the old town square. She gave me some simple directions. I thanked her and went out to the parking lot. It smelled like the desert outside—hot, dry, and clean. The heat was already starting up. That close to the border, it would probably go well over a hundred by noon. But it wasn't a sapping heat. It was more like the heat from an open fire. If you moved, it made you warm without burning you. If you stood still for too long, it began to hurt.

I started the Mustang up and followed the road that ran beneath the concrete ramps of the highway, along the eastern edge of town. To my right, residential streets, full of small ranch houses and Spanish bungalows, led across town. To my left, the desert extended all the way to the

240

El Capitan mountains. There were a few ranch houses scattered on the desert side and a few more at the foot of the mountains. I couldn't see much of them from the car—just stucco walls and window glass blazing in the sun.

About two miles up the road, I turned right, down one of the crosstown drags. The nearer to the center of town I got, the fancier the homes became. Some of them were very handsome. White haciendas with adobe walls—like thick slices of whole wheat bread—and belltowers and watchtowers rising from their flat tiled roofs. In the middle of town, the road narrowed to the width of an alley and the pavement gave way to cobblestone. I crept along behind a row of very old, weathered, one-story buildings. Then I saw the church belfries, soaring above the flat rooftops, and I knew I was behind the town square. I pulled over and parked. A pedestrian alley ran between the buildings. I got out of the car and walked up it to the square.

There was a promenade in its center, brown with grass, and an old bandstand painted white and red. A cobbled street circled the promenade, running past the row of beaten buildings, in front of the church, then down the other side of the promenade where a second row of one-story buildings formed the third side of the town square. Most of the buildings housed shops—restaurants, silversmiths, antique stores, a gun shop. The church dominated the square. It was massive, cut-stone, Spanish colonial, with a heavily ornamented portal in front and twin belfries on either side. There were a few steps leading up to it. I didn't see anyone standing on the stairs, but it was just ten of nine.

I wandered down the dusty sidewalk, reading the historical markers on the buildings. The store at the far end of the square—away from the church—was built like a stone garrison. It looked very old. The marker on the door said that it had been a jail at one time. At another time, it had been the seat of the New Mexican territorial government. Billy the Kid had been incarcerated there by Marshal Pat Garrett. And, before that, the Gadsden Purchase had been signed in the building. I went in.

It was an antique and curio shop now. A rugged-looking woman, her skin weathered by the sun, was standing behind a glass-and-wood display counter, full of silver belt buckles and silver and turquoise Indian jewelry.

"Was Billy the Kid really jailed here?" I asked her.

She looked at me disinterestedly. "That's what the sign says, doesn't it? He was jailed here before they moved him up to Lincoln county. That's where he made most of the trouble."

I knew a few of the names. Tunstall and Chisolm. I'd heard them in movies or read them in books. But the crowded little room, with its thick stone walls and worn beam ceiling, didn't look like anything out of a movie. It looked like a provisioner's store. Small, windowless, full of goods.

"How old is this building?" I asked.

"It goes back a long way," the woman said with a touch of pride. "To the Spanish missionaries. This used to be the chief city of New Mexico. Mesilla was the capital of the territory for a while." She sounded wistful and a little soured, as if she resented the fact that they'd moved the capital to Santa Fe.

"He was a right bastard, you know," she said as I walked back to the door.

"Who?"

"Billy the Kid. He was a liar and a killer. All that crap about how the Mexicans loved him? That was just crap. They hated him. They were afraid of him. He was crazy."

"I'm disappointed to hear it," I said.

"Most people are," the woman said.

I walked back up the sidewalk to the church. There was a man sitting on the steps. I couldn't see him clearly until I got to the head of the square. He was wearing jeans and a white cotton shirt. His hair was glossy black, parted in

242

the middle, and combed down flat on either side of his head. He had a small moustache and a lean, brown, pock-marked face. He wasn't very big, but he had big muscles in his arms. He looked as if he'd worked hard all his life. There was a mark on his face. I thought it was a birthmark until I walked up to him. But it wasn't a birthmark; it was a tiny teardrop, tattooed in fading blue ink at the corner of his left eye.

"Mr. Ramirez?" I said.

The man stood up. "I'm Jorge Ramirez."

"Harry Stoner."

I held out my hand and we shook. I towered over the little man. He couldn't have been more than five seven or five eight. His white shirt billowed at his belt, as if it were several sizes too large for him.

"How can I help you, señor?" he said.

"I'd like you to take me to Dover's ranch," I said. "Can you do that?"

"Of course."

"And would you mind answering some questions, too?"

"I wouldn't mind," he said placidly. "The ranch is in the hills. We need a car."

"We can take mine."

"Better take my jeep," Ramirez said. "It's pretty rough road out there."

36

I followed Ramirez across the promenade to another walkway that ran between a couple of buildings on the far side of the square. His jeep was parked in an alley, behind the gunsmith's shop. It was an open-topped jeep, with a rollbar on it. It looked fairly beaten.

As I got in, I asked him how far away the ranch was.

"Ten miles. Not far."

"And where's the airfield in Las Cruces?"

The man pointed south. "Same direction. 'Bout five miles."

"Did you pick Dover up at the airfield this weekend?"

He nodded. "On Friday night."

"Do you know why he came to Las Cruces?"

"He came about the ranch," Ramirez said. "We talk about it last week. It gave him a lot of trouble, with the floods and all. He made up his mind he was gonna sell it."

"And that's what he came here for?"

"Yeah," the man said. "He tol' me last week he'd got a buyer. A rancher from Texas."

I sat back on the jeep seat. "Did he sell it?"

Ramirez nodded again. "I think so. On Saturday. He didn' want to sell it—I'm sure. But . . ." Ramirez spread his hands in a gesture of helplessness.

"You were his overseer?"

"Yeah." He started the jeep up and we took off with a lurch.

The wind was too loud to hold a conversation over. So I just sat back and took in the view. Ramirez drove east to the road I'd been on, turned south onto it, and headed away from town toward Mexico. There was a mountain range on the southwest horizon. Eight miles down the road, Ramirez turned onto a dirt lane that led to the mountains. There was a ranch built on the side of one of the foothills. Even at a distance, I could tell that it was a big spread. A dry wash ran past it, coming down the mountainside and cutting across the desert floor. The dirt of the wash was yellow and cracked. The jeep shook as we crossed over it. The ranch house was a quarter of a mile further down the road. Ramirez pulled up in front of it. There was a "For Sale by Owner" sign stuck in the yard, with a "Sold" sticker pasted over it.

I stared at the sign for a second. I didn't know if it was my pride or my mean streak, but I felt cheated.

"He came all that way to sell his house?" I said. "That's what this was all about?"

"What what was all about?" Ramirez said politely.

I shook my head. "It's not important. Did Dover do anything else while he was in town—other than meet with the buyer from Texas?"

"I don' know. I didn' see him after I picked him up at the airport."

I stared at the house again. It was an elaborate thing for such a remote spot. Full of plate glass. Modern A-style, rather than the traditional Spanish of the haciendas in Mesilla. There was a pool behind it, covered with a tarp. And a tennis court, fenced in wire.

"How much did he get for it?" I asked Ramirez.

"I don' know. A hundred and fifty thousand, maybe. That's what he was asking. He was taking a beating, man. It cost him a lot to fix the place up after the last flood."

"Who was the buyer, do you know?"

"He say a man named Clark. Gene Clark. Big rancher from El Paso. He wanted a place to spend the winter— some place close to home."

"Did you meet this guy?"

"No. I don' see him. Señor Dover said he was gonna meet him at the ranch."

A gust of wind kicked up a spout of dirt at my feet, as if someone had taken a shot at me with a rifle.

I felt a little like I'd been shot at. "For chrissake," I said aloud.

"You wouldn't have a key to the place, would you?"

Ramirez shook his head. "Señor Dover took the keys."

"Chrissake," I said again.

I walked back to the jeep, Ramirez tagging along beside me.

"Do you know how to get in touch with Clark?"

He shook his head. "Señor Dover handled it. All I do is pick him up and take him back to the airport."

"Might as well take me back to Mesilla then," I said. "I guess I'll have to get in touch with Clark from there."

"Yes, Señor," Ramirez said.

As soon as I got back to the hotel, I called El Paso information and asked for Gene Clark's number. They didn't have a listing for him, under Gene or Eugene or G. or E.. I thought about calling Seth Murdock to see if he knew anything about Clark, but I was almost certain that he didn't—Dover hadn't mentioned him or the sale of the ranch to his lawyer. He'd just told Murdock that he was involved in some business deal. I couldn't really understand that—why he hadn't told Murdock about the ranch sale. I could see why he wouldn't have mentioned it to his mother or to Marsha. Connie, particularly, wouldn't have had a hard time putting two and two together, especially if Dover had been as sentimentally attached to the place as Murdock had claimed. She knew that her son was having problems on 'Phoenix'; the sale of the ranch would

246

have tipped her off to how serious those problems really were. But Murdock was a different case. He didn't know about 'Phoenix.' In fact, he'd been urging Quentin to unload the New Mexican property. There was no reason not to let him in on a possible sale, unless Dover's pride had kept him from admitting to Murdock that he'd been right about selling the ranch.

I didn't really believe that. No more than I really believed that Dover had taken all of those extraordinary precautions just to disguise the sale of some property. True, it was a large sale—a hundred and fifty thousand dollars, according to Ramirez. But Dover was well over a hundred thousand dollars in debt. Between the mortgage payments on his estate house and his mother's condo, fifty grand wouldn't have bought him much time.

I decided to phone around in Las Cruces, anyway, to see if a bank or savings and loan or realty office recognized Clark's name or knew about the sale of the ranch. I went through the Las Cruces phone book. There were only a couple of dozen banks and realtors. It took me two hours to make the calls. No one I spoke to knew anything about Clark. No one even knew that Dover's ranch had been for sale. All of them recognized Quentin's name and said some sad word about his death. They seemed to have liked Dover in Las Cruces—that's about all I learned. Ramirez seemed to have liked him, too. I remembered that Connie Dover had accused Ramirez of fooling around when he visited Cincinnati. But after meeting the man, I doubted it. Ramirez didn't look like the type who fooled around at anything. He struck me as being a tough little New Mexican cookie. But then most of the people I'd met or talked to in Las Cruces seemed hardboiled and tough.

At two o'clock, I gave up on my phone survey and decided to drive back out to the ranch. I thought there might be something inside the house that would lead me to Gene Clark—if there was a Gene Clark. I wasn't quite

247

ready to write him off as another one of Dover's inventions, aimed, this time, at keeping his overseer from knowing what he was really up to on Saturday. But I was leaning that way.

It was scorchingly hot outside by that hour of the day. I could feel the heat rolling off the parking lot as I walked to my car. The tar was soft and sticky underfoot. I rolled down the car windows, opened the doors, switched the air conditioner on full blast and started the Mustang up. When I could get inside the car without breaking into a sweat, I rolled the windows back up and took off, down the long dusty road on the eastern side of town.

It took me ten minutes through the desert to get to the turnoff. I babied the car across the dry wash and pulled to a stop in front of the ranch. The tires kicked up a mighty cloud of dirt. I waited for the dust to settle, then got out and walked up to the front door. The door was set in a low brick wall; a triangular picture window ran above it to the tent-shaped roof. I rattled the door but it was locked. Then I stepped back and tried to look into the high window. There was a heavy curtain hanging across it. I walked around to the west side of the house and continued along the brick wall to the back yard. There were a couple of smaller windows in the back wall and another door. I tried the door but it, too, was locked.

There was no way in, unless I broke a window or jimmied a door. I thought about it for a moment and decided that it was worth the risk. What I needed was a large rock or piece of timber. I scratched around the back yard looking for a crowbar. Eventually I settled on a long metal pole I found on the deck of the pool. I picked it up and took it back to the house. There were two small windows on either side of the rear door—probably bathroom or kitchen windows. I picked the one to my right and tapped it with the pole. The glass was thick and I had to whack it a couple of times before it shattered. I knocked all the loose glass out of the casement with the pole. Then I went back to the pool, sat down on the deck in the shade of a palo verde tree, and waited.

The window glass hadn't been wired or taped. But there might have been a vibration-sensing or photoelectric device connected to some alarm system that ran through the underground phone lines to the Las Cruces police department or to a private security firm. I gave the cops fifteen minutes to respond to the alarm. No one showed. I waited another five minutes just to be sure, then I walked over to the window and boosted myself in.

It was a bathroom, like I'd thought. The shattered glass on the tile floor gave me pause for a second. That was what it must have looked like in the Belle Vista on Monday morning, I thought, only there would have been blood everywhere and Quentin's torn-up body lying in the middle of it. I walked quickly over to the bathroom door and opened it. It was very hot in the house, and I broke into a sweat immediately. There was a short hall outside the bathroom, with a low ceiling overhead. The hall stopped abruptly at the rear of the living room—a huge room, with a cathedral ceiling that made it seem even larger. A balcony ran around the walls, like a cut-out second story. A staircase on the west wall led up to the balcony.

I went into the living room, dripping sweat from my arms. There was a huge stone fireplace on the east wall, with a thirty-foot-high chimney running up to the roof. An Indian rug was laid out in front of it with a couch and two chairs arranged around the rug. The rest of the flooring was hardwood, polished like gun metal. There was a study area on the east side of the room—a plexiglass desk and chair and a couple of wood file cabinets. The desk was littered with papers.

A small picture of Marsha Dover was propped on the edge of the desk. I picked it up and looked at it for a moment, then put it back down. Most of the loose papers were 'Phoenix' materials—breakdowns and scripts. But there was a xeroxed manuscript on top of the heap that looked too big to be a breakdown. It was stapled on the side and someone had written "Here it is" in the margin. I sat down and skimmed it. It was some sort of story line—not a very good one, as far as I could tell. But it was definitely a story line.

I folded it up and stuck it in my back pocket. Then I went upstairs. The balcony ran back to a small bedroom area at the rear of the house, above the john and what was probably a small kitchen. The bedroom was just a mattress on a wooden frame, a bureau, and a chair. The sheets on the mattress were rumpled, as if someone had slept in the bed recently. I went through the drawers of the bureau. They were filled with clothes, men's jewelry, and toiletry items.

I walked back downstairs to the study. My shirt was completely soaked by then. There was a phone on the desk. I started to copy down the number and then realized that I already had it—it was the same number Quentin had forwarded his calls to.

37

After checking out the kitchen, which was spotlessly clean, I went back into the bathroom and climbed
out through the window. The open air felt good after that
hot, cramped place. I could feel the sweat start to evapo-
rate immediately, as if the sunlight were a kind of breeze.
Dover had spent the night in the house, but as far as I
could tell he'd been there alone. There was no indication
that he'd had visitors—Gene Clark or anyone else. No
liquor glasses lying about. No cigarette butts in ashtrays.
No dishes in the sink or food on plates. It made me wonder
if Quentin had done anything more than sleep there on
Friday night and then go someplace else on Saturday,
after he'd spoken to Feldman and before he'd had
Ramirez take him to the airstrip. There should have been
at least one liquor glass in that house—Quentin's. There
wasn't even that small sign of habitation. Only the rumpled bedclothes and the papers scattered on the desk.

But as I was driving back to Las Cruces, I realized that
somebody else *had* been in the house—at least once, on
Monday morning. Feldman had talked to him—a man
who spoke Spanish and who hung up on Feldman when
he mentioned Quentin's name. Unless Ramirez had been
lying to me, it hadn't been him. He'd claimed that he

didn't even have a key to the house any longer. The house hadn't been ransacked—before I broke the window—so whoever had been there hadn't been there by accident. That meant that somebody else had a key and a legitimate reason to be in Dover's house on Monday morning.

I decided to talk to Ramirez again and see if he could explain it.

It was almost five when I got back to Las Cruces. I stopped at the City Hall before I went to the hotel—to make one last attempt at locating Gene Clark. I checked with a Mexican woman in the Office of Titles and Deeds to see if the sale of the ranch had been registered there. But she had no record of a sale and seemed surprised that Dover would have put the ranch on the market. He'd really loved the place, she said.

When I got to the Holiday Inn, I went up to "Maximilian," took the document out of my pocket, and put it in my overnighter. I took a quick shower, then phoned Ramirez. A woman answered the phone.

"Jes?" she said.

"Mrs. Ramirez?"

"Jes?" she said again.

"My name's Stoner, Mrs. Ramirez. I'd like to speak to your husband."

"He's no' here," she said and hung up.

I copied Ramirez's address on a Holiday Inn notepad, got dressed, and walked down to the lobby.

"Can you tell me how to find this street?" I asked the desk clerk and showed her the address I'd written down on the pad.

"Sure," she said with a smile. "I'll draw you a map."

She drew a diagram for me on the pad and printed some instructions beneath it. I thanked her and walked out to the lot.

It was cooling off outside. The heat had been so ferocious at the heart of the day that the sudden chill seemed

252

as miraculous as a change of season. I stared at the map and gazed into the desert. It was deep brown now, in the setting sun. The El Capitan mountains were still lit brightly on their peaks, but the slopes were beginning to purple into shadow. A few houselights flickered in the valley at their feet. According to the map, one of those lights was where I would find Jorge Ramirez.

I followed the instructions of the map, getting back on the expressway in front of the hotel and driving east ten miles to Exit 2-B. There was a Shell station at Exit 2-B and a paved two-lane road, running south parallel to the mountain range. I stayed on the two-lane road for about three miles, until I came to a four-way stop sign. I turned left at the stop sign onto another two-lane road that went east toward the mountains. There were a few deserted ranch houses along the road, with dusty, wind-bellied fencing surrounding them. Eventually the fencing disappeared and the road turned to hard-packed dirt and I was out in the open desert—among the sage and the agave—heading into the shadow of the mountains.

Five miles farther on, I could see the lights of a ranch house at the foot of the mountain range. An old, rusted horse trailer and a broken-down wagon littered the road leading to the house. The house itself looked adobe. As I drove up to it, I could see that it was a Pueblo house, with rounded doorways and rounded windows. Vigas projected out of the walls beneath the flat roof. The place was a little larger than Maria Sanchez's bungalow, but far more weather-beaten and run down. A maroon Chevelle, stripped of all its chrome, was parked in the front yard. I didn't see the jeep.

I pulled up behind the Chevelle and got out. It was cold in the shadow of the mountain, and the wind made me shiver. There was still enough daylight in the sky to see clearly, although everything looked slightly gray and washed out, like on a cloudy winter's day. I walked through clumps of sage to the door of the house. It was standing open. Through it I could see a truncheon table with a kerosene lamp on it. The lamp lit up the walls of the ranch, turning them yellow and casting deep shadows on the spots where the adobe was cracked or chipped. A woman stepped into the lamplight. She was wearing a gingham skirt and a sweatshirt. The sweatshirt read "Arizona State University." When she looked out the door and saw me standing in the twilight, she took a step backward. She had a high-cheeked, pretty face and long black hair, braided in back.

A couple of children came running to the door to see what had frightened their mother. They were small and brown—a boy of about six in underpants and a torn T-shirt and a girl of about four in a nightgown with ruffles on it.

"Mrs. Ramirez?" I said.

She nodded without moving from where she stood.

"I'd like to speak to your husband."

"He's no' here," she said.

"Do you mind if I wait?" I said.

"No. I don' mind." She stared at me for a moment, then herded her children back in the house.

I went over to the Mustang, sat down on the hood, and waited.

About ten minutes later, I heard the sound of an engine. The woman heard it, too. She came to the door and gazed into the desert. Far out on the plain a pair of headlights was making bright, jouncing flashes in the twilight. As the jeep got closer, I could see a plume of dust rising behind it, like the rooster tail of a speedboat. It took the jeep several minutes to get to the ranch. The woman watched it intently, glancing now and then at me. When Ramirez pulled into the yard, she called out to him in Spanish. He looked at me, then got out of the jeep.

"How'd you find us?" he said, walking across the yard to the Mustang.

"The girl at the hotel drew me a map."

"Yes?" He studied me for a second. He was dressed as

254

he'd been dressed that morning, in jeans and the over-sized white shirt, except that he'd put a cracked leather flyer's jacket over the shirt. His jeans were dirty and his hands were caked with dirt, as if he'd been digging. "What can I do for you, señor?"

"I've been checking around town," I said, "trying to get a lead on this man, Clark. Nobody I talked to ever heard of him. In fact, no one even knew the ranch was for sale. And Dover didn't register any sale with the county."

"Maybe he didn' sell it after all," Ramirez said. "Or, maybe Clark registered the sale in Santa Fe."

"I couldn't locate Clark in El Paso. He wasn't listed in the phone book."

Ramirez shrugged. "Coul' be he don' have a listed phone number."

"It could be," I said. "When did you say that Dover mentioned the sale to you?"

"On Wednesday," he said. "I come up to see him. In Ohio. Make my report. I come up twice a year, you know? This time, he say there was somethin' important we gotta talk about."

"And it was the sale?"

He nodded.

"Did Dover tell anyone else about the sale? His wife? His mother?"

"Not while I'm around. I think maybe he wanted to keep it a secret."

"Why do you say that?"

Ramirez stared at my face for a moment. "How well do you know Señor Dover?"

"I never met the man."

"He was a very proud man," Ramirez said. "When he had troubles, he didn' wanna worry other people. I think maybe he was havin' some trouble—that's why he needed to sell the ranch."

"I think he was having trouble, too," I said. It was fully dark by then and the only light on the whole vast desert

255

seemed to be the warm yellow light spilling out of the ranch house door. Ramirez's sober, inexpressive face was lit by it. "Did you see Dover at all on Saturday?"

He shook his head. "Only when I took him back to the airport."

"And you never actually met this man, Clark?"

"Like I tol' you this morning, I picked Señor Dover up and dropped him off. That's all I seen him. He tol' me he wanted to be alone."

"Is there any other place in Las Cruces that Dover might have gone to on Saturday? Outside the ranch?"

"He was meetin' with Clark, man," Ramirez said. "Where's he gonna go?"

"Did anyone else have a key to the ranch—outside you and Dover?"

"Just us," he said. "Señor Dover, he was a generous man. He let me stay at his casa when he was not there."

"You liked him, didn't you?"

He didn't answer me, but it was clear that he had liked Quentin Dover a great deal.

"Someone answered the phone in Dover's house on Monday morning," I said. "Was it you?"

"No, it wasn' me. I didn' have a key no more."

"You don't have any idea who it could have been?"

"Maybe, Señor Dover gave a key to someone else."

Ramirez's wife called to him in Spanish from the doorway. The two kids were sitting at the truncheon table. Bowls and plates of food were arranged in table settings.

"We gotta eat now," Ramirez said politely. "You coul' stay, if you want."

I shook my head. "No. Thanks for the invitation. I better be getting back to town."

"Señor," Ramirez said. "Señor Dover had some trouble, maybe. We all have trouble, you know? You don' judge a man by his troubles." He looked at me sadly. "You understan' what I'm saying? It don' make no difference whether the patron sold his house or not. Maybe he just wished he

256

could, you know? Leave it alone, señor. Whatever he done, it ain't hurtin' you. It ain't hurtin' nobody."

Ramirez understood Dover a lot better than I'd thought. "What *did* he do, Jorge?" I asked.

The little man shook his head. "I tol' you what I know. That's what I believe. What difference does it make now? We all gotta do things we don' wanna do."

He walked into the ranch to join his family. I opened the car door and sat down on the seat. Ramirez had been a good friend to Dover. And maybe, he was right—what difference did it make? I started up the car and clicked on the headlights. As I was backing up in the yard, the lights lit up the rear bumper of the Chevelle parked by the house. The license plate glowed like phosphorous.

It wasn't until I was a half mile down the road, with the lights of the ranch house already fading into the darkness, that I let myself admit that it hadn't been a New Mexican plate. It had been a California plate—BBB82305. I pulled over and scratched it down on a piece of notepaper. After what Ramirez had said, it made me feel bad to do it—the way I used to feel when I was a cop.

When I got back to the Holiday Inn, I ate some dinner in the little cafe—a steak and some of the spiciest gazpacho I'd ever tasted. I had to drink three Dos Equis to cool off. Well, I didn't have to. But I did it anyway. Then I went up to my room and phoned Seymour Wattle.

"Stoner?" he said with surprise. "I thought we were dealing through Jack Moon."

"We were," I said. "We're not anymore."

"Did he tell you the latest about the Pacoima killings?"

"I haven't talked to him in a while. What do you have?"

"The Pacoima cops say it was definitely a gangland killing—Mexican maf'. They think maybe the Ruiz kid is dead, too. There's been some talk on the streets that he got himself involved in a drug deal that didn't go down right. You know, they've been putting a lot of heat on dealers here in L.A. lately. And a lot of people are showing up dead."

"And that's why Maria and her son were killed? Because of a drug deal?"

"Apparently," Seymour said. "You never really know with these things. Maria and Ruiz lived together—part of the time, at least. So whatever he'd gotten into, she was probably into, too. They knew something they shouldn't have. They had something they shouldn't have had. They did something to make the wrong people nervous. What difference does it make?"

I laughed dully. "Someone said the same thing to me a couple of hours ago."

"How's it going in Beanville?"

"Dover got in on Friday night. His overseer picked him up at the airfield and dropped him off at his house. He told the overseer that he'd come to Las Cruces to sell his house—to a rancher from El Paso named Clark."

"Did you talk to Clark?"

"There is no Clark," I said. "At least, I don't think there is. The whole story was just more of the same—another alibi to fool the overseer and free up some time in Las Cruces. I think the overseer knows that, too. He just doesn't care."

"What was Dover really up to?"

"Some deal," I said. "I don't know if I'll ever find out, for sure. I don't know if I care, either."

"You sound kinda wore out," Wattle said.

"I am. I'm weary of Quentin Dover."

"Did Moon tell you that the Ruiz kid picked Dover's car up at the airport?"

"Yeah."

"I been thinking about that. Maybe you were right about the Sanchez girl. Maybe she was killed 'cause of Dover. Ruiz, too. I mean, if they were all involved in a drug deal, that could have been why the two greasers were bumped off and why Dover killed himself. Christ, what a bunch of amateurs. You know what I'm saying?"

"Yeah, I know. They're all dead."

"I gotta friend with the Texas state troopers," Wattle said. "You want I should have him check out this guy Clark for you?"

"Yeah," I said. "Do that. Gene Clark in El Paso." The California plate popped into my head. I pulled the slip of paper out of my shirt pocket and stared at it for a moment. "You better run a plate for me, too. California BBB82305."

"What's that?"

"Just call me in the morning, O.K.?"

I gave him my number at the hotel and rang off.

38

Before I went to sleep, I read the document through—the one that I'd found in Dover's home. It was a banal story about a man running from some crime he'd committed in his past. He shows up disguised as a lawyer in a new town and a local girl falls in love with him. Then another man shows up who knows about the lawyer's past. He starts blackmailing the lawyer. The blackmailer is killed; the lawyer is accused of his murder; and his secret past is revealed. It went on like that for almost a hundred pages. After about forty, it began to put me to sleep.

That night I had a very bad dream about Marsha Dover. I didn't remember all of it when I woke up, but the bad feeling lingered on. Around eight-thirty the next morning I phoned her. This time she answered.

"Yeah?" she said groggily.

"This is Harry."

"Harry?" she said. "Hi Harry."

"Are you O.K.?"

She laughed. "Sure, I'm O.K. I'm always O.K. I'm sorry about the other night. I fucked up."

"That's all right," I said. "Go back to sleep."

"Are you O.K.?"

"Yes."

"You didn't come back to see me—I thought maybe you were pissed. I wouldn't blame you if you were pissed."

"No," I said. "I'm not pissed."

"You'll come and see me?"

"Yeah."

"Maybe we can go on that trip. I think I'm ready to go, now."

"We'll talk about it. Go back to sleep."

"O.K. 'Bye, Harry."

"Goodbye, Marsha."

Hearing her voice made me feel better about the dream. Worse about other things. I tried not to think about any of it. After a while, the bad feeling went away.

Jack Moon called me around nine, as I was drinking coffee and staring out my hotel window at the bleak, sunny Las Cruces streets.

"I'm in Cincinnati," he said, after he'd said hello. "Frank ordered me back. He told me to tell you that you're off the case, Harry. He knows we've been in touch. There was just no way to keep it a secret."

"I'm off the case because of Connie?"

"Yeah. I told you this was going to happen. To be fair, it wasn't Frank's idea. But he's got people he's responsible to. And they don't want any trouble."

"What about Dover?" I said.

"He died of natural causes, following a fall in the bathroom. That's the way it's going to stay."

I sighed. "Maybe so."

"Frank would appreciate a call, Harry. He feels rotten about this. He really did want to clear everything up."

"I'll call him," I said. "I guess I'll fly back to Cincinnati tonight."

"You want me to pick you up?"

"No, I left my car at the airport."

"I'm sorry about this, Harry," Jack said. "You must think we're real shits."

261

"No, I don't," I said. "Maybe he did die accidentally. I found a document at his house here in Las Cruces. Could be he came out here to work on it, after all."

Jack laughed. "You don't really believe that, do you?"

"No," I said.

"What was the document about?"

"A man running from his past, who disguises himself as something he's not, then gets blackmailed for it."

Moon didn't say anything for a moment. "That sounds familiar. Must have been one of our old story lines."

"Probably," I said.

"I'll see you when you get back, Harry," Jack said and hung up.

I packed my overnighter and called the El Paso airport. There was a plane leaving for Cincinnati at four-thirty that afternoon. I booked the flight. It would take me about an hour to drive down to El Paso, the ticket agent told me. That gave me five and a half hours to kill. Checkout time at the hotel was two. I decided to wait until then to check out, in case I wanted to come back to the room to make a call or eat lunch. I left the overnighter in the luggage rack by the door and walked down to the lobby. It was funny but I didn't feel angry or disappointed about being taken off the case. I think I felt relieved.

I decided to do a little sightseeing—like any tourist. It was a very warm day. The sky was white hot overhead and pale blue above the mountain ranges. The desert was drenched in sunlight. I drove out on the desert for a while, then worked my way southwest to Mesilla. I stopped at the old town square again and took a closer look at the church and the shops. I ended up in the curio store at the end of the promenade—the stone building where the Gadsden purchase had been signed and where Billy the Kid had been jailed. The woman with the weathered face and the grudge against Santa Fe was waiting on a Mexican boy when I stepped through the door. The boy was about twenty-two and he wanted a silver belt buckle so badly that he could taste it. The woman took the one he wanted out of the glass case and he fondled it lovingly. He was a tall, skinny kid in a plaid shirt and blue jeans. His black hair was cropped so short in back that he looked like a Marine in boot camp. When he handed the buckle to the woman, she dropped it back in the display case and gave him a disgusted look. The kid looked embarrassed and walked out. As he passed by me, I noticed that he had a teardrop tattoo on his eye, like Ramirez.

"Goddamn Mexican trash," the woman said when the kid had gone. "Coming in here and wastin' my time. The only way he's gonna get seventy bucks is to steal it. And both he and I know it."

"Why do you say that?"

She pulled at the flesh beneath her eye. "Didn't you see it?"

"The tattoo?"

"Yeah. It's their macho mark. You can only wear that if you've done hard time. That's what they say, anyway."

"You know a man named Jorge Ramirez?"

She nodded. "I know Jorge."

"He's got that kind of tattoo."

"He did time," the woman said. "But he straightened himself out. He's one of your decent Mexicans. It's that wetback riff-raff I can't abide."

"What did Ramirez do time for?" I asked her.

"I don't remember. It's been a while. Like I said, he straightened himself out. Got married, went to work, had kids."

"Did you know Quentin Dover?"

"Hell, yes," she said. "I knew Quentin. Sorry he's dead."

"Ramirez worked for him, didn't he?"

"He not only worked for him, he worshipped him. Dover was good to Ramirez. Good to a lot of Mexican

263

families around here. He had a thing for the so-called disadvantaged."

"You didn't approve?" I said.

"Never said that," the woman said sharply. "He was just like a lot of Easterners who come out here and don't know what it's all about, that's all. He would have grown out of it, after a time. You gotta do for yourself first, mister. That's my motto. You can't depend on other people to do for you. They'll let you down every time."

"You think Dover depended too much on Ramirez?"

"I think he didn't depend enough on himself," she said.

She was the kind of woman who gave the frontier spirit a bad name. But she was honest in her own, bigoted fashion and what she'd said about Ramirez interested me. But not enough to do any more detecting. I was done with Quentin Dover. He'd been picked over enough, God knew, in life and in death. And I'd liked Ramirez enough not to want to know whether he'd been involved in Dover's final folly or in some folly of his own. I was just a tourist now.

I drove back to the hotel at one-thirty and went up to my room to get my luggage. The message light on the phone was blinking, so I picked up the receiver and dialed the desk. Sy Goldblum had called at twelve-thirty. He'd left a number where he could be reached and an urgent message that I return the call. I almost didn't do it. I almost tore the phone number up and walked down to the desk and checked out. What I didn't know wasn't going to hurt me—or anyone else. And I didn't want to hurt anybody, least of all Quentin Dover. Connie would have been proud.

I made the call anyway.

Goldblum sounded very excited. That in itself almost made me hang up the phone.

"My friend in Texas tells me there is no Gene Clark in

264

El Paso," Wattle said. "Thought you'd like to know."

"I already knew," I said.

"Now here comes the interesting part."

"Don't tell me," I almost said.

"That license number you gave me? Ran it through DMV this morning and guess what? The registration comes up Jerry Ruiz."

"Shit," I said.

"Why shit? Christ, man, we're really onto something!"

I thought of that broken-down ranch, the man, the woman, and their kids and felt sick at heart. If I told Wattle where I'd spotted that plate, he'd have cops swarming all over the Ramirez ranch in a matter of hours. And if the cops knew about Ruiz, the gang that killed Maria wouldn't be far behind. There'd be more dead bodies—more dead kids. And for what? Because Ramirez did a favor for a man he'd loved and admired. "Who have you told about this?"

"Nobody yet. I've been waiting for you to call back to find out where you spotted the tags."

"I want you to do me a favor, Sy. I want you to forget about the plates."

"Forget about them," he said with a laugh. "You're kidding."

"I'm not kidding," I said. "Forget I mentioned them."

"I can't do that, Harry," he said in a tough voice. "This ain't the sort of thing you can pass by. Somebody's got to look into it."

"*I'll* look into it. I give you my word."

"It ain't enough. This is murder, man."

"Look, you don't know that. I don't either. The Ruiz kid hasn't been directly related to the Sanchez girl's death."

But it wasn't the Ruiz kid I was thinking of.

"I can't forget it, man. Understand?"

"Two thousand," I said. "I'm sure I can get it for you, Sy. By tomorrow."

265

"Make it five," he said.

"I'll make it five."

He didn't say anything for a moment. "I don't understand this, man."

"I don't either," I said. "Is it a deal?"

"I'll have to think about it," he said, and hung up.

39

I called the El Paso airport and canceled my reservation for the flight to Cincinnati. Then I called Frank Glendora at the United American building.

"We've got a serious problem," I said.

"I'm really sorry about this whole thing, Harry," he said unhappily. "Connie's just being intransigent."

"That's not the problem."

"Well, what, then?"

I explained the situation to him. "Dover's overseer, Jorge Ramirez, is apparently harboring a fugitive—a kid named Jerry Ruiz. Ruiz is the boy who helped Dover get out of the Belle Vista on Friday night. He's probably also the one who picked him up at the airport on Sunday morning. The point is, Ruiz was heavily involved in Dover's scheme. And now it looks like Ramirez was involved, too."

"But we don't know what that scheme was, do we?" Glendora said innocently.

I was getting a little sick of that innocence. "At this point, I can make a pretty good guess. You must know that, Frank. Jack has to have told you."

"He told me some things," Glendora said.

"Frank, this isn't the time to kid around. Ruiz is connected to a killing. He may be marked for killing himself."

"I fail to see how that involves us."

"You do? Then let me make this as plain as I can. The Sanchez girl and her son were tortured to death. Cut and burned, Frank. Gangland style. They were made examples of, because they'd gotten involved in a drug deal that didn't go down right. You hear what I'm saying?"

"Yes," he said. "I hear you."

"It was Dover's deal, Frank. I'd bet on it now. I don't know the details, but they're bound to come out. Sy Goldblum at LAPD knows that and he also knows that I know where Ruiz is. He knows I'm witholding evidence in a capital crime, too. Now we can buy him off—maybe. But I wouldn't count on him staying bought and it's going to cost you a great deal of money."

"How much?"

"Five thousand, at least. It'll probably be more by tonight, once Sy has had some time to think about how serious this thing is. And something has to be done about Ruiz, Frank."

"What?" he said.

"I don't know. I won't know until I find out how deeply involved he was in Quentin's scheme and what that scheme actually was. If Quentin screwed with the wrong people, he could have sentenced everyone else who was connected to him to death. Maybe we can make it right again—for a price. But we have to know who to deal with."

"You're asking me to put you back on the case," he said.

I laughed. "You think I'm looking forward to this? I was just as ready to call it quits as you were. Quentin has that effect on me."

"Then why not . . . I mean could we just . . ."

"We could," I said. "But if it ever comes out that we did, you'd have the biggest scandal on your hands in the company's history. If I could make Ruiz's car, so can a state trooper. Goldblum already ran the license through California DMV, so somebody at DMV knows about it, too. And if the cops know about it, you can bet the thugs who killed Maria Sanchez know about it."

"God's teeth," Glendora said.

"There's something else," I said. "If I'm right about this thing, Ramirez, Ruiz, the Sanchez girl—they wouldn't have been involved if it weren't for Dover. Ramirez, in particular. I don't want to see anybody else get killed or busted, if I can prevent it. Not for Quentin's sake. And if I'm right and we don't follow up on this, I've got the feeling that there's going to be more death. Maybe United can live with that, but I can't."

Glendora took a deep breath. "Neither can I," he said. "Do what you have to do, Harry. I'll back you up on it. I'll go out to L.A. tonight to talk to Goldblum and to be available in case you need me."

"Good," I said.

"You may be costing me my job, old boy. You and Quentin."

"You shouldn't have cared about him," I said.

"I couldn't help it," Glendora said.

I didn't start thinking about what I'd bitten into until after I'd gone out to the car. Then everything began to seem very complicated. I hadn't wanted Ramirez to be involved in the case. But he was, and he had a criminal record, and he was harboring a boy who was either running away from a murder or involved in it himself. I couldn't wish that kind of trouble away, like Ramirez had said Dover was trying to do. I couldn't go out to that ranch armed with good intentions.

I drove the Mustang back to the town square and parked behind the low row of buildings fronting the south side of the promenade. There was a gun shop on that side of the mall. I'd seen it on Monday when I'd been waiting for Ramirez and again, that morning, when I'd browsed in the curio shop. I walked up one of the alleys to the sidewalk and went into the store.

"What have you got in .45 caliber?" I said to the stringy Mexican man behind the counter.

"Revolver or automatic?"

"Automatic," I said.

He took a blued Colt Commander out of the display case. I checked the magazine lips and the trigger pull. It had a five- or six-pound pull—a little heavy compared to my Gold Cup.

"That'll do," I said. "I'll need a box of .45 ACP, too."

"Twenty-five or fifty?"

"Twenty-five."

He took a yellow and green box of Remington 230 grain hardball off the shelf behind the counter.

"I'll need some I.D."

I got my F.F.L. out of my wallet and handed it to him.

"You're a collector, huh?"

"Something like that," I said.

"This ain't really a collectible," he said and winked. "But we'll make an exception."

I bought the gun and the ammunition and a belt holster, too. When I got back to the car, I drove down one of the sleepy Mesilla streets and pulled over in a gravel turn-around. There was some sparse shade in one corner of the turnaround, beneath a palo verde. I parked under the green-barked tree, undid my belt, and slipped the holster onto it. Then I got the Colt out, loaded the clip with seven rounds, and dumped the rest of the bullets in my pants pocket. I put the gun in the holster and pulled my shirt out of my pants. The shirttail covered the holster, or, at least, it would when I was standing.

I redid my belt, started up the car, and headed east, toward the El Capitan mountains.

It was about four when I got to the ranch. The Pueblo house looked grimier and more rundown in the light of day than it had at twilight. I drove past the abandoned horse trailer and the broken wagon into the yard. The jeep was parked by the house; the Chevelle was gone.

As I cracked the car door open, Ramirez stepped out of the Pueblo house. The vigas cast blunt, saw-toothed shadows over the doorway. He stood in the shadows—his hands at his side—and watched me walk up to him. He wasn't armed, or if he was, the gun was tucked out of sight, like my own.

"Señor," he said. His face looked sad and impassive. He hadn't shaved that morning and the day's growth of beard gave him a played-out look, although that could have been the way I was seeing him. He was wearing a collarless undershirt, stained yellow at the armpits and around the neck, and dirty blue jeans.

"We've got a problem, Jorge," I said.

"Yes?"

"The car that was parked here last night—the Chevelle? Where is it?"

"It's gone," he said. "I got rid of it."

I looked over Ramirez's shoulder into the house. There wasn't anyone else inside—no sign of his wife or his children.

"Did your wife take it?" I said, looking back at him.

He nodded. "She drove down to Juarez."

"I know about the car, Jorge. I know whose car it is. And I know that Dover wasn't going to sell his ranch. Whose story was that—yours or his?"

He took a deep breath and let it out slowly. "I knew you were gonna come back. I tol' my wife you were gonna come back."

"Is that why you sent her away?"

He nodded again. I stared at him for a moment.

"Don' worry, señor," he said with a polite smile. "I ain't gonna give you no trouble. I ain't gonna lie, either. It just don' work out. That's all. Not for Señor Dover. Not for me. He didn' wanna get nobody hurt."

271

"Sure he didn't," I said to the man. "Where's Ruiz?"

Ramirez pointed toward the mountains. "Up there. I got a lean-to. I let him stay there."

I looked over my shoulder at the mountain range. It looked gray in the late afternoon light. Gray and brown where the scrub pines grew below the timber line.

"Why did Ruiz come here?" I asked.

"He say he got no place else to go. They killed his woman and her kid. He thinks they were gonna kill him, too. He come down here 'cause that's where Señor Dover tol' him to go, if things didn' work out right. He's pretty scared, man."

"What about you? Aren't you scared?"

He shrugged. "What good's it gonna do? I ain't so happy about my life I care one way or 'nother. You know? I just don't want my old lady to get hurt. And my kids."

"What actually happened on Saturday?" I said.

"Like I tol' you—I picked Señor Dover up and took him to the ranch. Some men come there, up from Juarez maybe. I don' know for sure. He tol' me they were gonna buy the house. Only I knew that wasn't true. He just didn' want me to worry about him. He was scared, you know? He never done nothin' like that before. I tol' him I wasn't gonna let him down no matter what. I did what he said to do and pretended I didn' know what was really happenin.' But I kept my eyes open, you know, in case they tried something."

"Did they try anything?"

He shook his head. "They gave Señor Dover a suitcase. He had it with him when I took him back to the airport. He gave them some money, I think."

"The men Dover gave the money to—who were they?"

"I don' know. I never seen them before. Maybe Jerry knows."

"Did they see you?"

"Yeah," Ramirez said. "They seen me."

I stared at him again. He was a brave man—a good

272

friend. And he deserved better than he was going to get.

"All right," I said. "Let's go."

"I ain't gonna say nothin' to the cops about Señor Dover."

"I'm not taking you to the cops." I pointed to the mountains. "Up there. I want to talk to Ruiz."

"He ain't gonna talk to you, man. He's young. He don' wanna die."

"I'm not going to kill him. I just want to talk to him."

"He's gotta gun, man."

"I'll take my chances," I said. "Now let's go."

40

There was no road—at least, none that I could see. But Ramirez drove across the open desert as if he were navigating a familiar channel. The jeep filled quickly with dust thrown up by the tires. The dust was hot from the sun, like the sand of a beach. About ten minutes out, Ramirez pulled up in front of a talus at the base of one of the mountains to the east of Las Cruces.

"We gotta walk from here," he said.

I got out and followed him up the talus, picking my way through the hot rubble of stones. When we got about fifty yards up the hillside, the ground flattened out a bit. A narrow trail was cut into the hill, wide enough for two men to walk on. It ran parallel to the desert floor, a hundred and fifty feet up. I couldn't see where the trail led, because it snaked around the mountain into the shadow on the north face. Beneath us the desert stretched for miles. Las Cruces looked like a spot of green and adobe white from where I stood.

"How much farther?" I asked Ramirez.

"Not far."

I looked at the sun. It was about forty-five degrees above the horizon, just beginning to set for the day. I

274

wanted to get to Ruiz before it was too dark to see what he was doing.

I followed Ramirez down the trail, toward the north slope. We walked for almost ten minutes. Then the trail stopped and we came to a small clearing about thirty yards square, like a tiny plateau in the rock face. The clearing was surrounded by the mountain on each side. A small cabin was built into the west wall—the one facing the trail. The cabin was made of wood planks, with a corrugated tin roof and a stovepipe chimney. A trickle of woodsmoke was coming out of the chimney, grayish blue against the washed-out sky. There was one window and a door in the front of the cabin. I couldn't see into the window because the sun was glaring off the panes.

"You stay back," Ramirez said. "If he sees you . . ."

"I'll stay back," I said. "Tell him it's Harry Stoner. He knows me."

Ramirez started across the clearing and I sat down in the shadow of an overhang at the end of the trail. I could see the cabin clearly from where I sat, but I doubted if Ruiz could see me in the shadows.

I took the pistol out, cocked it, and locked it. Then I stuck it back in the holster beneath my shirttail.

I watched Ramirez go in the front door. He came back out a few minutes later and waved his right arm at me to come ahead.

"Keep your hands up, so he can see them," he called out.

I raised my arms and started to walk across the clearing. Something was gleaming in the sunlight in the doorway to the cabin. It wasn't until I got close that I realized it was a rifle barrel. I hesitated for a second when I saw it, then walked up to the door. Ruiz was crouching on one knee just inside, holding the rifle on me. Ramirez was sitting on a plank bench across from the door.

"Put the rifle away, Jerry," I said to him.

275

"How do I know that you didn't come to kill me?" he said nervously.

"Why would I want to kill you?"

"To get rid of me," he said. "Just like they got rid of Maria. So there won't be anybody around who knew what that fucker was doing."

"You're just going to have to trust me."

"I don't trust nobody." He stood up and waved the rifle barrel at me. "C'mon."

I stepped through the door onto the plank floor. It was hot and dark in the cabin. The place smelled like an attic. There was a wood-burning stove on the back wall, beside the bench that Ramirez was sitting on. A table by the door. A couple of ladderback chairs with broken rungs on the north wall. And a cot with a thin mattress on the south. It was a far cry from the Belle Vista Hotel.

The kid looked like he'd had a rough time. His hair was dirty; his handsome face was ragged with a five-day's growth of beard. His clothes smelled. He kept blinking his eyes, as if someone were shining a light in them. His eyelids were swollen and ringed with purple flesh.

"When's the last time you slept?" I asked him.

"I don't need to sleep." He wiped his brow with the back of his hand. "I'm all right."

"You're not all right," I said. "You're in trouble, and you know it."

He looked at me as if he wanted to cry.

"Whoever killed Maria Sanchez is going to try to kill you, too."

"Shut up!" he said. "How do I know that you're not one of them?" He looked wildly at Ramirez. "He could be one of them."

"He's not," Ramirez said.

"What do you know? You stupid beaner."

Ruiz was clearly paranoid with fear and fatigue. After five days on the run and a few nights in that deserted cabin with nothing to think about but Maria and her son, it was inevitable. It was also scarey.

"You should have seen what they did to her," he said with horror. "My God, my God."

"Who did it?"

"Some guys. From L.A. The ones that Dover sold the dope to."

"There may be a way out of this, Jerry. But I've got to know what happened before I can help."

"Why?" he said with a laugh. "So you can turn me over to the cops as an accessory? You're just trying to protect him, man. I know that. If you hadn't gone to Maria's house on Thursday, she wouldn't be dead. And I wouldn't be in this shithole."

I felt sick. "What are you saying?"

"They *saw* you, man. What do you think I'm saying? They know you've been snooping around. They were following you, you asshole. They're onto you."

"How did they hear about me," I said. "Did you tell them?"

"You think I'm crazy!" he shouted. "They're paranoid, man. They don't take any chances. When they thought Maria had been talking to you, they killed her. Then they came after me."

"Listen to me," I said. "How did they know about me?"

"Dover's pal," he said. "He told them."

"What pal?"

"The one he was doing the deal with!" he shouted again. "Don't you know anything? Big deal fucking asshole detective!"

"Who was he doing a deal with?" I said.

"The guy, man. The guy in L.A. The one who picked him up on Sunday."

"You didn't pick him up on Sunday?"

"Shit, no. He said he didn't need me."

"Did you see this guy?"

277

He shook his head violently. "No! How many times do I have to tell you? I heard them talking on the phone when I come to give him the key on Friday. He tells me he's doing a favor for his buddy. That it's gonna get him off the hook. But he has to get out of the hotel, you know, without anybody seeing him. I went along, that's all. For a few bucks." He started to sob. "That's all I did, man. Get him the key and pick up his fucking car."

"Then why did they kill Maria?"

"I don't know," he moaned. "They thought she knew something, I guess. Maybe, I told her something. I don't know."

"What did you tell her?"

"I overheard the call. And he's got maybe a hundred grand on his bed, for chrissake. You don't have to be a genius, you know?"

I turned to Ramirez. "Did Dover do any repairs on his house this year?"

"No, señor," he said. "We don' have no flood this spring."

"So that's where he got the money."

"Who the fuck cares where he got the money," Ruiz said. "If you hadn't shown up and started asking questions, they wouldn't have cared. You got her killed, man. You're gonna get me killed, too." He looked around the room. "They probably followed you here. Didn't they? They're probably out there."

He lowered the rifle to my chest.

"Jerry!" I shouted.

Ramirez jumped off the bench and tackled Jerry at the waist. As they went down, I pulled the pistol from my belt. The rifle went off with a terrific bang, shaking the walls of the cabin. Dust fell from the rafters, filling the room like thick smoke. I couldn't see anything for a second. When the dust settled, Ramirez was sitting on the floor about two feet away from me. There was blood on his shirt. Ruiz was lying next to him. The rifle was still in his hands and the barrel was pointed at his chin. The top of his head was gone above the eyes.

"Oh, my God," Ramirez said, staring at Ruiz. "Oh, dear Jesus!"

He touched the blood on his shirt and threw up.

I pulled him to his feet and pushed him out into the yard. He was weeping hysterically.

"I killed him!" he cried. "I killed him!"

I grabbed him by the shoulder and shook him. "Stop it!" I said.

He worked his mouth noiselessly a couple of times.

I glanced back at the cabin door. There was blood on the floor, flecked with pieces of fractured bone. There was no question about what had to be done.

"Who else knows about this place?" I said to Ramirez.

It took him a moment to answer. He wiped his nose and mouth with his shirtsleeve. "My wife," he said. "My children."

"Is there a shovel in the cabin? Something to dig with?"

He looked at me with horror. "You gonna bury him, man?"

"Would you rather call the cops?"

"But I killed him," he said.

"Don't be a fool," I said. "He killed himself."

He shook his head slowly. "It's not true."

"What difference does it make?" I said. "He's dead, and unless you want to go to prison, you're going to help me bury him."

"Madre de Dios!" Ramirez said.

I went into the cabin and dragged Ruiz out into the yard. His brains made a long smear in the dirt. Then I went back in the cabin and searched it. I found a shovel in the corner by the stove.

"Can you clean up in there?" I said to Ramirez.

"I don't know."

"Then dig." I jabbed the spade into the hard-packed dirt.

279

I went into the cabin a third time, pulled the sheets off the mattress and blotted up the blood and tissue from the cabin floor. I took the sheet out into the yard, wadded it up, and tossed it beside Ruiz's body. Then I took a couple handfuls of dirt from the hole that Ramirez was digging and spread it over the cabin floor. The first few handfuls turned pink. But after six or seven trips, the floorboards looked the way they had before Ruiz had died. It wouldn't have fooled a cop, but it would fool Ruiz's wife and kids or anybody else who happened to wander into the place.

When I went back out to the yard, Ramirez was leaning on the spade handle—knee-deep in the hole he'd dug. He was weeping again. The sunset colored his face and hands; it had turned the whole clearing a golden brown. Within another hour, it would be fully dark. I helped Ramirez out of the hole, then stepped in and dug some more. I dug for thirty minutes. By then the hole was fairly deep.

"Take off your shirt," I said.

Ramirez pulled the undershirt over his head and tossed it into the hole.

I got out of the grave and rolled Ruiz's body into it. I threw the bloody sheet in, too.

"When you get the car back," I said. "Take it some place and ditch it. Some place no one will find it. Understand?"

He nodded. "Why do you do this, señor?"

"I don't know," I said. "C'mon, let's bury him before it's too dark to see."

We finished just as the sun set. I scattered some unturned dirt on the grave. It didn't really make a difference. In a few days, it would all be covered with dust again. I left the shovel where I'd found it, in the cabin, then followed Ruiz down the trail to the talus above the desert floor. We half-slid, half-crawled down to the jeep. When we got to the car, we sat down beside it to catch our breath.

"What did you go to jail for, Ramirez?" I said, after a time.

"When I was much younger, I stole something—some money from a gas station. You ever been in jail?"

I laughed. "No. It just looks that way."

We got in the jeep. Ramirez started it up and clicked on the lights. The engine thundered against the mountainside.

"I don' come back here no more," Ramirez said over the roar of the motor.

I nodded. "Maybe, that's best."

We drove through the pitch dark back to the ranch. The Chevelle was parked in the yard. Ramirez's wife was standing in the lighted doorway of the Pueblo house, wiping her hands on a dish towel. As we pulled up, she called out to her husband in Spanish. He said something back to her, then translated for me.

"She wants to know what happened. I tol' her everything's O.K. We been up in the hills."

"Does she know about Ruiz?"

He nodded.

"How much does she know?"

"Just that it's his car. And that he's a friend of Señor Dover."

"Tomorrow morning, you take that car and ditch it— like I told you. When you come back, tell her Ruiz is gone. That he took the car and left."

He nodded again. "What about you? What are you gonna do?"

"Go to L.A., I guess, and find Quentin's pal."

"He called somebody on Saturday. I don' know who. Maybe it woul' help to find out."

"He called from his house?"

"He called twice—once before the men came. And once before we left for the airport."

"That's a help, all right."

I got out of the jeep and walked across the yard to the

Mustang. Ramirez watched me from where he was sitting in the jeep—his arms folded on top of the windscreen.

"Señor," he called out. "Go with God."

"You, too," I said.

I got in the car and drove back to the hotel.

41

The lobby was crowded and my clothes and skin were covered with dirt. I walked past the front desk as quickly as I could, went up to my room, and called the valet. I didn't know if there was any of Jerry Ruiz on my clothes or not. But I felt dirty—an under-the-skin kind of dirtiness—and I wanted the clothes cleaned. A kid came up to collect them. I handed the bundled-up jeans and shirt to him through the door, then went into the john and took a good, long look at myself in the mirror.

I ordered a bottle of Scotch from room service and spent the next hour steaming myself in the tub and drinking. Around nine-thirty I called Glendora at the Belle Vista. I was more than a little drunk.

"It's all coming back to roost, Frank," I said when I got through to him.

"Are you O.K.?" he said with concern.

"Just great. How'd it go with Sy?"

"I think it went all right. I'm rather a novice at these things. He asked for ten, and I gave it to him. How'd it go with you?"

"Marvie," I said. "Did you know that we got Maria Sanchez and her little boy killed?" He didn't say anything. "No, I guess you didn't know that. But it's a fact. We got them killed. You and me and good old Quentin."

"How?" he said.

"Oh, fuck, I don't know how. How? Quentin let Jerry Ruiz know too much—sloppy planning on our boy's part. And Jerry let Maria know. And when I came snooping around her house, the wrong people found out and killed her. Take a guess how they found out."

"Why don't you tell me?"

"No. Take a guess."

"Harry," he said. "Tell me."

"Someone told them about me, Frank. Someone told them I was investigating Dover's death. Someone who was just as nervous as they were about what I might find. You see, Quentin didn't go to New Mexico to do a deal for himself. He went there for someone else—someone in L.A. He wasn't trying to make money on the deal; he was trying to win friends and influence people."

"Oh, God," Glendora said. "Which people?"

"I don't know for sure, but I can make a guess."

"Make a guess," he said hollowly.

"Who had the power to keep Quentin's career alive? At least for another thirteen weeks? Whose cooperation was absolutely essential if Quentin was to continue as head writer on 'Phoenix'? Who had a boyfriend who was a snowbird? Who knew how to get the shit or how to point Quentin in the right direction? Who knew from the start that I was investigating Dover's death? And who didn't want his contacts to be jeopardized or anyone to get wind of what he and Quentin were really doing? Sound familiar, yet?"

"Are you sure, Harry?"

"Let me ask you a question, Frank. I found a document in Quentin's ranch house. I thought it was an old story line, but let me paraphrase it for you, and you tell me how old it is."

I told him the story of the man running from his past and of the other man who blackmailed him.

When I finished, he sighed. "It's Walt's document, all right. Or rather Russ Leonard's. I don't suppose Quentin could have picked it up someplace, could he? Or stolen it?"

"There was a note printed on it—'Here it is.' Does that sound like a pickup? Or more like a gift? A fair exchange for services to be rendered? Face it, Frank. Walt was the only one who could have saved Quentin's bacon. He was the only one with that document that Quentin had promised everyone."

"Oh, God," Glendora said again. "But if you're right, why would Walt have given Quentin the document before he . . . before the deal was made. And why would he have needed Quentin at all, if as you say he had the drug connections?"

"It wasn't the document itself that mattered," I said. "It was Walt's willingness to go along with Quentin—to share the credit for having written the document, or to let Quentin take the credit for himself—that was really at stake. I assume he gave Quentin a copy of the document sometime on Friday, as a show of good faith and to give Quentin the chance to familiarize himself with the story line before the staff meeting on Monday. As to why he let Quentin handle the drug transaction, rather than handling it himself . . . I don't know. Maybe Walt wasn't sure of his connection. Or maybe he just wanted to put Quentin through a little more hell before finally coming across. He did have a long-standing grudge against him, because of Leonard."

"You think Walt was that vindictive?"

"Call your friend at Ma Bell. Have him call a friend in New Mexico and have that friend call me. Quentin made two calls from here in Las Cruces. They'll tell us if I'm right."

"I'll make the call in the morning," he said. "I hope you're wrong."

I hoped I was, too, because I'd told Jack Moon almost

the same thing that I'd told Glendora and he hadn't mentioned Walt's document. I didn't want to know why.

I did some more drinking before I went to sleep—enough to make me sick in the middle of the night and leave me badly hung over in the morning. I went down to the lobby about nine-thirty and sat in the cafe, sipping coffee and smelling the wet pool smells of chlorine and tile. Business in the cafe picked up around ten. I couldn't stand the noise or the faces, so I went back to my room and called the El Paso airport. I booked an L.A. flight departing at five Mountain time and arriving at LAX at five forty-five Pacific time. I called the Marquis, too, and reserved a room. The bellboy came by with my jeans and shirt—all neatly pressed and spotless. I threw them in the overnighter, packed the gun in its case, and the ammunition in its box. Then I sat down by the phone and waited.

Around one, the phone rang. I picked it up, thinking that it was someone with the New Mexico telephone company, calling to tell me what I already knew. But I was wrong. It was Glendora again.

"Harry," he said heavily. "I just heard some very bad news. I thought I'd better tell you."

I held my breath for a second. "What is it?" I said.

"Marsha Dover is dead. They found her in her bedroom this morning. They think it was . . . well, too much alcohol and too many sleeping pills."

"It was a suicide?" I said.

"Harry, I don't know," Glendora said.

"I'll call you later, Frank." I hung up the phone.

I sat there for awhile. Then I called a friend in Cincinnati—a newspaperman—and asked a few questions, because you're supposed to ask questions, even when there aren't any answers. She hadn't left a note. She'd been drinking. She'd taken some Nembutols. And she'd gone to sleep.

I got the bottle of Scotch out of the suitcase and poured

286

a drink in one of the bathroom glasses. I sat there drinking for a long time, until I was numb. I tried to think about the way she'd looked—about how beautiful she'd been. But I kept remembering how I'd felt when I'd left that house for the last time, practically running away from her, the way the phone guy had run away from me. I thought of what Helen Rose had said about Quentin—about how we fuck with other people's lives. Christ, how he'd fucked with hers. How he'd fucked with his own.

The phone company man called about a half hour later. I was so drunk by then that I had trouble concentrating on what he said. He gave me two numbers. I copied them down. One was an L.A. exchange—Dover had made that call at eleven P.M. on Saturday night. The other, made early on the same day, I didn't pay attention to, until after I'd hung up. When I did take a look at it, I started to feel bad all over again. It was one more thing that I hadn't wanted to know.

I dialed the number, anyway, from the phone by the window. His wife answered.

"Where is he, Liz?" I said.

"I thought he was with you," she said with surprise. "In California. He left this morning."

"Did he say where he'd be?"

"At the Belle Vista, I guess. That's where he usually is. What's wrong, Harry."

"Liz," I said. "This is important. Did Quentin Dover call Jack on Saturday?"

"Yes. He called him on Saturday afternoon. Jack hadn't gotten back from New York yet. So I took a number and left a message for him to call. Why is that so important?"

"Do you remember the number?"

"It was a local number."

"In Cincinnati?" I said.

"Yes. I don't remember it exactly."

"Did Jack return the call?"

"Yes. Late that afternoon. Harry, would you please tell

me what's going on. First Jack starts acting strangely and now this."

"How was he acting strangely?"

"He seemed upset with himself the last time he talked to you. You know how he gets—little attacks of conscience, like hot flashes. He started berating himself for letting you down. That's why I thought he was with you. He said he was going out to the coast to put things right."

"Christ," I said. "If he calls, tell him I'm on my way to California. Tell him *not* to do anything until I get there. Tell him I said everything was all right—that there weren't any problems."

"O.K.," she said uncertainly. "But what's this about?"

"I'm not sure, Liz. Something to do with Quentin."

As soon as she hung up, I called Glendora at the Belle Vista.

"Is Jack Moon with you?" I said.

"Why, no," he said. "He's in Cincinnati."

"No, he's not, Frank." I hesitated a moment. If I told him what I suspected—that Jack had somehow been involved in Quentin's deal—it would have meant Jack's ass. There had to be some way around that, I thought. There had to be a way to get someone out of this thing unscathed. I decided not to tell him. Instead, I put him on mild alert. "If you see Jack at the hotel, I want you to collar him, Frank. I want you to order him to stay put until I get into town this afternoon."

"Why? What's he doing out here?"

"Some amateur detective work," I said.

"That's unlike Jack. He's usually such a prudent man."

"Today he's not," I said. "I'll be in at five forty-five."

"What are we going to do about Walt?"

"You let me handle it. Just find Jack, all right?"

"About Marsha . . ."

"I don't want to talk about that," I said and hung up.

I dialed the other number I'd written down—the California one. Walt Mack answered the phone.

288

"This is Stoner," I said. "I'm coming into town tonight. I want to talk to you."

"I'm busy," he said curtly.

"Well, make yourself unbusy, Walt. I know about the drug deal and I know about the document."

"Bullshit," he said.

"Mack, if you know what's good for you, you'll stay in your house until I get there. Don't go out. Don't let anyone else in."

"Why? What do you mean?"

"I mean your friends killed a girl because you told them that she knew about Quentin's deal and because I was getting vaguely close to finding out about it. I'm a lot closer now, Walt. And if they'd kill her for next to nothing, just think what they'd do to you."

"They won't do anything to me," he said calmly. "But there are some others who might be in jeopardy."

"You mean Jack, don't you?"

"I mean if you're thinking of going to the police, think again. You're way out of your league on this one, sport."

"How deeply was Jack involved?"

"Just deeply enough." He laughed. "If I go down, he's going with me. I'll see to it. So let's stop threatening each other, all right? I've got a soap to write."

He hung up.

42

Talking to Mack and Liz Moon sobered me a little. A quart of hot coffee and a handful of aspirins helped, too. By three-thirty, I was steady enough to drive. I checked out of the Holiday Inn and drove south on the expressway to El Paso. The heat in the car helped sweat the booze out of me. By the time I got to the airport, I had a raging headache and was drenched in perspiration, but I was sober. I dropped the car off at a Hertz stand and picked up my pass at the American window. I had to go through a special procedure to take the gun with me. They made me disassemble it, unload the magazine, and stick it in my overnighter. They tagged the suitcase with a special red "Firearms" sticker and stowed it in a pressurized compartment in the cargo hold. That special tag was like an engraved invitation to any sticky-fingered baggage handler. I fully expected to find the gun or the suitcase gone when I got to L.A.

I didn't drink any booze on the plane ride. I was afraid to—afraid I'd make myself sick or drunk again. It wouldn't have taken more than a couple of drinks to do both, even on airline Scotch. When we landed, I went to the baggage pick-up and got the overnighter. It felt as if the gun was still inside. To be sure, I went into one of the

290

johns in the terminal, and took a look in the bag. The gun was still there, boxed and disassembled. I put it back together, loaded the clip, and cocked and locked it. Then I stuck it back in the bag and walked out to the taxi stands.

It took twenty minutes for the cabbie to drive to Mack's house on Highway One. On the way there, I thought things out. I decided to kill Mack. All things considered it was probably best for everyone. If I killed him and made it look like a suicide, I'd get the thugs off Ramirez's back. And, maybe, off Jack's. I was sure they'd feel a lot safer with Mack out of the picture. He was the only direct link between them and the cocaine, except for Dover, who was already dead. It hadn't been just their own asses they were covering when they'd killed Maria Sanchez and her son, it had been Walt's. Jack Moon could be next, if he was more directly involved in Quentin's deal than Maria had been. The alternative was to pay the hoods off in some way that would make them feel reasonably secure. I didn't know how much money that would take—probably a great deal. It would be simpler to kill Walt. After Marsha, I wanted to kill someone, anyway.

The sun was beginning to set over the ocean when we got to Pacific Palisades. It was turning the breakers gold and lighting up the cliffs and the bungalows built into the hillsides. The cabbie pulled over at the turnoff and I stepped out into the sunset. I paid the cabbie and told him he could go. He sped off in a little cloud of gravel dust. When he was gone, I took the pistol out of the suitcase and tucked it in my belt. Then I walked up to the buzzers and rang. No one answered. I pressed the buzzer again. When no one answered the second time, I started to worry. The fence was over ten feet high—impossible to climb without a ladder or a boost up. I tried my shoulder against the gate, but it was locked with a dead bolt.

I was about to go hunting for something I could use as a step ladder—some concrete blocks or two-by-fours when someone pressed the buzzer. The gate fell open. I walked through it into the courtyard. I looked up at Mack's second-story balcony. The sliding glass door was open and a stream of dust was blowing out of it and falling in the narrow court. It looked like gold dust in the sunset, but it tasted like snow. I ran up to the front door of Mack's house and tried the handle. The door was unlocked.

I went inside, up to the circular stairway at the end of the hall. There was blood on the bottom steps. It looked as if it was dripping down from the landing. I pulled the pistol out of my belt, unlocked it, and slowly climbed the stairs. I could hear the surf pounding through the open balcony door in the second-floor den. When I got to the upper steps, I craned my neck and peeked over the landing. Walt Mack was lying on the floor right across from me. His eyes were open and staring into mine. There was blood coming from his nose, ears, and mouth. It had pooled around his head, soaking the carpet and dripping down onto the bottom steps.

I walked quickly up to the landing, flattened myself against the wall, braced the pistol with both hands, and swung around into the entryway of the den. Jack Moon was sitting on the floor by the sliding glass door. His legs were stretched out in front of him. He seemed to be staring at them. He was clutching his stomach with his hands. There was blood on his hands and everywhere on his shirt front. A gun was lying on the floor in the middle of the room, by the overturned Parsons table. A cellophane bag full of cocaine lay by the open door. It had spilled open and the cocaine was blowing out toward Highway One.

Jack looked up at me, glassy-eyed.

"Oh, God, Jack," I said. I went over and kneeled down beside him, dropping the pistol on the floor.

"It doesn't even hurt," he said with a weak smile. "I thought it hurt getting shot."

I went downstairs to the phone and called for an ambulance, then I went back to him.

"It was Walt's gun," he said. "I didn't even know he had one. Came here to tell him that I was going to go to the police. That I'd figured it out."

"Don't talk," I said.

He smiled again. His teeth were stained with blood. "I didn't know about the deal, Harry. Really, I didn't. Didn't want to know. When I talked to Quentin, he said that Walt wanted me to do a favor for him—the sort of thing I used to do for Russ. Just an errand boy, again. Executive producer. Should have guessed what was going on when Walt didn't call me himself. Maybe I did guess."

He coughed up some blood and his pupils dilated and his eyes opened very wide. "I take that back about it not hurting," he whispered.

"Jack, shut up," I said to him. "Please."

In the distance I could hear a siren screaming toward us, down the coast highway.

Jack swallowed hard. "Just wanted the money, that's all. Got hungry—tired of waiting. Tired of not having. I was supposed to carry some of it to New York—for Helen and her friends. Quentin said it was for Walt. Poor Quentin. I finally figured it out when you told me about the document. Knew what Walt had done. What a bastard—Walt. He made Quentin go through all that hell and gave him Russ's document at the end of it. It would have gotten him fired anyway. Can you beat it? After all that. Maybe Quentin figured it out for himself on Sunday. Maybe Walt told him—it was his style. Poor Quentin."

The siren noise got very loud. Jack looked up. "Tell Liz," he said.

Two paramedics came into the room, carrying a folded-up gurney.

"Christ," one of them said.

They lifted Jack onto the gurney and carried him downstairs. There were cops and flashing lights everywhere. I tried to get into the ambulance with Jack, but one of the cops stopped me.

"You're not going anywhere," he said.

The ambulance flew out of the turnaround. I watched it disappear down the coast highway. I didn't find out until early the next morning that he'd died on the way to the hospital.

The cops kept me for ten hours. I didn't tell them anything I didn't have to. It was about three A.M. when Glendora finally managed to spring me. I still don't know how he did it. They weren't about to let me go on their own.

As we were walking out to his car, he said, "We're going to have to keep Quentin's name out of this. If we don't, Goldblum will blow the whistle on all of us. He told me so. The Pacoinia police are just too close to making a connection between the Sanchez girl and Ruiz and Dover."

"What about Jack?" I said.

He shook his head. "They found him there. With the cocaine and a dead man. It's out of our hands now."

"You're going to let him take the fall for this?"

"Harry," he said painfully. "I haven't got a choice."

"And what about Helen Rose? She was connected, too. Jack was supposed to deliver some of Walt's cocaine to her in New York."

"I'll take care of it," he said. "I give you my word."

"And the thugs who killed Maria Sanchez and bought Quentin's dope?"

"That's up to the police, I guess. Maybe they'll find them."

"It isn't right, Frank," I said. "None of it is right."

"I know."

"Dover risked his life for a stupid document. Then killed himself when he found out that Walt had double-crossed him. And all those others—they died for nothing. For a dumbass soap opera. And nobody's ever going to know."

"We know," Glendora said grimly.

294

The LAPD wanted me to stay in L.A. until they'd sorted everything out. But Frank made some calls and I ended up flying back to Cincinnati with him the next day. I wanted to be at her funeral—he knew that. As it turned out, Frank and I were the only ones there.

I thought maybe some of her relatives would come. But nobody showed. It started to rain after the service. We walked back through the rain to the parking lot.

"The L.A. coroner has released a final verdict on Quentin's death this morning," he said.

"What was it?"

He laughed dully. "Natural causes. They say he had a coronary and fell in the shower."

When we got to the lot, he said, "Can I give you a lift back?"

"No," I said. "I think I'll stick around for awhile. I've got my own car."

He held out his hand. "Goodbye, Harry."

"Frank."

He got in the car and left.

I stayed for another half hour or so. Then I drove over to Jack's house in Hyde Park—to try to explain it to his wife and son.